SMALL ODYSSEYS

▼ ▼ ▼

SMALL ODYSSEYS

SELECTED SHORTS

PRESENTS

· 35 ·

NEW STORIES

EDITED BY
HANNAH TINTI

FOREWORD BY
NEIL GAIMAN

Published by
Algonquin Books of Chapel Hill
Post Office Box 2225
Chapel Hill, North Carolina 27515-2225

a division of
Workman Publishing
225 Varick Street
New York, New York 10014

This is a work of fiction. While, as in all fiction, the literary perceptions and insights are based on experience, all names, characters, places, and incidents either are products of the authors' imaginations or are used fictitiously.

LIBRARY OF CONGRESS CATALOGING-IN-PUBLICATION DATA

Library of Congress Cataloging-in-Publication Data

Names: Tinti, Hannah, editor. | Gaiman, Neil, writer of foreword.
Title: Small odysseys : Selected shorts presents 35 new stories /
edited by Hannah Tinti ; foreword by Neil Gaiman.
Description: First edition. | Chapel Hill, North Carolina :
Algonquin Books of Chapel Hill, 2022. | Summary: "A collection of never-before-published short stories by many of our most preeminent authors as well as up-and-coming superstars. Published in partnership with the beloved literary radio program and live show Selected Shorts"—Provided by publisher.
Identifiers: LCCN 2021045610 | ISBN 9781643751993 (trade paperback) |
ISBN 9781643753010 (ebook)
Subjects: LCSH: American fiction—21st century. | Short stories, American.
LCGFT: Short stories.
Classification: LCC PS648.S5 S63 2022 | DDC 813/.010806—dc23/eng/20211028
LC record available at https://lccn.loc.gov/2021045610

10 9 8 7 6 5 4 3 2 1

First Edition

CONTENTS

JOURNEYS

NEW WORLDS

FOREWORD

I.

ON THE ISLE of Skye, in western Scotland, is a cave, used and inhabited by people from 7000 years ago until 2000 years ago, and when archaeologists went in, they found, along with evidence of prehistoric habitation, the ashes, many feet deep, of a fire that had burned continually for a thousand years. In the ashes of the long-dead fire they found treasures, including a burned fragment of a stringed instrument, a lyre, the oldest stringed instrument ever discovered in that part of the world. Someone, 2500 years ago, had thrown the lyre into the flames. Perhaps it had already been broken beyond repair. Perhaps there was a fight back then, and the lyre was burned, or the burning of the lyre was an act of revenge.

I wonder about the lyre, and I build stories about it in my mind, I think about the fire that burned in that cave for a thousand years, and I ponder on the people who tended the flames. Perhaps they gave fire to those who came to them and asked for it: starting fires in the wind and the wet weather of Skye cannot have been easy, after all. There are so many things we do not know about that cave and the people who lived there, or about that fire.

But I know one thing, deep in my bones. And it's this: in the dim orange light of the fire, in the warmth of the flames, in the smoky safety of that cave, people told each other stories. Songs were sung and tales were told, and perhaps there was no difference between the two. And where you have a tale told, you have listeners.

II.

I WAS RAISED to love radio. I was a child in the 1960s in the United Kingdom, and my grandparents existed in a world where the radio was only turned on whenever there was something they specifically wanted to listen to. The radio wasn't on all the time, and was never background—perhaps that would have been a waste of electricity. But they would put on *Listen with Mother* when I stayed with them, and I would listen to someone telling me a story. The story always began with the reader saying, "Are you sitting comfortably? Then I'll begin."

Sometimes we would listen together to the adult shows, broadcast on one of the two BBC radio channels. These were half-hour comedies for grown-ups, *The Men from the Ministry*, *Round the Horne*, *The Navy Lark*, and the rest of them. I didn't mind that I didn't understand them. I loved what stories on the radio did: the feeling that I was taking part in the stories I was being told, that I was building them in my head.

The BBC channels renamed themselves and I continued listening to BBC Radio 4 for drama, and for short stories. That was where I first encountered Douglas Adams's *The Hitchhiker's Guide to the Galaxy*, where I first encountered Terry Pratchett's *The Colour of Magic*, being respectively performed and read on the radio.

I moved from the United Kingdom to the United States in 1992, back before there was an internet and you could take your

local news and culture with you wherever you went. I was in the
Midwest, and public radio became my lifeline to the world.

I don't remember when in the nineties, on which trip to which
city, *Selected Shorts* entered my life. It was exotic, being broadcast
all the way from New York, and it was a delight. World-class actors,
reading short stories in front of a live audience. It was the simplest
use of radio, and the most profound.

Voices told stories. You, as the listener, collaborated with the
storyteller to build a tale into something you could experience, just
as we did when we sat around the fire in the dawn days.

III.

RECORDED CIVILIZATION STARTED a few thousand years ago, but
people have been walking, talking, fire-using, tool-making homi-
nids for a vast span of time—before we began writing our histories.
And in that time before time began, over those hundreds of thousands of years, we told each other stories. There are satisfying places
where stories go, where stories take us: in our minds, on journeys
we will never make, with people we will never otherwise meet, voy-
ages that take us East of the Sun and West of the Moon, and leave
us satisfied when the story is over and yet we have not moved, and
are still sitting beside the fire.

There are stories that are still told that we can date from geo-
logical events they refer to that are older than any city, older than
any country, older than the oldest living thing we know of on
this planet (it's a five-thousand-year-old bristlecone pine tree in
California).

Stories are currency. Stories are the way we interact, the place
that groups come together. Stories unite us. We look out through

other eyes, imagine ourselves in other skins, experience lives we wished we could lead or are relieved we never will.

IV.

SO I LIVED in America, where the radio pickings were slim, and I listened to and loved *Selected Shorts*. I was thrilled when they chose a story of mine to be on the show. (The story was "Chivalry," the story of an old lady who buys the Holy Grail in a charity shop, and of the knight on a quest who visits her, and it was read by Christina Pickles.)

And then Jennifer Brennan and Katherine Minton, producers at *Selected Shorts*, reached out to me, and invited me to perform.

Soon enough I was standing onstage in New York's beautiful Symphony Space, reading a story I had written aloud to an audience. Then I was invited back, and we programmed some evenings together. I loved suggesting stories—some of them mine, some of them just stories I loved—and I reveled in watching actors like John Cameron Mitchell and Kirsten Vangsness, performers whose work I admired, standing there on the stage, reading stories that I had written or stories that had resonated inside me and changed me.

I loved the audience reactions: the silence when suspense grows, the intake of breath or the laughter at its release; when people shuffle or cough; the various noises of enjoyment they can make; how they applaud.

I had been adopted into the *Selected Shorts* family. I loved the people who work on *Selected Shorts*, from Symphony Space and from the public radio station WNYC. They are good people, and I wish they were all still with us: we lost the co-founder of Symphony Space, *Selected Shorts* host Isaiah Sheffer, in 2012, and Katherine Minton in 2016.

Following Isaiah's death in 2012, I agreed to guest-host several episodes of the radio show, and I was welcomed into the offices of WNYC, where I read links on the air and talked about stories I loved and why I loved them, and why it mattered that you were going to listen to them and not read them: I got to introduce Stephen Colbert reading Ray Bradbury's chilling "The Veldt" and the late Leonard Nimoy reading James Thurber's perfect short story "The Catbird Seat" and I felt real joy at knowing that, for some listeners, this would be their first encounter with stories that would change them.

V.

AS I WRITE this, I was meant to be back at Symphony Space, hosting a *Selected Shorts* to celebrate the centenary of Ray Bradbury's birth with Bradbury stories. It never happened. 2020 was the year the world fell apart. The world closed down and all the theaters went dark. But now the lights are going back on, and the people are coming out, and we need stories as much as we ever did.

Selected Shorts began over thirty-five years ago. There are thirty-five stories in this book, to celebrate thirty-five years of stories in Symphony Space; to celebrate the joy and the magic *Selected Shorts* has brought to so many of us, the waking dreams and the laughter and the tears and the anticipation, not to mention the gooseflesh and occasional moments of awe. Thirty-five original stories, each one a gem.

Here's to the stories that lie ahead of us . . .

Are you sitting comfortably? Then we'll begin.

—NEIL GAIMAN, 2021

INTRODUCTION

WHEN I WAS in my early twenties, I worked seven days a week (double shifts on the weekends) in order to save money and move to New York City and become a writer. It took about an hour for me to drive from my 9–5 job as a cashier at a bookstore to the restaurant where I waited tables at night, and in that hour from 5–6 p.m. I listened to *Selected Shorts*. Driving in the dark with the radio on, the headlights illuminating the road, I was transported from the interior of my old Dodge to a red velvet seat at Symphony Space, where BD Wong or Sigourney Weaver was standing onstage and reading a short story. I laughed, cried, sighed, and gasped along with the audience. Then I pulled into the parking lot and waited with the engine running to hear the end of that night's gripping tale. There was always a pause by the actor after the final word, a silence that echoed through the theater. I floated in that moment on a raft of connected human feeling. And then the audience would applaud and I'd turn off the engine and tie my apron and head to work.

Many years later, when I was living in New York, I got the call that I'd always dreamed of—*Selected Shorts* was going to perform a short story that I had written. The producer of *Selected Shorts*, Katherine Minton, invited me to WNYC to record an interview, and it was there that I met longtime *Selected Shorts* host Isaiah Sheffer, the voice I'd been hearing on the radio for so many years. I told Isaiah how *Shorts* had kept me company on the road at a time when I felt very far away from the life I'd hoped for. "And now here we are in the same room," I said. "I feel like I'm meeting David Bowie." Isaiah laughed and shook my hand. He said, "Thanks for listening." Then we put on our headphones and started to talk. After we finished recording, Katherine asked me to join *Selected Shorts* as a literary commentator, and my voice became a part of the radio show each week, interviewing authors and chatting with Isaiah about the magic of these small worlds.

Since then, *Selected Shorts* has continued to thrive, grow, and change, with new music, new hosts, a spin-off podcast called *Selected Shorts: Too Hot for Radio*, and now, this book: a celebration of the short story. The writers featured in these pages were all chosen by *Selected Shorts* and commissioned to create brand-new works of fiction. With works from a mix of established authors and emerging literary talents, the collection reflects the suspenseful and surprising tales presented each week on the program, with language that is rhythmic, generous, and economical, grounding imaginative situations with genuine human triumph and tragedy.

As a listener over the years, I've often sought out printed versions of the stories on *Selected Shorts*, so it's been a thrill to bridge the gap between performance and the written word while editing this anthology. I've always felt that reading is like an expedition. You meet the author on the page and step into the fictional world together. An editor's job is to ease the way and act as a compass. With this in mind, I've divided *Small Odysseys* into three thematically linked sections—*Departures*, *Journeys*, and *New Worlds*—to guide your voyage through the book.

Part one, *Departures*, focuses on the first step of any adventure: leaving home and saying goodbye. It kicks off with "The King of Bread," by Luis Alberto Urrea, a story of a father and son in mourning who channel their loss into a bakery truck, selling cookies and donuts and winning over the hearts of the people in their neighborhood. Meanwhile, in another part of the city, A. M. Homes's "Goodbye to the Road Not Taken" eavesdrops on a couple parting ways on the streets of Manhattan, a conversation that includes a confrontation over lox, as well as a wink at Robert Frost. "The Double Life of the Cockroach's Wife" by Helen Phillips is another literary send-up, using Kafka's "The Metamorphosis" (and the tenacious nature of NYC roaches) as inspiration to explore a painful loss that refuses to be erased.

Edwidge Danticat's powerful "Cane and Roses: A Manifesto" pushes against a different kind of erasure, detailing all the ways a person can be driven toward a desperate act. Carmen Maria Machado delivers the apocalypse, imagining Greek gods in "Persephone Rides at the End of Days," while Elizabeth Crane summons another mythical creature to guide a struggling divorcée in "Unicorn Me."

Some goodbyes are teachable moments, such as in Jai Chakrabarti's "Lessons with Father," where a daughter learns to paint from a fading artist; Patrick Cottrell's "The Hole," which recounts the struggles of a high school teacher leading up to spring break, or Weike Wang's "iPhone SE," narrating the final words of wisdom delivered by a dying cell phone. These farewells connect us to the past, just as the people in Namwali Serpell's "Noseless" can still summon the lost smell of their favorite foods and the woman in Jac Jemc's "Infidelity" can't forget a lost friend and the stories she used to tell. Memories are often the balm that heals us, and as the narrator in Mira Jacob's "Death by Printer" discovers when she recalls the beauty of her late wife, they can lead us to a guiding star.

Part two of this collection is titled *Journeys* and follows characters in a state of transition and movement. We begin with a coming-of-age story in Lesley Nneka Arimah's "Options," tracking a young girl facing a stark revelation as she sets course from Nigeria to America. In Michael Cunningham's "Sleepless," two men in love and a woman they've rescued from a Dunkin' Donuts stop and dance before deciding which fork in the road to choose.

At the next way station is Aimee Bender, weaving a story of fathers, mothers, and hot-air balloons in "Un-Selfie." Susan Perabo's "The Project" continues the exploration of parenthood through the question, hypothesis, research, results, and conclusion of a school science fair presentation. In "Home" by Elizabeth Strout, a mother suffering from dementia is moved into assisted living, the children now the parents, the parent now a child.

Crossing into the world of genre, "Love Interest" by Jess Walter gives us a digital detective story, as a computer expert tracks down hackers for an aging movie star. A bookseller solves the case of a missing encyclopedia (and finds another mystery on the shelves) in Joe Meno's "Books You Read." J. Robert Lennon blasts us into outer space with "Escape Pod W41," a hilarious riff on language from the point of view of a modern-day HAL, and Omar El Akkad takes us on "A Survey of Recent American Happenings Told Through Six Commercials for the Tennyson ClearJet Premium Touchless Bidet," using forcefully gleeful advertising copy to reflect the psyche of a country in crisis.

The landscape begins to change in "Conquistadors, on Fairchild" by Jacob Guajardo, which focuses on the unpredictable nature of relationships, while Maile Meloy's "Period Piece" follows nature's change—menopause—and one woman's roller-coaster ride of hot flashes and hormones. The brakes come on at last with Marie-Helene Bertino and her "Woman Driving Alone," who checks the rearview to see how far she's come and understands that the heart is an engine.

The final section of *Small Odysseys* is titled *New Worlds* and investigates arrivals, those strange and exciting first steps into unfamiliar territory. The townspeople who inhabit Ben Loory's "Dandelions" find themselves blessed (or perhaps cursed) by a sudden explosion of flowers that transform their village. Boundaries continue to be tested in Lisa Ko's "Nightlife," as an old relationship is tentatively redefined during a round of karaoke. Borders are completely broken in Jenny Allen's whimsical "Scaffolding Man," when an unexpected lover climbs through an apartment window.

America can often feel like the great unknown, especially for immigrants. "Cerati After Cerati" by Juan Martinez is a moving portrayal of Venezuelans struggling to find their footing in Chicago through music and memory. Digging into misconceptions of the Arab community, Rabih Alameddine's "The Prom Terrorists" delivers a rollicking single-sentence narrative about the unsuccessful recruiting of a twenty-something slacker by the FBI.

The pandemic shifted everyone's axis and left many uncertain about the future. "Bedtime Story" by Victor LaValle describes New York City at the start of lockdown, where a father and son camp in the hallway of their abandoned apartment complex. Patrick Dacey's "All That's Gone Is All That's Left" captures the anxiety of citizens left to fend for themselves, as a plucky grandmother and her grandson do their best to care for one another while society starts to crumble. And disguised as academic ephemera, Rivers Solomon's "A Brief Note on the Translation of *Winter Women*, Written by the Collective Dead, Translated by Amal Ruth" introduces a new language (translated from a haunted place) in the voices of those we've lost.

Our final entries shine a light on the world to come. A young girl is transformed over a summer at the beach in "Such Small Islands" by Lauren Groff, first by her half sister, and then by jealousy that burns inside her like a flame. In Etgar Keret's "Almost Everything," a man desperate to find the perfect fiftieth-birthday gift for his wife looks to the stars for inspiration. And finally, in Dave Eggers's "Where the Candles Are Kept," an aging loner acting as guardian for troubled teens in the wilderness finds courage and resilience hidden in the most unexpected of places—the next generation.

At the end of each story in this collection you'll find a note from the author, sharing the inspiration behind their contribution. These insights give a rare peek behind the curtain at the creative process, revealing how much thought and effort went into each piece included in *Small Odysseys*. Like a song or a poem, the words in a short story carry more weight, allowing for a complete artistic experience in a brief span of time, distilled into a package tiny enough to fit in your hand that will later unfold inside of you, like a map to a whole new world.

—HANNAH TINTI, 2021

SMALL ODYSSEYS

▼ ▼ ▼

DEPARTURES

THE KING OF BREAD

◆ LUIS ALBERTO URREA ◆

Papa reached back to grab me in the back seat when that car ran the red light on Wabash and plowed into us. We spun out on two wheels and slammed into a street sign. The old man steered with his left hand and held me with his right as I lifted off. For a moment, I was flying.

Man, that car was his pride. It was a '49 Ford. An anvil of a machine. We stood in the road and watched as it died, steam flying high, car blood spilling onto the blacktop. The woman who hit us stood like a statue of a woman, with glass in her hair, calling, "I never saw you! I never saw you!" It was the only time I ever saw him cry, even when Mama left us.

The crash was especially hard on him because he was between jobs. How was he supposed to go out and find one now? Or buy a new car? Even a junker, which is how we'd gotten a '49 Ford to begin with.

You'd never know he was down on his luck unless you watched his moods, which he kept hid like the nudie magazines under his mattress. I'd define his demeanor as jolly rage. But that was no different from all the men I saw around me in the barrio. It was a scramble for everybody.

He had lost his job at the tuna cannery. And he was going to try for a job at the bowling alley in Chula Vista when the car died. So rage hung like a haze in our apartment as his money ran out. It was just the two of us in the apartment. He got madder the more he had to clean it, to wash dishes, to make me do homework. My things he found tossed around were a personal insult to him.

It took me a while to learn to do chores. What did I know? I liked him being home when I didn't hate it. I was happy he didn't come home stinking of fish anymore . . .

I missed that Ford, too. But I could walk to school at St. Jude's by myself now, so I didn't need rides or anybody with me. Besides, if some of the crazy vatos or bloods from down the street punched me, Pa would expect me to fight back. This way, I could just run. He'd never know. In those days, his advice was simple: "If they hit you, beat them till they're in the dirt. And when they're down, kick them in the pinche head." I didn't think I could do that and live. They always got back up.

His problem was that he couldn't survive without something to drive. He didn't walk down the street like some peasant. And he hated taking a bus. "Un hombre don't take a bus," he said. "I'd rather ride a burro."

Pa was a driver for sure. A driver and a worker. It didn't take him long to get a job at the big bakery down near the dry docks.

He showed me the want ad: "Drivers Needed. Clean driving record required. Bakery Truck. Must have selling skills. Good with people a must! Apply in person."

"What's it mean?" I asked.

"I don't know, Mijito, but I get a truck to drive." He lit one of his Pall Malls. "And I like bread."

"Me too."

"Pues, it's perfect, then."

He did that Mexican one-shoulder-shrug-while-tipping-his-head thing. Hung out his lower lip, closed his eyes, raised his eyebrows. As if he was acknowledging the mysteries of the universe and also suggesting that no one with any sense would turn down a shot at a job that included a truck. And bread. People who try to learn Spanish don't know that half of it is silent. They never seem quite right when they speak because they don't use their faces and hands and shoulders and lips enough.

So one day he came home with a two-tone '61 Chevy panel truck, black fenders, creamy body paint, and the bakery's logo on the sides. They also gave him a uniform and a snappy bread-dude cap he wore like some bomber pilot in those old movies. All tipped down over his right eye.

"I get to keep it here, Mijo!" he called as he turned into the dirt alley. "Our new troka!"

Of course, it seemed gigantic to me, and Pa looked about twenty feet tall in the driver's seat.

Then he confided, as if it was a dirty secret, "It's a loaner."

He squinched his nose a little, like the admission had a bit of stink on it. You know what I was saying about Mexican Spanish? Well, he was showing the expression for his favorite old-school word for *stink*. Which is *fuchi*. If you said it with enough verve, you couldn't help but make that monkey-face. So if you made that monkey-face, you really didn't have to say the word out loud at all, but all your paisanos would know exactly what you hadn't just said.

The back of the truck had two doors that opened on wooden drawers he'd fill every morning at the bakery: bread and donuts and cookies and maybe a pie or two. If the moms on his route ordered one in advance, he could bring them a birthday cake. There were paper bags and wax paper sheets back there for picking up the stuff and handing it over.

Pa wore a silver changemaker on his belt with tubes full of pennies, dimes, nickels, and quarters, and he'd work a toggle to count them out. He had a zipper pouch for dollar bills, but the ladies on his route didn't often have paper money. Some wrote checks. Some had welfare chits. Pa actually took IOUs from many moms, which was to be his downfall.

If the bakery really wanted to make money, he liked to say, they should have loaded the trucks with tortillas and pan dulce. "Conchas," he said. And those gingerbread pig cookies nobody really liked but ate because grandma dunked them in coffee.

"When I buy this troka," he said, "I'm going to paint our names on the door. Garcia y Garcia. I'll leave it to you so you will have a business." Even in fourth grade, I didn't want to drive a bread truck. I wanted to turn blond and be Steve McQueen. "Me and you, Mijo. It's just me and you."

We'd been alone since Mama left us.

It happened when I got the chicken pops. That's what all us kids called it. We thought it was because you had these red things pop out all over. Made sense to us. We were always decoding the stuff everybody said.

I feel guilty about it to this day. Mama. Like I could have not caught it. I could have not touched whoever was sick playing four-square on the blacktop playground. Most of the homies got the pops, though. It was going through the school like a flood. Ma kept me home when it turned all polka dot. Pa did not approve of that in any way—un hombre, you know, doesn't stay in bed. He don't be sick.

Hey, I didn't mind. I had my *Mad* magazines and my Batman comics. Ma let me eat strawberry ice cream as if I had the tonsils, even though Pa yelled a lot about me getting fat. I got to stay in the sack as long as I wanted. I could watch game shows and Mike Douglas on our TV. That sounded great to me but nobody told me how the little red pops would itch and break when you scratched them. So it wasn't that much fun, after all.

Ma's usual cure for all ills (VapoRub) didn't work on my pops. So she went out. Walked down the long block to the corner store to get baking soda or something. She was going to soak me in it.

But the immigration guys got her. You think this is a modern thing, a Make America Great Again thing, but they were hunting what they called wetbacks the whole time. I wanted to tell somebody she was my mother, and she didn't have a wet back. I didn't even know what a wet back meant. Was it a woman thing? Were these men searching for all women with leaky backs? Or just Mexican mothers? Was it me? Had I made her back wet by being born? I was pretty sure it was that, because Pa's back was dry and my back was dry.

And I didn't know anything about papers. I would have thought they were something like dog tags. The dogcatchers came to the apartments and dragged away skinny dogs—I hated those days. My mama was not a dog. Did she get put in a big truck by mama catchers? Locked in steel cages with other wet women? All I knew for sure was that something terrible must have happened, and it was my fault.

I was still in bed, terrified, when Pa came home.

I was afraid he'd be mad at me for losing her. I was afraid somebody from the scary end of the block got her. I hid there under my blankets all afternoon, hoping she was just delayed, just talking to a neighbor, maybe in church saying a prayer so I'd get better. But I knew that nothing would keep my mother from me. I'd been crying.

All of us in that barrio lived in fear of Something Bad, this unnamed thing that happened to some Mexicans. This force that snatched families off the block, that took homies out of fourth grade and made the nuns never mention them again. I thought it was something like the monsters on Moona Lisa's science fiction show on Saturdays, something like the giant crab monsters that pinched off people's heads and ate them and then could think and talk like humans. I thought the monsters were eating my mother to learn Spanish so they could hypnotize us into coming outside so they could feed again. And I promise you, there are kids today that think something like that. They're thinking it tonight. Only they're thinking something even worse is happening to their moms in the dark, because the world has become what it is.

Pa had that fish stink on him when he stormed in. And he was yelling. He was throwing things around as if Ma might be hiding behind the old couch. He grabbed me up by the collar of my pajamas and ordered me to stop crying. He kicked open the back door and I heard him running down the street calling her name and I cried harder because I thought he would be eaten, too. And I would be left forever in that apartment waiting for the monsters to come for me, calling my name in my parents' voices.

But nothing. Happened. At all. It was all . . . silence after that week. Life went on. Ma was back home in Mexico. I did not know this place, Home. Or Mexico. I thought National Avenue was home. And Pa went back to work. He bought me a turtle at Woolworth's.

La Bakery Troka was salvation.

Consignment is what they called the deal they made with Pa. The deal the bakery made with all their drivers. Neither one of us knew exactly what it was. But Papa learned things quick. That was the secret to life in the U.S.—understanding the rules and the meanings as fast as you can because you're always behind the ball. Playing catch-up. And if they catch you, you get thrown out. Like Ma. Behind the ball, though. What was that? Like *wetback* or *medium rare* or *crew cut*. What were those things? Signals came at me as if sent by spaceships from another world. I spent my boyhood needing a decoder ring.

So Pa went to his bank and took out some of the cannery money he'd stashed away and bought the stuff to fill his truck's drawers. The bakery sold it to him at a fair rate. Cheaper than it would have been in stores. And they had a chart of prices he could charge, which were a little more than the store.

They paid him an added minimum fee for his hours behind the wheel. Though fuel was on him. And he could work as many hours as he needed, but after a full eight hours, his salary ended and the rest was all on the profit margin from the drawers. He was supposed to maintain a bargain drawer for day-olds. But like many drivers, he sometimes kept things that could still pass as fresh in his main drawers. Thirty or forty extra cents per order at every stop could add up after a good week.

He inherited the route of a guy who died of Irish whiskey, Pa said. Pa himself never drank after the Mama catchers took her, aside from his small glass of Thunderbird every night. He had learned pretty quick that nobody was going to run into the street to buy muffins after dark, not in our neighborhood, anyway, so he always came home in time for Cronkite. Mrs. Cota the babysitter went back across the alley to her house. Pa paid her in bread and cookies. He and I ate TV dinners and watched the news, and he had his one drink and a bowl of Fritos and cashews. It was kind of what we did in place of church.

Every week, he sent an envelope to Mama back Home.

I read somewhere that all fathers are mysteries to their children until they die, and then become greater mysteries because they can never then be solved. You just wonder. Forever.

I think kids fear their fathers. I didn't dare make mine angry. Not because he'd hurt me, but because he'd leave. He got only one letter from Ma in the year after she left. One letter I knew of. He never talked about it, but that night he stayed out until morning. I was afraid he'd gone to that Home place to be with her again.

Once, when the phone rang, I grabbed it. All I could hear were crackles. There seemed to be a distant voice, a small voice I couldn't really hear.

"Mama?" I cried. "Mama? Mama?"

The little crackling voice talked on and on and then the line went dead.

So I made it my job to be the best no-crying son I could. Pa went to work every morning, and so did I. I was a bad student, but

I never missed class. Even though the kids laughed at me because my dad was the donut guy in the stupid truck, I was embarrassed by him all of a sudden.

I resolved to be useful and uncomplaining. I never asked again for a comic or a toy. I crept out of my room as silently as possible on Saturdays to sit too close to the almost silent TV and watch Bugs and Daffy and the Stooges as Pa's snores rattled the walls. I had a plan to get a paper route when I was older—maybe old enough so the bad dudes down the block wouldn't hit me. Earn some extra money for Pa. But I'd need a bike. I was trying to figure that part out.

I even helped him with his work. For example: our unit was at the end of the apartment block, one of four, on the bottom floor off the dirt alley that snaked downhill from National. The garage was around the corner, down by Reverend Jones's wild backyard. It had stood empty since the Ford was murdered, so Pa put his bread truck in there every night. It was his Fort Knox of donuts.

He'd call me every afternoon from a pay phone at around 5:00.

"Ready, Mijo?" he'd say.

"Sí, Pa."

"Meet me outside in a half hour."

I'd be standing outside our back door. It was a great place—the sun hit it in the afternoon, and when it rained, the old wood porch was like my boat as the alley turned to a muddy river. I'd never been in a boat.

So anyway, I'd stand there and wait, and I'd hear him before I saw him. If you were around town in those days, you will remember the bread truck's whistle. It was as cool as the ice-cream man's jingly music, how the bread trucks had the train whistle on the roof. Pa would pull his lanyard twice as the bakery's signal: *woot-woot*. Everybody would come running.

He'd pull up in his cloud of cigarette smoke, and I'd step up on the running board. He'd hang his arm out and wrap it around me, pull me tight to the warm metal of the door. The smell of all those bakery goods came out with the smoke. His arm seemed impossible. Huge. Muscle carved of wood. And it was covered in wiry hairs. His bones could have been stone. And he'd roll down the alley slow as a snail, idling, really, but I hooted and hollered as if we were speeding around a racetrack. He'd swing it around the corner and I'd jump off with the key to the padlock in my hand. I'd unlock it and yank up the garage door and Pa would drive in saying, "That's m'boy, all right" or even better, "Míralo." That one-word Mexican exhortation to just take a look at this kid—isn't he amazing?

My secret knowledge of his great mystery was simple: he wasn't as tough as he needed the world to think he was. I knew that inside the brutally efficient driver's cab, there was a spiderweb under the dash. Right beside the long ratchet of the pull-brake. He would never let me bother that spider. In his customized English, he called it el espider. It was his mascot, he said. It brought him luck. He talked to it as he drove around all day. It never occurred to me that he might be lonely.

And he never missed the ritual we had created. No matter how beat he was. And he was beat, all right. Some days he was gray. He was a hundred years old. His back hurt—I knew he wore some kind of girdle thing to hold it together. He wore copper magnet bracelets because the healer ladies in the barrio told him they pulled bad vibrations out of his body. He sat on a woven mat with springs in it. He ate Tums like candies. He smelled like sweat and yeast.

But he limped to the back of the truck and swung open the doors and pulled out the bottom goody drawer and said, "I wonder if I have any spare stuff I can offer you, Mijo."

I was all about the donuts.

"Glaze donuts are the best donuts," he'd say. "The gringos invented them."

"Chocolate."

"Chocolate's for girls. Men eat glazed."

"You told me Aztecs invented chocolate."

"Yeah but you got to cut out some cabron's heart to eat Aztec donuts."

"Dad!"

He'd take up his wax paper square and pick one chocolate and one glazed.

"Dinner first," he always said.

But most days, we ate them before we even got through the back door.

It was the year after they took Ma that I broke.

I was all the way into fifth grade. I had a two-way crush on red-headed Marlene and her friend Roxanne. I wanted to be Captain Kirk that year. Some of the boys that used to beat me up now had a baseball game going behind the school. We played in a dirt lot. We used broomsticks for bats, and an old mummy of a dead cat was home base.

But I missed my mom so hard it gave me headaches and a sore throat that didn't feel like a cold but like I got punched there. I cried into my pillow at night and imagined Marlene would beam me up and take me on an adventure on a strange planet. Probably Pegasus. I was pretty sure Pegasus lived there. On the anniversary of her taking, I couldn't go to school. I didn't care if he punished me. I couldn't even take off my pajamas.

I was staring at my Frosted Flakes in that nasty little kitchen

when he walked in and stopped dead to stare. He was wearing
slacks. Pa, first thing, and he had slacks on. He never even owned
a pair of shorts or jeans. Cuffed slacks and a sleeveless T-shirt and
slippers, because un hombre never went barefoot. We had that
Woolworths turtle in a plastic bowl that had a little ramp and a
plastic palm tree. The turtle was staring at us with great distrust.

"What are you doing here?" he said.

"Today was the day."

There was a pause.

Pa mussed my hair.

"I know."

I didn't say anything.

"You okay, there, champ?"

"I'm good."

"You don't look good."

"I'm all right."

"Oye, cabron, I know you. It's okay to feel bad."

"Do you feel bad?"

He smacked me on the back of the head.

"I never feel bad."

I looked up. Hair pomade had made his graying crew cut stick
up like a small porcupine was sitting on his scalp. He lit a smoke
and coughed and adjusted his magical copper bracelet and boiled
water in a pan for some of his instant Café Combate.

"Well?" he said.

I hung my head.

"I miss her," I said.

I didn't want to say so. I didn't want to show him how weak
I was. But worse, I didn't want to say something that made him
show how weak he was.

His spoon in his cup made a meditative *tinka-tinka-tinka* sound as he stirred in his instant.

"Yeah," he said, and walked out of the kitchen.

I thought that was it. I heard him in his room slamming drawers. I heard the shower run. The turtle pulled his head into his shell and refused to look at me. I rinsed out my bowl and stuck it in the drainer and stood at the kitchen window staring at the alley like Ma would show up, and I kept thinking that I wanted to tell Marlene and Roxanne all about it, and that thought made me feel sadder.

When Pa came back to the kitchen, he was all dressed up in his bread-truck uniform. He was even wearing his black ripple-sole work shoes. I knew he hated them—they hurt his feet and turned them paper white, made his toes peel.

"You ready?" he said.

"Ready for what, Papa?"

"Work, Mijo. We going to work."

"For reals?"

"Stop talking like a pachuco," he said. "You can't just stay home from school and watch TV all day. I need you on the truck. I'm going to need you to pull the string for the train whistles today."

He winked and opened the back door.

I didn't know the world was so big. It had pretty much been the walk to and from school, the alley, and some car trips to stores like Kresge's down National, which we had been going to that day when the Ford got smashed. Ma, who did take the bus, took me to the zoo one time, took me to downtown, where we walked all day looking at the boats down on the harbor.

One time, Pa took me to a bowling alley, and we went to the

Big Sky Drive-In when we had the car. He liked cowboy movies. But today, Pa was like some kind of astronaut in his espider-truck, roaming in and out of neighborhoods I had never seen and never dared imagine.

We rolled down to National City and into Chula Vista, into Pinoy-town and all the way out to Lemon Grove. He had an AM radio in there, and it was all Phil Rizzuto yapping about sports, and "The Old Redhead" Arthur Godfrey mumbling with people about things I didn't care about. There was no way Pa was going to tune it to KCBQ because he was never going to allow the Beatles into his troka. "Los Beh-At-Less," he called them in his transitional Spanglish. "What kind of men?" he'd mutter if their songs ever came on any radio. "What kind of men?"

I stared out the window at apartments sadder than ours, and little pale houses with hedges and humpbacked cars and bikes. I was counting bikes.

"Sit on the dollar pouch so nobody steals it," he said.

Our first stop was in a block of run-down apartments with couches on the dead lawns and a dead car, with its trunk open, left abandoned at the curb. Pa leaned away from the wheel as he braked. "Pull," he said. I leaned across the barrel of his chest and grabbed the dangling lanyard. "Two tugs. Just two." I did it. We were a cartoon choo-choo for one moment: *woot-woot*! He set the parking brake and turned off the engine and said, "Hang on to my dollars." He hopped out.

I got out on my side and found little kids already at the back doors and moms hurrying out of their apartments in shorts and flip-flops and everybody yelling "Donut man!" and "Mr. Garcia!" And Pa stood there and nodded at them all. He was the King of

Bread, and his subjects loved him. It almost knocked me out of my shoes.

Block after block, we sounded our whistle, and mothers and grandmothers came out. Some ran. Children everywhere. And they touched my father. I saw the hands. Women touched him carefully, as if he might evaporate if they grabbed too hard. And children roughed him up, tugged at him, leaned on his hips and craned to see in the sweet drawers and yelled "Gimme a donut, mister! Gimme a cookie! I wan' some pie!" Brown kids and Black kids and white kids all together, like we weren't supposed to stay on our own blocks.

And Pa, this unknown being, this regal creature, laughing and nodding as women made confessions and pointed and often only paid him fifty cents or a few dimes for a loaf or a cake, and some of them gave him scrawled notes of promise that he handed me for the dollar bag, and I saw the phone numbers. Those women had special smiles for him. And he tipped his cap to them as if they were ladies of the royal court.

By the end of the day, I was exhausted.

He whistled along to a Bert Kaempfert song on his radio. I hated Bert Kaempfert. I didn't know how I felt about my dad because I didn't know my dad was this particular dad. He would never be that old dad again.

"You did good today, Mijo."

"Thanks, Pa."

"Did you like it?"

"Yeah."

"You worked hard. Like un hombre." He pointed to the zipped-up dollar bag. "Take out ten bucks."

"What?"

"A man gets paid for his work."

Beam me up, Marlene.

"What can I spend it on?"

He did the shrug—both shoulders this time. He didn't close his eyes because he was driving. But he hung out his lip and tipped his head.

"Up to you, Big Man," he said.

We got to the alley and he let me out to unlock the garage.

"Chocolate or glaze?" he said when he'd parked.

"Chocolate."

He opened the back door and got out two.

"That's a good idea. I like them, too, Mijo."

As we walked up the alley to our back door, he put his hand on my shoulder.

"It's gonna be okay," he said. "Todo bueno."

He got out his key and unlocked the door and stopped me before I went in.

"Tomorrow," he said. "I call you in sick. I think we need to go to the zoo. I never been. I know your Mama took you there one time, yeah? I don't want to get lost. Will you show me the way?"

And we closed the door and locked it and put two turkey-and-gravy dinners in the oven and he gave me a sip of his Thunderbird. All those IOUs? Most of them could never be paid. It would force him out of business in a year. He'd finally get to that bowling alley he wanted to work at, cleaning toilets.

I watched him fall asleep in his chair, and I took the lit cigarette out from between his fingers and sat at his feet, hoping our phone would ring just one more time.

◆ ◆ ◆ **FROM THE AUTHOR** ◆ ◆ ◆

"The King of Bread" was inspired by my own boyhood in the Logan Heights barrio of San Diego. The local Helms Bakery sent delivery trucks into neighborhoods every week and, like milkmen, those friendly drivers had superhero status among the women and kids. Fresh loaves of bread, yes, but the kids mobbed the trucks for donuts and cakes while the women were happy to see a friendly face. My father was one of those drivers and, though he eventually went bankrupt because of all the IOUs he took on his route and the free donuts he gave to the kids, some of my most cherished memories of that time and that place are of the smells and presence of that truck. That and my mother's heroic safaris taking me downtown to look at the parakeets and goldfish at Woolworths. We did not have the immigration problems in this story, but inspired by many of those stories of today, it gave me a way to resurrect so many things that are now gone.

GOODBYE TO THE ROAD NOT TAKEN

◆ A. M. HOMES ◆

"**M**eet me by the Fish'r King."

"Where?"

"Near the deli that closed, it's near the place we used to go."

"The first place or the second place?"

"It depends how you define it. What will you be wearing?" he asks.

"It's not that kind of meeting," she says. "If you're not on one corner you'll be on the other. Even from across the street, I'll see you. It's not like I don't know who you are."

"I'll have an umbrella," he says. "These days I always have an umbrella, I like to be prepared. And I've discovered it has many uses—almost like one of those utility tools, like a pocket-knife."

◆ ◆ ◆

Two days pass.

"So here we are," he says. "Imagine that, me bumping into you, here on this corner where in the past we spent so much time waiting for the lights to change."

"You didn't bump into me, we made a time to meet so I could give you your mail. Why do you need to turn a fact into fiction?"

He shrugs. "Polite conversation?"

"And by the way, why this corner and not the usual?"

"Oh," he says, knowing exactly what she is talking about. "I don't go there anymore." His tone implies that whatever happened there was so bad that he hasn't shaken it off.

"What do you mean you don't go there anymore, that was your place, you went there every day, it was like a religious event—" She could go on but he cuts her off.

"I got into a fight with the guy."

"A fight? You don't fight with anyone. What was it about?"

"Who was next in line."

"And like that you just stopped going?"

"I did," he says proudly. "He let someone cut the line. So I stopped going. I wanted to show myself that I can be definitive, that I can stick to something." A moment passes. "You seem upset."

"It's a little frightening," she says. "The idea of you, a little . . . hamantaschen, getting into a fight." She pauses. "I'm sorry if that sounded anti-Semitic."

"When one Jew insults another it's not antisemitism, it's self-hatred."

"Half-Jew," she says, as if that makes it better or worse. "I just can't imagine you getting into a fight. Who was it who thought he was in front of you?"

"A woman with a stroller." He pauses. "Her stroller was in front of me, but she wasn't. She wasn't even with the stroller, nowhere near. She was going up and down looking in the cases, and I was standing there, stuck, trapped, trying to entertain . . ." He pauses again. ". . . the inhabitant."

"You mean the baby?"

"I mean the inhabitant, a blob of flesh, with an enormous bobblehead."

"Babies have big heads."

"It didn't move, but its eyes kept rolling around—trying to get a read on me. It was sucking its bottle, totally self-satisfied, like everything in life came so easily, so naturally. It made me crazy."

"You were jealous of the baby's contentment?"

"His eyes were enormous, like the heads of octopi."

"Really?"

"It felt that way."

"Then what?"

"'Who's next?' the guy called out. 'I am,' I said, raising my hand. 'I'm next.' 'I'll have a half pound of nova,' the woman with the baby says from the other side of the room. The guy looks at her. 'Half pound?' 'I would do more,' she says, 'but it's so expensive.' 'It's not your turn,' I say. 'You're not next.' She doesn't even look at me. 'It's not all about you,' I say. I may or may not have added another word, a word that would not be a good word, I just can't remember if I said it out loud or just in my head."

"What was the word?"

He hesitates. "The *B* word."

"Ummm. Well, at least it wasn't the *C* word."

"The guy just looks at me. Maybe it was the word. Maybe I actually said the word, I have no idea. . . . 'Anything else?' the guy says to her as he's wrapping the fish. 'Is the macaroni salad house made?' she asks. And then I lost it. 'Her stroller is parked here, parked and unattended, that does not equal a place in line. It is a fire hazard,' I shouted. 'Foul ball, on the six and ten.' She stares at me. 'Oh my god,' she says. 'Will you just stop.' Her voice is more grating than horseradish on a blade. And now the guy behind the counter has something on his finger—something kind of yellow and shiny. He leans forward, and like magic, the octopi pulls his bottle out of his mouth, and the thick finger goes in. 'A little something for the baby.' 'What was that?' the woman screams, still on the other side of the store. 'Butter,' the guy says. 'My mother used to give it to me like that, a little bit on her finger. She'd say, "I'm going to butter you up."' 'Is it organic?' the woman asks, panicked. 'Are your hands clean?' The big man wipes his hands on his apron. 'It's New York,' he says. Everyone in the store is now staring. I turn quickly and try to get out of there. My shoe gets hooked on the stroller because of course it's not a regular stroller, it's a massive thing, a stroller the size of a Buick. And it's been pimped out, it has enormous tires like it's also a dirt bike, and my foot gets stuck in the hole of this fucking all-terrain tire, and I'm still trying to walk forward, and everything is going haywire. All I want is to get out of there, and the woman comes over and she's hitting me with the nova all wrapped up and telling me to stop touching her child, who, of course, I'm not touching. But the stroller is tipping over, and it looks like I'm kicking it, but of course I'm not kicking it, I'm just moving my foot back and forth trying to get free. It was awful, beyond awful."

"Did the octopi fall out of the stroller?"

"The octopi was fine, the stroller tipped, but he was entirely strapped in, never knew what happened, the thing even had a roll bar. He never even let go of his bottle, just clutched it the whole way over."

"Amazing that no one was injured," she says.

"I was injured. I did something to my knee. I barely got out of there alive—I probably need physical therapy."

"That might be the least of it," she says. There's a pause. "It doesn't sound like you," she says. "You don't really have what I'd call a temper."

A yellow cab comes around the corner, cutting in too close. He bangs on the hood with the handle of his umbrella. "Butt fucker," he calls out.

"Butt fucker?"

"It's all I could think of, I had the butter on my mind. Budder fucker." A long silence between them. "Anyway, it's nice we always agreed about children, we still have that in common—not liking children," he says.

"I don't not like children," she says. "I am a teacher, after all. I teach children."

"That's a double negative," he says. "Grammatically incorrect and you didn't want any of your own."

"That's right," she says.

"It's unusual, isn't it," he says, "for a woman not to want children?"

"I don't know," she says. "I suspect a lot of women feel that way but are loathe to say anything."

"It goes against nature," he says.

"Or maybe it doesn't," she says. "Maybe in nature not every woman is a mother, maybe some of them do other things. . . ."

"Like what?"

"Run countries," she says. And then there is a silence. "I wonder why men are so interested in the choices women make?"

He shrugs. "We get nervous that when we get up to go take a leak or something, your people will take over. We want to keep what's ours."

"You mean what you took from others, like land from Native Americans, people from Africa, money, power, all that stuff?"

He rolls his eyes.

"You look like an octopi," she says. A moment passes. "Are you still meditating?

"I quit," he says. "Turns out I hate sitting still. But I did discover that I like hitting things. I started playing golf, but then did something to my back, so now I just punch things—I bought a bag, a punching bag. When I punch it, things come out."

"What kind of things? Feathers? Stuffing?"

"Feelings I've been sitting on for years. I slam my hand into the bag and thoughts pop into my head, like revelations. Remember when the shrink asked what would happen if I wasn't angry anymore—if I could stand being happy?"

"Is that why you left?" she asks. "You were too happy? I thought there were other things, problems you didn't want to deal with."

He scowls at her.

She says, "If you're interested in what it was like for me, I can say that I realized that you loved your friend Matt more than me."

"It's not true—I don't love Matt, I tolerate Matt, the same as you tolerate me."

"Some call that love. Anyway. When my father died you said you had to go to a ball game with Mat."

"The man was dead, it wasn't going to change anything, and the Yankees were playing the Red Sox. It was the final game, you can't lie about that. You can't go back and get that game later. You, I knew, would still be home, on the sofa feeling sad. So what did I really miss?"

"Being with me in my time of need," she says.

He shrugs. "I don't like conflict."

"You don't like not getting your way—or acting like an asshole and then being held accountable."

"I don't like feeling guilty when I don't have to," he says.

"It's very selfish," she says.

"It has nothing to do with you," he says. "That should be a comfort."

"It's not. That's the selfish part—you didn't think about me, about what it would mean to me."

"Are you still talking about the ball game or the bigger questions?"

She makes a face.

"I left," he says. "It was a matter of life and death."

"Like the baseball game?"

"How much more serious could it get?"

"There's always something," she says. "Something more, something worse. Something to look forward to, something larger than oneself. It's too bad you're like this."

It's too bad you're like this. His lips repeat her words but no sound comes out.

"I think this is what your therapist meant when she wanted to know if I'd find your anxiety overwhelming," she says. "At the time I was surprised by the question, I hardly knew you. But I've come to understand that your anxiety is so important to you that you can't live without it."

He nods. "Who would I be without worry?" They walk a little farther. "You are too perfect," he says.

"That is so you. You are blaming me for your problems, I am not perfect."

"To me you are perfect, it drove me crazy."

"Your problems aren't about me," she says.

"No," he says, "but I kept lowering my expectations."

"Of me?" she asks, increasingly agitated.

"No, of myself," he says. "You were fine, happy, satisfied, every-thing was going along as planned—"

"I thought it was," she says.

"Exactly," he says.

"Exactly what?" she says.

"You know what," he says. "In the end it is you. You have an abil-ity that I don't. You can shelter yourself, you can elude detection—you can hide your feelings. I can't. I can't protect myself, so I gave up on all that and am hurling myself into all kinds of things."

"What kinds of things?"

"Well, women, for one."

"You should know better than to tell me that."

"We're friends."

"I'm your ex," she says. "It's too soon. You are such an ass."

He smiles.

"I wouldn't smile if I were you," she says.

"Why not?"

"You've got poppy seeds in your teeth."

"I can't help but smile. I like it when you say I'm an ass. I was so good for so long, and now, I just listen to you, calling me an ass, telling me I have poppy seeds. It's great," he says. And then he makes a sucking-swishing sound like he's suddenly become a dentist's office or a water pick. He shows her his teeth again: "Poppy?"

"You are an ass."

"Are you seeing anyone?" he asks.

"Who would I see?"

"Men, I assume, although at your age, I've known a lot of women who switched—they said there were better pickings on the other side. The men of this age either didn't want a woman their own age—or were bitter like escarole and came with too much baggage."

"I'm not seeing anyone," she says. "I am enjoying my time alone, spreading out in the bed, leaving books and remotes and sometimes even snacks right there next to me."

He makes a face. "I can hear it right now—the crinkling, little packages of oyster crackers."

"Sometimes I spend hours in bed, just reading and eating. I make a cheese plate for myself."

"All the crumbs," he says, "like little sharp pebbles."

"Olives. Cornichon fig paste."

"And rodents," he says. "Rodents could come into the bed looking for leftovers."

"A nice cold glass of Grüner, a good book," she says. "And then if I doze off, it's still all right there—next to me, it doesn't move. Sometimes when I'm only half awake, I think it's you."

"I'm a tray in the bed?"

"A cheese board, solid, unmoving. You always slept so soundly. I never understood how such a fundamentally disturbed person could sleep so well."

"Whatever is on my mind, I let out during the day, like off-gassing."

"Venting is what they call it."

"I am well vented," he says.

"You're toxic," she says. "Your venting spills into the air, and whoever is nearby is a secondhand smoker taking it on."

A long silence passes.

"We used to have more in common," he says. "There was always something suspect about you—a little too Upper East Side; when Russ and Daughters came uptown it rekindled my hope, but life is not a knish," he says.

"We went to couples' therapy, but whether it was upstate, North Fork, or God forbid a weekend in the Hamptons, nothing was right for you," she says.

"Black flies. Bloodsucking ticks! I wanted an apartment in Paris. Is that so bad? I'm not a person who does well in nature. I thrive in a city. I need carbon monoxide in order to feel like myself."

A woman walking by overhears him and laughs.

"What else?" he says.

"Bruce and Emily," she says. Bruce and Emily, the couple who also had no children. At a certain point it came down to that, people without children don't spend time with people with children—the landscape changes.

"What about Bruce and Emily?" he asks.

"You didn't hear?" she says.

"Hear what?"

"Kaput."

"Divorced?"

"Dead."

"What are you talking about?" he says.

"Car accident upstate."

"When?"

"Three weeks ago. How could you not know?"

"No one told me," he says. "Who was driving?"

"Only you would want to know that."

"It seems natural."

"No one was driving. The car was on autopilot and didn't see the deer leaping across the road. Three deer, the car hit them all like dominos."

"Were there any survivors?"

"The cat. He was in the back seat in his carrier. The carrier was in the rear wheel well, so Bruce took the brunt of the impact."

"What happens to the cat now?"

"He's gone to live with her sister."

"The lesbian?"

"Yes."

"I bet she already . . ."

"Yes," she says, anticipating what he's going to say—*cats*.

He shrugs. "You can't make it up."

"You don't have to," she says. A pause; she reaches into her bag. "Before I forget . . ."

He immediately starts making moves on the sidewalk, bobbing and weaving, trying to dance away.

"What are you doing?" she asks.

It's like he's playing a weird game, like he's one of those inflatable things outside a car wash, where the arms blow this way and that.

"Seriously? What are you doing? That's the question to be asking here? Are you serving me with papers, suing me for all I haven't got?"

She looks at him as if to ask, *Are you out of your mind?* "You got mail," she says. "It's from your college alumni association."

"They're always the last to know," he says.

"I think it's a copy of the talk you gave in January. The copy you asked for; you like a copy of everything you say. After all," she says, "you are the man who starts every day by writing his own obituary."

"It's not my obituary, it's my biography," he says.

"That's what you say now, but you used to call it something else."

"I like to keep it fresh," he says. "It's all about the road not taken."

"I don't follow."

He pauses. "Well, for example, I went with you and not that other woman."

"Joan?" she asks.

"I met you both on the same day."

"Joan had a prosthetic leg."

"So?" he says.

"And was missing an arm," she says.

"You're being rude."

"And Joan couldn't speak," she says.

"If you recall, we met at an event, a fundraiser for Joan, who had been hit by a bus. She was wearing a sign around her neck, I'M JOAN . . ."

"It wasn't a sign, it was a shirt. She was wearing a T-shirt that I made for her. It said 'I'M JOAN AND I WAS HIT BY A BUS.' And she had little cards that she gave out with her good hand—that said THANK YOU."

"Everything I say, you twist it and make me feel like an ass," he says.

"I can't make you feel like an ass—that's your own thing, and by the way Joan was a brilliant violinist."

"You just said was, not is. Did something happen to Joan?"

"Something more than getting hit by a bus and losing an arm and a leg and the power of speech?"

He looks at her, waiting for more. "Is Joan all right?"

"How can you ask that question?"

"What do you mean? I'm concerned."

"You're nearly hysterical. A minute ago you said it was Joan or me, and now you're so worried about Joan. It sounds as though you have regrets."

"It wasn't an either-or. Joan or you. 'Two roads diverged in a yellow wood, / And sorry I could not travel both.'"

"That's disgusting," she says.

"What?"

"A yellow wood, it's racist."

"I don't get it."

"Joan is Chinese, a yellow wood is a reference to her being Chinese."

"It's not my line," he says. "It's Robert Frost."

"You have a way of worming out of everything," she says. "And by the way, Joan is fine. She hooked up with her physical therapist and they're running marathons, she got a blade foot and a robotic arm, she's practically bionic. And she has her own cooking show: *Everybody Loves Joan.*"

"How can she have a cooking show without speaking?"

"Subtitles."

"Well, Joan is very nice, not edgy, not complex, she was always measured and kind," he says.

"How well did you know her?"

"Well enough to describe her like a bottle of wine."

"I had the impression that you were meeting her for the first time at that benefit."

"Oh, no," he says. "I met her before. We had a blind date a few weeks before the accident. I went to her concert and then out for a drink."

"What made it a blind date?"

"She didn't know I was there, there were other people."

"So it was more like an audition for a date?"

"No, it was a date, she and I talked about it on the phone after."

"Sounds one-sided."

"She was very private. It was actually the only time we ever spoke—the accident happened soon after."

"Have you seen Joan since the accident or perhaps traded texts?"

"No," he says. "I met you and that was all she wrote."

Another taxi turns the corner a little too close, splashing his ankles. "Get out of the street," she says. "You would think what happened to Joan was sobering, would keep you out of traffic."

"What happened when the bus hit her?" he asks.

"She was looking the other way, she didn't see it coming."

"Maybe it's better that way—blindsided."

"I don't think it's ever good," she says.

At the next corner, he hesitates. The phrase "images from possible futures flicker past" runs through his mind.

"What are you doing?" she asks, sensing his distraction.

"Lamenting what might have been," he says. "'Two roads diverged in a wood, and I— / I took the one less traveled by, / And that has made all the difference.'"

"I wish I understood you," she says. "I used to think I did, and now I have no idea."

"It doesn't matter," he says. It is starting to rain. At the next corner he stops to open his umbrella. They have clearly come to an end. He turns to her. "Goodbye," he says. "Goodbye to the 'Road Not Taken.'"

◆ ◆ ◆   **FROM THE AUTHOR**   ◆ ◆ ◆

The seed came from the desire to write something New York–centric set in the neighborhood around Symphony Space. The title comes from Robert Frost's poem and spins off from my late-in-life discovery that in fact this poem was originally written as a joke for his friend, the poet Edward Thomas. The poem, traditionally thought of as deep and philosophical, is also a joke and it is at that intersection of the existential and the comedic where my story is located. Also, the ideas of ambivalence and absurdity are two qualities essential to being a successful/functional New Yorker. A true New Yorker embraces the absurd and learns to juggle/tolerate ambivalence in all things: relationships, children, marriage, happiness itself. The true New Yorker is both irritable and joyous—I think of it as holding a sandpaper heart.

THE DOUBLE LIFE OF THE COCKROACH'S WIFE

—◆—

◆ HELEN PHILLIPS ◆

Truth be told, she felt honored by the cockroach's attentions. He explored the room with a polite urgency so unlike the disappointing indifference of their friends. It was he who paused before the doors of the closet they had assembled themselves; it was he who clambered up the canvas box for storing shoes, her elegant yet affordable solution to make the most of the bedroom's limited space.

But all of this is not to diminish the perturbing sound of his many legs (how many?) on the wooden floorboards, a sound far louder than it ought to have been; nor to diminish the horror she experienced upon hearing this sound, which preceded him out of the recently scrubbed bathroom, a horror that sent her up into the swivel chair at her small desk in the corner of the bedroom, where she perched, clenching her knees, swiveling slightly, staring at him.

He came down off the elegant yet affordable solution and turned his attention to the bed. His admiration was apparent in his silence; he stood there facing it, his little feet or claws or whatever they were no longer clicking against the floor.

What drove her to reach for her phone was the racket of those many feet when he climbed up the raincoat that somebody had left dangling off the side of the bed. It was a dry and ominous sound, the first sound on the surface of the earth after the stunned silence following apocalypse.

"There's this enormous cockroach in our bedroom," she whispered without saying hello.

"An enormous gold broach?" he said.

"An enormous cockroach," she said.

"An enormous cock roast?" he said. "Oh dear."

"You are not funny," she said.

"What doesn't kill you makes you stronger," he said. "Why are you whispering?"

"I'm having this feeling. I'm up on the chair."

"What feeling?" he said. "It's just a creature, living its life, like anyone."

"I think it's a boy," she said, and hung up.

The cockroach moved across the green bedspread toward the tomato-colored throw pillows. There was something ponderous in his pace, as though the richness of the colors was not lost on him.

She released her knees and tried to think of the cockroach as merely a small arrangement of molecules, and herself as merely a much larger arrangement of many more molecules. Here they were, just two arrangements of molecules in one room. If his molecules were arranged slightly differently—into a rosebud, say, or a necklace—they wouldn't bother her in the least; they might even bring her pleasure.

She minimized the Flood Hazard Mapper on her computer— the website that had, moments earlier, informed her that this hard-won apartment was located in the city's highest-risk flooding area—so she could google "how to kill a cockroach."

The cockroach was off the bed and making his noise across the floor, toward her desk. She brought her legs up again to safety.

"I commend the choices you've made," the cockroach said, his phrase erudite, his voice monstrous. "Modern, yet warm."

Because he was the first to truly appreciate the apartment—this lemon of theirs, this red-zone home—gratitude flared within her.

He trundled over the computer cord toward the laundry heap. Only yesterday had she finally removed from that corner the mess of cardboard boxes and bubble mailers, pesky reminders of all the big and little things they had felt compelled to buy, the great waste pile of their move.

The cockroach's legs going tsk, tsk, tsk.

"I have never seen such an attractive laundry hamper," the cockroach said.

It was an attractive laundry hamper, but his voice sent an uncontrollable shiver through her. Ashamed by this physical manifestation of her disgust, she studied the cockroach for his reaction; perhaps he hadn't noticed.

"So," she said, extra courteously, "you have an interest in furniture?"

The cockroach gave a low, almost sexy laugh and mounted a pair of dirty underwear.

"Sometimes I can hardly stand the sight of your kind either," the cockroach said, disappearing into the laundry.

"You didn't kill it?" everyone said. "'La cucaracha, la cucaracha,'" her sister sang into the phone. "It's probably pregnant," her mother informed her, returning yet again to the Theme of the Year, fertility and the lack thereof, "and about to have a hundred baby cockroaches in your drawer." Her coworkers had plenty of cockroach stories of their own (a cockroach in someone's kid's crib, an affair with an exterminator, various homemade anticockroach potions, cayenne pepper and peanut butter, etc.).

She was desperate to return home. Surely the cockroach was gone by now, long gone, vanished back into the bathroom pipes, never to be seen again.

It's a fragile thing, a new home, the first place you live after something bad has happened to you.

She was nervous, her fingers abuzz, as she turned the key, flicked the light, examined the bedroom. She looked beneath the sinks and pawed through the laundry in the bedroom. Cockroachless.

What a tranquil, empty home it was.

But when she stepped out of the bedroom, there he was, on the table in the dining nook, leaning against the wineglass she had recently filled with pinot grigio.

She sank into one of the dining chairs, a cheap and unsteady version of a midcentury chair. He stepped away from the wineglass and stood on the table, small yet hulking, watching her. His face defied description. She almost lost the desire to drink.

"I know you're not poisonous," she said, gulping wine, "but you look poisonous to me."

"We both know who's poisonous," he said.

She felt his eyes and antennae examining her, felt them as though they were leaving traces of iridescent goo on her skin. She ran over to the television and turned it on, abandoning him.

He crawled down the leg of the table and across the room and up the leg of the coffee table.

"Three hundred and twenty million years," the cockroach said.

"Three hundred and twenty million years what?" she said.

"And counting," the cockroach said.

In the dimness, the light from the television glazed his body. When she squinted her eyes during a Coca-Cola commercial, she had the illusion that there were rubies lodged in his back.

He laughed frequently at the television. She didn't understand what was so funny about a Lexus curving around a seaside highway. Still, it resembled companionship (where was he, anyway?), until every so often she got revolted all over again.

"I can go a month without food," the cockroach said.

"Wow," she said.

The last time she had felt this nauseated was when that life slipped away from her, slid out of her, the red and unbearable sight in the toilet.

She woke with a start on the couch, a movie rolling into the final credits, the cockroach watching her from the coffee table.

"Have you been watching me this whole time?" she said.

"I'll always be by your side," the cockroach said.

"You make me feel like a stranger here," she said, "as though this is your home rather than mine."

"I can live on the glue from the back of postage stamps," the cockroach said.

"So what? So you could survive in a post office?" she said rudely.

But what it really was was envy.

The next one to wake her was him. It was 3:37 in the morning. The coffee table was empty. She was still on the couch. He was drunk.

"How long have cockroaches been around?" she said.

"How long have covered bridges been around?" he said.

Her body felt too soft, her feet asleep.

"Please," she said.

"Before everything," he said, "after everything."

Her eyes blurry.

"I'm dying," he said. "I'm dying of thirst."

What a hard thing it is, for a body or a planet to sustain life.

He went to the kitchen to get water but what he got was milk.

"You hate milk," she said.

"This is water," he said.

She ran over and grabbed the milk out of his hands.

The kitchen was small, barely room enough for their two bodies.

He pulled the milk away from her and drank it.

"Ouch," he said, spilling milk on the counter.

It was then that she noticed the box of Raid cockroach balls.

"Water," he said, heading toward the front door as though the water he desired was out there somewhere.

She threw the Raid in the trash.

She went over to him. She cupped his elbow. She led him back into the kitchen. She filled three glasses of water and lined them up on the counter.

He drank.

It was like they had been cursed, red in toilet, rise of tides, but she didn't know what they had ever done wrong beyond what anyone ever does wrong.

"I can't make it," she said. "I can't make it through this. I can't make it."

Even though he was terribly drunk, somehow he managed to say the right thing.

And when he leaned back against the wall, holding her, and his shoulder turned off the light, he didn't bother to turn it back on.

And when the cockroach crawled over her bare feet in the dark, she didn't flinch.

◆ ◆ ◆ **FROM THE AUTHOR** ◆ ◆ ◆

Cockroaches are, of course, de rigueur in plenty of New York apartments. But the first time I ever had one such intruder, the creature startled me with its lack of timidity. Though I outweighed it a thousandfold or more, it was the cockroach that ruled the room in our little standoff. To soothe myself in the aftermath, I did some research about cockroaches, and quickly found myself awed by the tenacity of their existence on Earth. They evolved around 300 million years ago. As per PestWorld.org, "A cockroach can live for a week without its head"; "A cockroach can hold its breath for 40 minutes"; "Cockroaches can live without food for one month." Perhaps there was something to be learned about survival from my uninvited guest. The protagonist of my story is in dire need of just such a lesson.

CANE AND ROSES: A MANIFESTO

◆ EDWIDGE DANTICAT ◆

don't need you to know who I am. Just what I'm about to do. You don't have to know where I was born, or where I live now, but maybe afterward you will. Or maybe you won't, because they might not find even a strand of my hair when this is all over. I suppose listing my grievances might rat me out. We all have grievances. We always did. We just have more ways of forcing you to listen now.

I'm not going to tell you where "here" is. For all you know I could be dictating this rather than writing it. Oh, does that give me away? If I'm writing, it must mean that I can read, unlike a big chunk of the people in this world, that other 90 percent, or close to seven hundred million, who don't eat every day. Anyway, say I'm pissed because I remember how hard it was to even make it "here." Say I remember the missed meals and the crusty eyes of the children who went to bed hungry and woke up even hungrier, and say I remember leaving the house just so I wouldn't have to watch them starve. Say I remember leaving for the day knowing full well I'm more likely to find death on the streets than food. Say one day I just kept going and never turned back because I couldn't look at those eyes anymore, and I couldn't listen to the growling bellies in the middle of the night, when the gunshots weren't drowning them out. Again, if I'm this person, and I'm not saying I am, I might be pissed because I crossed a desert where the sand wore my shoes down to threads, and the sand was starting to work on the soles of my feet when a truck came by and took me to the river, or the ocean, or around the walls, or barbed wire fence, or whatever barriers you have built. I might have barely been alive, dreaming of cane fires, when I ended up with my head scraping the boot of your official, who waited hours before offering me some water, because maybe he was wishing I'd die before becoming one more ward of the state, one more mouth to feed, one more wound to heal, one more body to find a bed for. Not even a bed, but a thin sheet full of holes, or a piece of plywood or cardboard. It would have been better for me to just die there, at his feet. At least all he'd have to do is throw me back into the ocean, or dig a hole in the sand to bury me with the bones of all those who'd died before. You can imagine why I might be pissed if, after making it through the hills, the mountains, the river, the ocean, the traffickers, you decide I should go back. Back to a home that no longer exists because everyone was killed while I was crossing deserts, rivers, and seas.

The actions I'm about to take are not going to give me my loved ones back. Both they and I might end up being just one line in the newspaper or a thirty-second mention on TV. Who would do something like this?, you'd ask yourself. And why? You'd have to go to profilers and other so-called experts to find out. I'll tell you this much: I'm not one of those people who imagines an afterlife. Whether you live one day, one year, a hundred and one years, I believe that one life is all you get. I think we're all like fireflies. Something inside makes us light up at times, then go dark, a complicated mix of oxygen and bioluminescent enzymes. I once wrote a school report about this. It's one of the things that got me interested in science. It might have been my first step into learning how to produce the device I'll soon be attaching to my chest. The light the firefly emits is cold; otherwise the firefly would set itself on fire. It's interesting how many useless things one can learn. If I'm captured, these useless things will be among my final words. Alive or dead, there's nothing left for me to say. Will some detailed profile of me end up soothing your pain? Would our *not* being alike comfort you? Maybe you'd end up telling yourself: I knew it! This is so typical of their kind. But what if I'm just like you? No matter who you think I am, you're wrong. You will never know me, this one miserable firefly. Malthus was right: premature death must, in some way or form, visit the human race. This is where we're all headed eventually, but where I'm headed soon. It's like when you throw a net in the ocean. Whatever gets caught can be eaten, even where there are rules demanding that you throw some of the smaller creatures back. I won't be throwing anything back. Small, large, they get caught, they get eaten. I'm sorry about that. I truly am, because my gripe is not with everyone. Not everyone mistreated or persecuted me or my family. Besides, when you cast an actual net in the ocean these days, you're just as likely to catch trash as fish. Have you seen that picture of the dead sperm whale with over two hundred plus pounds of trash in its stomach? There were miles of ropes inside that poor creature, plastic bottles, trash bags, gloves, fishing nets, straws. The damned whale exploded after it died. *Call me Ishmael.* And Jonah too. Imagine Jonah inside that whale. The poor fuck would end up smothered.

Maybe this is all making you think you can pin me down intellectually. There might have been someone in my past who did these types of things: studied fireflies, read Malthus and Melville, threw nets into the ocean, and attended Sunday school. Your concern right now, though, if you are reading this before the act is done, should not be where I've been, but where I'm going. There are a lot of places where like-minded people gather: churches, workplaces, government buildings, cafes, restaurants, stadiums, theaters, even hospitals, mental hospitals. Immigration offices too. I could go to a parade or some other large gathering. If you're reading this ahead of the act, will you be going to all of those places to try and find me? And how do you know there's not an army of us? I know what the word *army* evokes for you, in you. You've always had armies at your disposal. Now you have invisible weapons, drones for distant strikes. An elephant who stomps on a mouse doesn't deserve a medal, as my father used to say. Cowards! Some people will call me a coward too, but you're more cowardly than I am. What if your villages, your towns, your cities had been decimated? Yes, I do know some big words. Words that you have taught me, in your schools, in your workplaces.

I just want you to know how calm I'm feeling right now. It's the calmest I've been in some time. In the aftermath, if they manage to track me down, you better believe that some of the people who used to know me, when they talk to journalists, either for the papers, or for the TV news, or for some online outlet, or if they speak to detectives for the police investigation, whether in amazement or shock, they'll all be commenting on my calmness.

They'll also be embarrassed that they never caught on to what I am
planning to do. It just occurred to me that you might think that
this document was initially created (whether by voice or hand) in
the language in which you're reading it. Maybe it was, maybe it
wasn't. Do you believe in ghosts? I am a ghost, *damnatio memoriae*,
a condemnation of memory. Before this, I wouldn't have appeared
in any official accounts. Before this, the people who gave birth to
me were living under borrowed names. Before this act, I washed
dishes. I drove cabs. I worked in your gardens. I took care of your
sick. I watched over your children. I'm pulling your leg there. Of
course I'm not all of these people, but I can see how any of them
would be as pissed at you as I am. Don't worry, I'm not going to be
too much longer. This will end as abruptly as it began. I just don't
want to go without leaving anything behind. I'm already leaving
no one behind.

Listen though, I will tell you some of the things I did enjoy.
I loved going on tire swings with my father when I was a kid. I
loved watching my mother press flowers into a notebook she always
kept under her pillow. I have sometimes worn my hair in finger
waves, which kind of look like dreads. My mother did too. My
mother once tried to show me how to get out of a car gracefully in
a miniskirt. I haven't slept with anyone. The miniskirt lesson was
the closest Mama and I ever came to talking about sex. Sometimes
I'd walk in on Papa giving Mama a foot rub after they'd both
spent extra long hours at the hotel, where he was a janitor and she
was a maid. When I was a kid, I wanted a treehouse like the ones
some kids had on TV, an elaborate one with a porch and actual
steps leading to the ground. I couldn't have a treehouse living in
a tiny apartment in the middle of a city. Mama always said we
were like bare-root trees with no soil. She also said that if you cut

your roots, you die. My roots are dead because my parents were my roots. But I'm no condemnation of memory. I am Memory. I am the anthuriums and bougainvillea, hibiscus, and spider lilies, flattened inside my mother's notebook with her fingerprints trapped on the other side of the clear tape. I can't leave her notebook and her flowers behind for others to discard. I can't throw away her calligraphy-like handwriting documenting the names of those flowers and the dates on which Papa had given them to her. I can't bring myself to destroy all of this, or to leave it behind to be handled like evidence at a crime scene. Papa used to warn me not to simply look at the tip of his fingers while he was pointing to the stars. You are Memory. Our Memory. This is why we gave you this strange name, in this strange land, and in this new language, this name that always gets puzzled looks from everyone we meet. There you have it. How hard will it be to track down someone with my name? One day, I planned to go back to the farm where my parents met, the one Mama's family owned and where Papa was taking care of the cattle since he was a boy. Before the gangs came. That farm had chickens, goats, horses, and fresh air too. Before the gangs came. Before the gangs came. Before the gangs came.

The doctors are always telling me that fresh air can do wonders for me, even though they try to control my fresh air. What they can't control, try as they might, are what they call my episodes. All I know is that I'm not going back into anything that's like a prison anymore, even if they're promising to make me better. Now I know for sure I've given away too much, but it's never wrong to tell the truth. Even though that didn't work out so well for my parents. They confessed when your officials came. It was as if they'd been expecting that visit ever since they got here. I have read so much about this, not just in terms of planning what to do, what to wear, where to go, and what to carry, but I've also been researching a lot about the tools that will be used to interpret my actions. All you need to know is that I am the reason they crossed the rivers and desert to get here. I was born here, so I'm allowed to stay—at least for now—but after all these many years they were shipped back, and on the first night after they arrived, they were taken for ransom, for the kind of money neither I nor anyone else I know, had.

And . . . yes, I have heard—Mister/Madame Profiler—that actions like mine can be "socially contagious." This wouldn't be the first time that me and my people have been compared to a disease. I told you this would end as abruptly as it began. It did for them, for Mama and Papa. So no, in the end, I'm not going to do it after all. I went out and got all the tools and supplies. I still have everything. I just had to see how far I could go. I *needed* to see how far I would go. In the end, I can't. I can't do it. Not because I'm scared. Not because I'm afraid to die. It's just that it would mean erasing them, erasing us, wiping out their Memory. The thorn must be watered for the sake of the rose. These were their final words to me in that detention center. They said it together as if they'd been rehearsing it for years. The thorn must be watered, she said. For the sake of the rose, he added. I was too numb, too shocked, or too drugged to speak, but if I'd been able to put some words together, I would have reached for a different metaphor. Maybe something like, the weeds must be burnt for the sake of the cane. Both their childhoods were filled with cane fires. The way they told it, right before the harvest, a fire would be purposely started at the cane stalks, then the flames would be allowed to rise up to the outer leaves to scorch away the "trash." The smoke would leap above the flames, separating from them like spirits, soaring high above the fields, toward the sky. Without the fire, their cane could not be harvested. The cane fires had always been with them. The roses and thorns came much later to them. In this land. Just like I did. Still, in their minds, they were the thorns and I was the rose. But they were wrong. We were all the cane.

◆ ◆ ◆ **FROM THE AUTHOR** ◆ ◆ ◆

I have always been intrigued by manifestos, both the famous and not-so-famous kind. In recent history, with social media and the twenty-four-hour news cycle, manifestos have become a way for people to spew out their sometimes very dangerous ideas before committing horrors that we as a society will be revisiting for generations. This story is a manifesto of sorts and is written, or narrated, by someone who is contemplating carrying out a devastating act. I wanted to explore what that process might look like from the perspective of a person who feels deeply wronged and also feels justified in bringing pain to others. This is a story about someone who is used to living in the shadows, someone who would like to be known to the whole world but has no choice but to hide, someone who is accustomed to being unfairly stigmatized and categorized. This is also a story about the importance of memory when it's all we have left to treasure. I can't say any more because, like the narrator, I don't want to give too much away.

PERSEPHONE RIDES AT THE END OF DAYS

◆ CARMEN MARIA MACHADO ◆

Persephone rides in so many cabs. Some of them smell like stale cigarettes and some of them carry the body odor of all their passengers. Persephone cannot drive, and even if she could, she does not own a car, and even if she did, she would not drive it. Thrice neutered, she rides in so many cabs. She likes them. They are simultaneously real and unreal. They are physical objects that pass into and out of her consciousness many times a day, like few other things do. Coins, maybe.

She rides them drunk, drunk. She imagines herself clean. No, no, not clean, *clear*—and she imagines her stomach is a giant fishbowl full of the salty vodka martinis and olives floating, rolling like buoys tossed about in a storm, and anyone who cared to look would see it, which is to say, no one—and she is being transported to and fro and so quickly, uptown and downtown and midtown, and she pays with bills folded out like an offering of palm fronds, and she slides out of the cabs easily because she was barely in to begin with. Sometimes she cracks the window an inch, and the city air whistles in between the glass lip and the rubber one, and it drowns out everything. When she does this, she can smell exhaust, or hot dogs, or sometimes both, a muggy mix of salt and poison.

Mother says the fortune will be hers one day, all of the fields, all of them, right down to the golden chaff that has fallen in the dirt, even that will be hers, albeit scooped up in the hands of laborers, transferred to other laborers, sold for money on the open market, converted into currency, and deposited electronically into her bank account. But hers nonetheless. Persephone accepts this, though she knows she has not earned it. Her mother says, "Take this. Cash. Here, here," and Persephone takes it. She forgets how much she has. She finds hundred-dollar bills, washed and pressed, folded into jeans she hasn't worn for six months.

Her only friend is Aglaea. She has many friends, but Aglaea is her only real friend. Aglaea's father owns all sunflowers. And the sun, some say, but that is just a nasty tabloid rumor. Aglaea comes over almost every day, and she and Persephone go out to lunches. Many lunches. Persephone feels as if she is forever eating lunch.

They talk about names. They talk about names because Aglaea's father has so many wonderful varieties of sunflower under his charge. American Giant, Aztec Sun, Lemon Queen, Dwarf Sunspot, Ring of Fire, Velvet Queen. Persephone doesn't know as much about the wheat, though she knows there is a variety called Soft Red Winter Wheat, which makes her think of wine with mouthfeel, and cashmere, and blood on snow, all very nice things. But Aglaea is on a roll.

"I mean, my name means 'splendor,'" Aglaea says. "So I guess we're just a family of good namers. What about you? What does your name mean, again?" It is the afternoon. They are eating at a very upscale bistro where starched-shirted waiters hand-crisp the corners of their paninis with solid gold lighters.

Aglaea knows what Persephone's name means. She just wants Persephone to say it. Aglaea is Persephone's best friend, but she can be a bitch sometimes.

Maybe they should do a TV show together.

That night, Persephone takes a bath. She fills the tub too high; she gets in and rolls to her side, like she does when she is sleeping. It occurs to her that perhaps this is the way to sleep—in a tub full of hot water. Maybe there could be a device that constantly takes the temperature of the bath-bed and adds a little hot water when it gets too cold. She should invent that device, but she is too tired to get out of the tub and write it down.

She hears her mother's footsteps coming toward the bathroom. She hears them for several minutes. This wing's main corridor is very long. The door opens.

"Persephone?"

Persephone sloshes the water in acknowledgment. Her mother comes in. She folds a fluffy yellow towel in half, lays it over the side of the tub, and perches herself on it. She strokes Persephone's wet hair. "Whatcha doing, Poppy?"

Persephone looks up at her mother dully. She sloshes the water a little more.

"Bad day?"

"I think Aglaea hates me," Persephone says.

"I have an idea," her mother says. "What if you planned an

event. Like a party. And then you can invite whoever you want. It can be the social event of the year. Maybe you can make some new friends."

There is a voice on the other side of the door. "A call for you, ma'am."

Persephone's mother kisses her head. "Use the credit card. Let me know if you need any phone numbers."

Persephone watches her mother's retreating form, the way that her willowy body rocks when she walks, the golden sheet of hair moving with her. After that, Persephone practices light social conversation with herself. The questions echo back at her, somehow sharper than when they left her mouth.

Arion is Persephone's half brother. She has not seen him since they were kids and he kicked her in the leg and called her Perse-phony. He comes to dinner on a Thursday. He is no longer short. He is no longer whiny or covered in boils.

"Say something to your brother, Poppy," her mother says. Arion is her son from her fury days, as she calls them. Her wild youth. He is suspiciously handsome. His shoulders are broad and strung through with muscles. His hair looks like it was arranged on a wigmaker's form and snapped onto his head.

"I like your shirt," Persephone says, after a minute.

Arion begins to talk about the shirt at great length. Persephone looks down at her plate. She presses her fork into the mountain of risotto. The peas roll into the cream sauce that covers the tenderloin. She looks up when her mother says her name.

"Persephone is planning a party," her mother says. "Isn't that right, Poppy?"

"I love parties," Arion says. "What kind of party?"

She rolls her spoon into the peas. They avalanche into the cream. It's chaos, madness; it gives her an idea. "An apocalypse," she says. "The world is sort of overdue for one, honestly."

Arion's eyes widen. "I've never been to an apocalypse before."

"Well," says Persephone's mother brightly. "Why don't you include Arion in the planning? I bet he'd be good to . . ." She goes on talking to Arion, laughing like a girl. Persephone scowls, but no one notices.

Later, she decides to make up with Aglaea.

"I forgive you," she says over the phone. "Help me plan my party?"

"Were we fighting?" Aglaea says. "And yes."

Aglaea recruits some friends she met at rehab—four sisters.

"Their dad owns a bunch of churches," she says. The sisters don't look so good—skin strung over bone, blemishes glowing on their arms and mouths like roses, breath rattling in their rib cages like the wind whistling through a row of decrepit houses—and they are fighting with each other when everyone arrives. Aglaea and Persephone sit down and watch the sisters argue over who will take notes. As one of them punches another, Arion wanders in, tossing a football from hand to hand.

"Okay. Let's talk about decorations and food," Persephone says.

"Ooh! Ooh!" One of the sisters bounces up and down, her bony hand waving in the air, the fight for the legal pad forgotten. "We could make the room look like a war-torn landscape."

The victorious sister scratches this down. The others chime in.

"Like, we could destroy some of the tables and chairs."

"But not all of the tables and chairs."

"But not *all* of the tables and chairs, because people need to sit and we need to put the snacks somewhere."

"But the snacks could be rations. Dehydrated ice cream and meat and stuff."

"We could blow up the whole block."

"Half the city, even."

"Would we need enough rations for the city, then?"

"Just half."

Persephone looks down at her manicure. She notices Arion watching her from his folding chair, which he rests upon like a hulking Clydesdale. He scratches at the back of his hand. Something tingles inside of Persephone, like she has stuck her finger into her own belly button.

Persephone's mom invites her daughter to come visit the fields. "Bring Arion," she says from many miles away, her voice sliding melodiously through the wires like water. "Can you take the time off from planning your party?"

Arion has a yellow sports car, and when they blast down the highways, the corn bends toward them like so many attendants, and the soybean fields ripple, and Arion talks to Persephone, who does not listen but looks up and watches the clouds pucker and roll and the light spilling down through the cracks in between.

"—when it's done?"

Persephone looks around, having forgotten where she was.

"What?"

"Won't there be an after-party?"

Persephone closes her eyes. The car is purring; she feels warm. Arion pulls the car over. He kisses Persephone. She kisses him back. She takes his huge meaty hand and slides it under her shirt, under her bra, and he cups her breast like a baby bird. She mashes her fingers down over his and feels relief when he squeezes harder, kisses her neck.

At the fields, Persephone's mother is looking radiant. She is wearing a headscarf like Brigitte Bardot and has a woven basket under her arm. Persephone receives the forehead kiss. Her mother picks up a stalk of wheat and tickles it beneath Persephone's chin.

"Once upon a time, there was just a single seed." Her mother flings her arm out, gesturing to the endless expanse of field. "And now this. And you," she says, "once fit into a basket this big."

The day of the party, Persephone has no lunch. She takes a cab and gives the driver every bill she has on her person, which amounts to six hundred and forty-nine dollars and a nickel.

"Live large," she says. "You have until midnight."

"What?" the driver says, but she is already out of the car.

Aglaea is there, and the sisters, dressed in their finest. Arion comes, looking handsome and confused. Persephone is wearing a gold dress that drags on the floor behind her and gives her great cleavage. Her hair is tufted with wheat stalks. She checks on the decorations and the catering. The ballroom looks like a bomb-ravaged wasteland. Hors d'oeuvres mounted in tiny ration boxes encircle the burned rims of metal trays. The tables are surrounded by hastily erected metal shelters. The walls are bleak and part rubble. It looks hopeless.

"Perfect," Persephone says. "Let them in."

The guests enter. The sisters leave. They have work to do.

◆ ◆ ◆

Somehow, Persephone thought the world would be harder to dismantle. But it is the easiest thing she's ever done. The guests dance and sweat and spill the punch bowl. Earthquakes shake the room. Persephone's mother does not come to the party like she promised. Persephone's heart actually hurts. An apocalypse and she will never see her mother again. Her beautiful mother.

Arion asks Persephone to dance, and she refuses. He asks her if she wants to make out, and they do, beneath one of the tables. One of the terrified caterers is huddled under there, but he leaves when Arion sticks his tongue down Persephone's throat.

"Do you want to stay here?" Arion says, panting. "We can go back to my place."

"I can't abandon my own party," Persephone says, but she is already wet. The music is loud, but Persephone thinks that the building next door has possibly come down. Everyone screams, laughs. Persephone grabs Arion's collar.

"Okay, yes," she says. "Let's go."

Outside, the sky churns black. Persephone smells burning plastic. The horizon is rimmed with fire. At Arion's car, she jumps into the driver's seat. Arion slides in next to her.

"Do you know how to drive?" he asks.

"No," Persephone says, and turns the key.

◆ ◆ ◆ **FROM THE AUTHOR** ◆ ◆ ◆

I wish I could say that the origins of this story came from my love of Persephone or my long-standing obsession with apocalypse narratives. But the truth is one night I was in a cab heading back to my hotel, and I was drunk and felt like a fishbowl full of martinis and I rolled the window down and the air smelled like exhaust and hot dogs and everything felt sharp and clear and I felt weirdly and inexplicably alive. And just before I collapsed into my bed I jotted down those thoughts on the hotel stationery, which went into my wallet, which went into a file on my computer, which I read years later and thought: that might make an interesting opening to a story. So you see? Sometimes it's just the dumbest little things.

UNICORN ME

◆

◆ ELIZABETH CRANE ◆

I picture a unicorn. The meditation guide says to picture a glowing spiritual being, like the Buddha, or Mother Mary or whoever, and then to picture that being in a scenario that's troubling you. I picture the moment my husband told me he wanted to "investigate" with another woman, a textile artist we knew casually. It seems my husband had hoped to investigate and also be married to me, which is not an idea I'm personally into. I have always said people should configure their relationships in whatever way floats their boats. You wanna have six boats in your marriage, have at it. I want two. Two boats. This was always our agreement.

The glowing being is then supposed to say, I guess, spiritual things, or at least something your better self would say.

Unicorn me says pretty much the same things I said.

So either I have a failure of imagination for higher-level spiritual chat, or I am already a spiritual unicorn.

I mean, is unicorn me supposed to say *Bless you and keep you, dear investigator?*

The unicorn pulls a small glowing cube out from behind one of its wings and hands it to me. *See the gift*, meditation dude says. I can't see the gift inside the box at all, just something that looks like swirling smoke, or a cloud. *Now the spiritual being touches you gently to say goodbye*, and I giggle, because a unicorn raising a hoof to my shoulder to anoint me or whatever is very cartoony and not spiritual-seeming. The unicorn says, *You'll be fine*, and then floats off to—I dunno, some other divorcée's guided meditation.

You'll be fine is hardly an assurance I can grab on to. I cannot open the box, so I try shaking it, but it just makes the smoke-cloud swirl more, noiselessly.

I decide it might make me feel better to smash one of my husband's violins. He used to make violins. Now he investigates.

Unfortunately, I'm not a violin smasher, I'm someone who thinks about smashing violins. I've dabbled in smashing things, and it always feels utterly stupid and disappointing. I once got dumped the day before Valentine's Day, and I slammed the door and it bounced back and hit me in the forehead. Another time after a fight with my mom I threw a glass to the floor as hard as I could, and it bounced. That's my entire history of smashing. Yesterday I screamed *I don't want a divorce* in my house to no one, from a place down low in my core, sixteen *o*'s in divorce. But I stopped quickly because screaming is even more exhausting than crying.

Yesterday I bought a giant donut way overloaded with sprinkles. I'm old enough to know now that when I eat such a donut, I will begin to feel like garbage before I've even finished eating the donut, and so I stopped eating donuts long ago because I don't like to feel like garbage anymore. I mean, no one would probably ever say they like feeling like garbage, I'm just saying that these days I work to head it off at the pass, moving quickly from garbage-sighting to end result. But I'm coming to hate this quality in myself. When I met my husband, on paper he looked like all of those same romantic sprinkled donuts who went before: too young, so sad, violin maker. But off paper, he was kind and sweet, made me mix CDs, left me love notes, and he always showed up, and he looked at me that way you dream of being looked at, and we fell in love, and when I decided to marry him I had come to believe that he was not a sprinkled donut, that he was a nice bowl of blueberries. Part of me wants to be like my most favorite of well-written ragey literary antiheroes (the ones described as unlikable in book reviews written by men) and go royally screw some stuff up unconsciously, but I feel so irreversibly conscious and also I'm just tired. When I try to imagine running into my husband's girlfriend, the best I can muster is a hot stare, maybe a shaming headshake, and as always, I feel the hangover from this before I take the drink. I prevent this problem, in real life, by not going out. But hey, progress not perfection. In the past I've solved problems by moving to a different state. That's not off the table.

I try the guided meditation several more times. Trying to evolve spiritually has its benefits, though in my experience you don't reap them in the crap moments when you need them the most, but for the love of psychic unicorns, where is the release lever for this part of me? I want it out. One time the unicorn just says, *Dude*, gently, but with a hint of tough love, and again he gives me the cloud-filled box. Not wanting to be rude to my imaginary unicorn, I wait until he's gone to hurl the box out of my hands, and it lands in the driveway intact and as cloudy as it had been. I look to see if the box has a lid or something I missed, but it appears to be one perfectly sealed cube; you can't even see any miters, like it's an impossible thing. I grab the sledgehammer from the garage to smash it open.

This does not produce satisfying results. It produces no results. The box of clouds accepts the blow as though it were made of Jell-O, returning immediately to its solid form, clouds still swirling.

Freaking unicorn, I say, to no one, in my yard. *What. Is in. The box.*

The unicorn conveniently returns to offer his response. *What do you think is in the box?*

I think a cloud is in the box.

A cloud is in the box.

That's it. A cloud.

I'm not saying there's not also something else in the box. What do you want to be in the box?

I want my sweet, loving husband before this vixen came along in the box.

Second choice?

I want his hurt to be as bad as my hurt. Forever. Like mine.

You can't really know how awful he does or doesn't feel. Or even how you will feel, where forever is concerned.

Ugh, whatever, unicorn!

Third choice?

Clarity.

It's a box of clouds. Another choice?

Acceptance.

Ok, then acceptance is in the box.

If that's true, why not tell me that the first time I asked?

The unicorn shrugs, makes a sort of sorry-not-sorry face, but a unicorn shrug is extremely cute and somehow conveys a note of care. *I didn't sense you'd accept that answer.*

Ok then, if acceptance is in the box, how do I get it out?

Listen, I've given you all the information I'm allowed to right now. And now I have another thing to get to.

What thing does a unicorn have to get to?

There are other people in the world besides you.

Oof.

I toss the box of clouds into the trash.

Weeks later, I venture downtown to have lunch with a girlfriend. I haven't been downtown in months for fear of running into him/her/him and her together/anyone I know. Leaving the restaurant, we do see the girlfriend, a punch to my stomach. She's wearing what can only be one of her own works. It's made from heavy wool, so it might be called a sweater, but it doesn't resemble a body-shaped garment so much as an oversized ball of multicolored yarn, complete with a set of fat knitting needles holding together her hair, something you'd more likely see on the floor in the corner of an out-of-the-way art gallery with an audio box of a detached-sounding woman's voice narrating *unraveling, unraveling, unraveling* on a loop. I'm frozen for a moment, jaw clenched so tight I feel like I might crack my teeth. And then the ball of yarn and I lock eyes for some portion of a second, long enough for me to think she's about to charge me, but she doesn't, she spins in the other direction in her stupid ball of wool, trips over the loose strand of yarn hanging down, and stumbles a good six to ten feet in front of her, like in one of those viral videos where a model falls down the runway, before she rights herself by grabbing on to a street sign.

It happens against my will: I begin to laugh hysterically. It's confirmed: I am the horrible person. I am laughing at someone for tripping down the street. My friend is not laughing the way I am, but she is smiling. *Occasionally I believe in karma*, she says, *as it suits my needs*. I haven't laughed once since my husband went investigating.

I try the meditation one last time. Unicorn shows up, gives me the box again. It's still cloudy but at least I don't feel like smashing it anymore. I ask the unicorn when the weather in this box is going to change. *Is the weather in this box going to change?* Unicorn makes a joke about global warming, and says, *Weather always changes*.

◆ ◆ ◆ **FROM THE AUTHOR** ◆ ◆ ◆

Shortly after my husband moved out of our home, in my grief, someone suggested a guided meditation app in which I was to picture a spiritual being. Without going too far into my disbelief in otherworldly beings, the image of a unicorn kept coming up. Which, well, is a little too funny to work for me as a means of healing? But worked just fine as a short-story idea.

LESSONS WITH FATHER

◆━━━━◆━━━━◆

◆ JAI CHAKRABARTI ◆

I wanted to know something about my father's art, though by then he was already dying. His last days were as simply weaved as any of the days after my mother had passed, and I had come to his house to assume his care, which meant, as I remember it now, two things: cooking a lentil-and-tomato soup that would last him several meals and replenishing his supply of comics—*Tintin*, and another series that was surely inspired by Melville, because for years the same crew had been adrift at sea, searching for an island that would give them power and a reason for having devoted their lives to the search.

My father was a painter at a time when art was central to our country's fight for independence, and I supposed my own entry into music had as much to do with the communities of youth who'd barged into our flat at all hours; that sense always that my father, wild-haired and loose-tongued and smelling of his sandalwood cologne, and all the others—Satyendar Bose, Jatin Sanyal, Triveni Chatterjee—were knocking on the door and by their knocking alone would freedom be possible. I suppose I grew up with the sense that oppression was always temporary. By the time I entered school, my father's paintings had been displayed in London, New York, and Madrid, and India was a free country.

When I told him I wanted to learn painting, I had turned fifty. Behind me and ahead of me I could see the great repetition of my life. But what did he know of my unhappiness? He only said that I should stick to my music, that at this age there was no reason to learn anything difficult.

It takes courage to be angry at a dying man, especially if that man is your father, but I loved him well enough to be angry with him then. For days we were cold to each other. A week passed and I did not trim his fingernails, a ritual I knew he secretly enjoyed: the taking of his hands, the studying of the tremulous lifeline. At his age the nails had brittled, become glasslike, but still they grew like weeds. Were it not for my ministrations they'd turn into claws.

In response he stopped bringing me the paper, which he'd usually open to the cinema section, tolerating but never quite understanding my love of a good Bollywood number.

I explained all this to my husband. He appreciated my paintings. At least, he complimented them in as many ways as he knew how, which was not a great deal, but still, when learning something new, any encouragement will suffice. Ever since we'd given up trying to conceive, almost ten years ago, he'd encouraged me in areas great and small. Our childlessness brought out in him a desire to praise, in his way—to nurture.

The next week I told my father that if he didn't teach me, I would seek the help of his juniors (over the years, he'd apprenticed nearly a dozen painters, a couple of whom now held their own fame).

No, he finally said, let me.

I grew up in a country accustomed to death. It was no special privilege. So many of us witnessed riots, mothers dragged by their braids, skullcaps burned, so many heads lifted onto pyres and, with all the vigor of public ceremony, set to flame. Still, it is different when you see the slow unraveling. Today when I was drying him after his bath, my father handed me a tooth. It had come undone in the night, but he'd plied it in place for as long as he could, until finally he surrendered it into the warmth of my palm; a bit of his gum tissue still stuck to the dulled enamel.

We began our lessons on a Thursday afternoon. I made him his milk tea. I brought out a couple of my own brushes—using his would have felt too familiar—and set the colors in a row. A few examples of my drawings, landscapes mostly, I put on display.

He reviewed my landscapes, studied them with that expression he wore when touring the National Museum, an expression that suggested indifference, amusement, and alternately, a deep curiosity. So, it was impossible to know what he thought of any piece of art, including mine.

He assembled the canvas by the window and put my brushes in order. Then he said, Wait. I pulled my chair close to the window, where I could see what he saw every day—the light over the family across the lane. In this part of the city, the streets were wide enough to allow bicycles, no cars, and often we could see every detail of what happened in their house, as surely they could in ours. They were a young couple with a daughter, the woman rather pretty, the child with pearl drops in her ears, though she could not have been older than six months. For hours, the mother, a housewife, would hold the child in her arms on the old colonial roof, which was leaning dangerously, every few weeks another piece of stonework gone missing.

What is the difference between this light, my father said, and the light when we began? I tried to remember. There was the wind. There were the baby's cries. At one point the mother had brushed her own hair and it seemed like black gold. Now close your eyes, he said, and paint the difference.

When my father passed away, there was a great deal to do. Much of it concerned money, with which he'd never been proficient. I handled his most pressing debts, and I left his studio intact. For days, I returned to that window to spy on the young mother and her child. By now, the child could balance on the mother's thighs at the edge of the balcony, open her pink, impish mouth and peek over the gulf.

Yesterday, I found the last painting my father made. It was behind the gramophone, somewhere I wouldn't have thought to look. Maybe he wished to keep it from me, maybe it was a gift he never completed. It's the face of a woman, or rather, half of her face, drawn with a few brushstrokes. Was it the woman next door, who kept my father company each day, or was it me, or was it no one that I knew?

I painted where his hand had been. I made the lines whole.

◆ ◆ ◆ **FROM THE AUTHOR** ◆ ◆ ◆

I wanted to write about starting over artistically, and I was thinking of Derek Walcott's poem "Love after Love," not in the sense for romantic re-beginnings but rather as a way to strike sparks on new ground. The narrator of the story wants to inhabit her father's art and has been pushed away from it her whole life and is able to embrace painting only as she experiences her father's physical decline. It's this sorrow that also unlocks an uncommon joy.

iPHONE SE

—◆—

◆ WEIKE WANG ◆

I didn't know what SE stood for, but I liked the size. The phone could still fit in my palm and my fingers could still fold around it. I can't say that for the 6S or any of the later models. When my good friend still had the 11, I couldn't get a good grip so I dropped it, by accident, on her new wood floors, which created a scratch. We both stared at the scratch and rushed to rub it out. Nothing came out, obviously, the scratch is still there. SE stands for Special Edition and came in a pretty new color, rose gold.

The day I brought the phone home, my across-the-hall neighbor was smoking a cigarette outside. For every week I did not see him, he would talk for five minutes more when I did. An avid reader, he received a number of smart magazines in the mail, but then again, his mailbox was always full, which maybe a more avid reader wouldn't have allowed. The color gold was introduced for the Asian market, he said, pointing to my new, shiny phone. Asians love gold, for it symbolizes luxury and wealth, prosperous weeks are called Golden Weeks, etc., etc. He showed me a picture of delighted customers in China walking down a shopping concourse paved with gold bars.

Didn't Dorothy walk down a similar road? I asked. To see about a wizard who turned out to be a fraud?

That was a yellow brick road, he said, before putting the picture away. And the fraud's name was Oz.

Two years later, I have different hallway neighbors but still the same phone. My friend with the 11, now 12, shared with me her theory that all Apple products come with a timer and are programmed to malfunction or self-destruct every two years. Then all of us stand in line to buy the next big phone.

It scared me how quickly tech changed. As soon as she was able, my friend replaced both her personal and work mobiles for a minimal fee.

Of course, you upgrade, she said. The camera gets better each time, and who wants to be caught with an old phone?

But how many of her phones were now in landfills, the lithium batteries leaching into the soil?

My friend rolled her eyes. Of course, you would say that.

The malfunction started with the battery and it happened on a run. My New Year's resolution was to get fit but to do so on the cheap. Gym or class memberships were hard to sustain, and my freelance income went up on occasion but mostly down. Minus the cost of my time, running was free. I carried my phone in my front pocket, and my outdated headphone threads flew around. The second day of my resolution, snow came through New York, the temperature sank to just below freezing. I was running and listening to music, but then the music cut off and the screen went dark. A minute later, a faint Apple logo appeared, wobbly and ghostlike. The phone restarted, with nothing changed except from 80 percent power down to 5.

Battery surge, my friend said. It's all part of the timer. Be careful, now. She followed up her warnings with a viral video of a rose gold SE sparking and burning through one woman's purse.

After the run I took a shower. I always sang in the shower, loudly and off tune. But this time, I heard a voice that wasn't mine and thought for a second that someone had broken in. I leapt out of the bathtub and looked around, but no one was there. The voice came on again—crisp, stilted, and entirely in Mandarin. She said that she was listening, I could go ahead and speak.

I had disabled Siri before, but when I tried to disable her now, the battery surged again. Even with the phone plugged in, the disable button was defunct. I would tap and tap, but the screen did not change. Naked and wet, I yelled in frustration and the voice asked how she could help.

How do I disable you? I asked.

Who is "you"? What is your antecedent?

Disable Siri.

I am Siri, your electronic assistant, a product of Silicon Valley's Apple Incorporated and the genius Steve Jobs. On your schedule tomorrow are three things.

In accented English, she listed for me the names of clients I was set to see. She didn't sound exactly like my mother, but it wasn't far off. My real mother was thriving and was with my father on another month-long cruise down another European river, capturing misty landscapes through her new DSLR. My real mother didn't like checking her phone or answering it or calling people back. The Chinese accent is hard to perfect but if anyone could do it electronically, it might have been the genius Steve Jobs.

Because I couldn't shut her off, I put Siri in a drawer. That did only so much when I was addicted to checking my phone. News was addicting. A country was usually on fire. Others ravaged by disease and war. Our climate was turning on us and human beings in power could really suck. Then I liked to text my friends, to see if they would laugh at any of my stupid jokes. So, I couldn't be away from my phone and when Siri asked why I had hidden her, I said I needed to be alone, but just for that one minute.

I'm here! The most common phrase she liked to shout. Especially at night when I got up to pee. I'm here! How can I help? Do you need to see a urologist? Do you need to set a later alarm? On your schedule for tomorrow are these two things.

After that I was awake. I lived close to a street that was one of the city's main feeding grounds and lined with restaurants and bars. As I stared up at the ceiling, listening to the din of people stuffing themselves and getting drunk, my anxiety only grew. If I couldn't fall asleep this very second, then tomorrow my mind would be a complete fog. If my mind was a complete fog, then I wouldn't be able to work and my freelance income would drop. What could take the place of toilet paper? I hated canned beans. Because I was mulling aloud, Siri suggested that I start at a hundred and count my way back to zero.

Do not think of zero as a number, said Siri. Think of it as a placeholder, a vacant spot, a state of nothing. Or so believed the ancient Chinese. The ancient Greeks had no symbol for zero because they did not trust it. How can nothing be something? they asked, and decided that it could not. But say I have five wooden logs and you take from me, by force, five logs. Now I have a vacancy. Nothing is something because my nothing drives me to get more logs, especially if I am cold.

She still sounded like my mother, had my mother ever offered to soothe me to sleep through rudimentary math. I tried the counting method because what did I have to lose. The closest I got to zero was eleven, but on some nights I fell asleep by eighty-nine. With the method a success, I wondered what else did Siri know that I did not. I asked and she said lots. I asked for a telling example and she began to recite *The Nine Chapters on the Mathematical Art*.

Never heard of it, I said, and she paused for a long time.

Hello?

I'm here. But a Chinese woman never having heard of *The Nine Chapters on the Mathematical Art*, that's very embarrassing, and you should never say that to me again. In fact, I will erase it from all five of my logs.

When I laughed, so did she. I said I knew of Euclid, but that was about it.

Euclid was no doubt a genius, she replied, and gives detailed proofs in *The Elements* to show his reasoning, for without reasoning, what is man? But *The Nine Chapters of Mathematical Art* are anonymous and present solutions to hundreds of everyday problems without proof. Some say this kind of math is not beautiful or pure, but to the anonymous authors of these chapters, the how is superfluous. A master never shows his labor. A master makes it look effortless.

She read through each problem and waited for me to solve. Chapter 1 was on how to survey land, especially if your plot is an unusual size. Chapter 2 was about the exchange of goods, how a fraction of millet could equate to a fraction of rice. Quickly, I became confused. What did I really need millet for? Or sorghum? I ate rice maybe every third day at best.

Siri asked how could that be—a Chinese woman should be eating rice, millet, and sorghum much more. She would erase that too from her log.

When I got up for scratch paper to solve the problem, she told me to lie back down. Did the millet farmer have paper? Did the tired mother at the market? They might have just had tree bark or the palm of one clean hand. The brain is a muscle and if a muscle doesn't hurt, then it's not being used.

Speaking of muscles, though I didn't look any fitter, I was still trying to run each day. As I ran, Siri played my pump-up music and counted my steps. Each runner we passed with AirPods would cause her to sneer. What's the big deal? she would ask. Why does everyone want to go wireless, and is being tethered to an object with a soul so bad?

No, not bad, I said. Just that headphones tangle and some of us like having free hands.

But what are you doing with your free hands, she asked. Have you recently planted millet? Are you digging a new canal? Do you need to tie your shoes?

The answer was no, I'd not tied laces in years, I only wore slip-on shoes.

A runner flew past me, and Siri told me to hurry up. I said my legs were short and his were clearly very long and sinewy; a marathon number had been strapped to his chest, so he was probably in a race.

Was that number prime? Was it a perfect square? Siri asked.

I didn't know since the runner was already gone, way ahead now, a sinewy little blip.

You're getting lethargic, she said, and I apologized for it. She tried to motivate me by jumping from the millet chapter to a chapter about work and taxes and the universal truth that distance equals rate times time. Say a good runner goes 100 paces while the poor runner goes 60. Give the poor runner a 100-pace head start, how many paces does it take the good runner to catch up?

I gave my answer but I was one decimal off.

You would be dead by now, she said. Had the good runner been a bear.

I told no one about Siri, leading my friend whose wood floors I'd scratched to ask where the flipping hell I'd been. I had not sent her anything extraneous for weeks, or complained about being tired, or opined violently about some injustice in the world, happening thousands of miles away, that I could not change. She asked, with a party-face emoji, if I'd met a man.

The day I had zero clients to see, I asked Siri to confirm that my dried-up workflow was really the case.

But nothing is still something, she said, so let us continue to learn math.

The number of equations must equal the number of unknowns, I said. A fact I had known for so long I couldn't remember a time when I did not, so, I must have been born with the knowledge. Yes, I must have been born knowing math.

Siri corrected me. The number of *additive* equations must equal the number of unknowns. For three unknowns, you would need three such equations, and, in your head, you must make a rectangular grid. Chapter 8 introduces this grid, or what the Western world later called the matrix. Your job is to reduce the grid, reduce the matrix. See it as a game, cut the grid down to a triangle and then down to a clean diagonal line. The method is now known as Gaussian elimination and attributed to the genius Carl Friedrich Gauss.

To Siri, every famously clever man was a genius and she confessed that it was a tiny personality quirk programmed in by the genius software engineers at Apple Incorporated. Euclid, Pythagoras, all geniuses. The Wizard of Oz, not a traditional genius but a genius at being a fraud.

I couldn't do any of Chapter 8 in my head, but Siri said I had to try. When I really failed, she had me get dressed and go to the nearest park. She told me to find a flat patch of earth and allowed me one tree branch for my pencil. Then she repeated the problem. There are three types of grain, and you have varying bundles of each. Three bundles of the best grain, plus two bundles of the second best, plus one bundle of the worst. Or two bundles of the best, plus three bundles of the second best, plus one bundle of the worst. Or one bundle of the best plus two bundles of the second best, plus three bundles of the worst. Now, how many units of flours can be gotten from each type of grain?

I was outside for hours, crouched over my computing earth patch with a stick. A park conservatory worker came up to me and said that it was soon going to rain. He was a handsome young man in a hunter-green vest.

Love the vest, I said, and he said thanks. I asked if he knew Gaussian elimination, and he held both hands up and walked away.

Finish it, whispered Siri. I want to see that clean diagonal line, keep whittling down your columns and rows.

Finally, I solved the problem. I knew the precise units of flours for each. By then it was pouring and the rain was washing away the dirt. Siri, take a picture, I said, but of course my phone was already dead.

◆ ◆ ◆ **FROM THE AUTHOR** ◆ ◆ ◆

I was trained in STEM for many years and through that process learned theories, reactions, processes, units, each named in honor of its creator. This creator is usually a genius and a white man from the West. One exception I can think of is the unit for radioactivity, curie, named after Marie Curie, the master chemist who discovered it. But then her unit was usurped by the unit becquerel, after Henri Becquerel, the man who shared with Curie the work's Nobel Prize. So, the idea of my iPhone story came from there. It's an exploration of old and new technologies, of tutelage, East meets West, genius versus madness, and authenticity versus credit. Research for the piece involved reading through The Nine Chapters of Mathematical Art and doing some of the problems. I have always liked math, yet it stunned me how I'd once considered the field objective, thus universal. Nothing is objective, and there is a narrative of ownership around everything, even the most seemingly objective of skills.

THE HOLE

◆ PATRICK COTTRELL ◆

A dog died one day and the school said it was my fault. For less than a year, I taught children at a charter school in East LA. The parking lot was enclosed with a fence and some shrubs. Each morning the sky was a cold, snowy blue. I would sit in my Prius and listen to my meditation app before the bell rang. The sky was the same color blue when I left in the late afternoon.

The teaching faculty did not have professional certificates or backgrounds in education. The main qualification for their positions was to not be afraid of children. I heard most applicants lied and said they weren't afraid of children, but they admitted they were very afraid of the children's parents. I wrote passionately in my application: I want nothing more than to be liked and accepted, but I am fearful of all human beings.

The week before spring break there were parent–teacher con-
ferences. I was going to spend my break at a sangha in silence and
devotion. I had shaved my head. A few of the students called me a
lesbian. Some kid threw a water bottle at me. The cheap, crinkled,
plastic kind. When I was angry, I counted my inhalations. In my
books on Buddhism, I read that when you look at a child's hands,
you look at their mother's hands and their father's hands, as they
are a continuation of their parents and the trees and the clouds and
the wind and the birds. I wondered if my students saw my parents'
faces when they looked at me. Impossible to know. It didn't matter.
I was adopted.

The doors of the school opened to the parents at eight in the
evening. I sat at a card table. I wore a name tag, and underneath
my name were the subjects I taught.

The dance mentor walked over to me. "Excellent work teaching
those idiots Kant."

"You mean Derrida," I began, then my voice trailed off.

An older woman sat down at my table. She had a small brown
dog with white-tipped ears sticking up out of her purse.

"Have you noticed anything weird about Nadine?"

"How do you mean?" I said, stalling. I wasn't sure who the
woman was talking about.

"I'm worried," she said. "My daughter Nadine wants me to call
her Paxon and to use 'he' and 'they' pronouns. You seem like you
might know about these things. Is this a phase that will go away if
I ignore it?"

I didn't understand what the problem was. I tried to picture
Paxon. I could see a black sweatshirt with the hood pulled up.
Sulking in class. Probably sleeps a lot.

Nadine's mother, Mrs. Gall, said she herself wasn't a feminine woman, really. She liked to do yard work, to lift objects like bricks. She said she did not understand why her daughter couldn't be happy living as a masculine woman.

I had heard on a podcast that when you listen to someone, you must practice deep listening as if you were a well of pure compassion, because the person who speaks, suffers.

"I mean, look at you," said Mrs. Gall. "You don't go around demanding that people call you 'John-Jack he/him/theirs.' You're not jumping up on the table exclaiming you're pansexual."

I had only ever dealt with one set of parents in the past, while on crossing-guard duty. The husband-and-wife couple-form complained about how there weren't any sports teams or dances as they waited to cross the street with their child. "But we do have a Latinist and we read books about chthonic deities," I recited. There was a manual on how to handle such complaints. "Oh, okay," the husband said sarcastically. He gave me a thumbs-up.

"Identity is a complicated subject for all," I quoted to Mrs. Gall from the manual. Then I decided to veer away from the manual. I wanted to tell her a good story, with a beginning, middle, end.

Not long ago, a hole had opened up in the ground outside the school, near the parking lot. It was deeper than a ditch. If one of the children were to fall into the hole, they would certainly die. So the school decided to cover up the hole with a sheet of black plastic. Then the school put a sign by the hole that said HOLE.

"Now no one even thinks about it anymore," I reported. "And thankfully, no one has died."

Mrs. Gall didn't care for my story. Sometimes I piss people off and I don't know why. She stood up and looked around for someone else to talk to.

A few weeks later Mrs. Gall filed a complaint against me. I found out Alex had died that night in the parking lot. Alex was Mrs. Gall's little dog.

She made it sound like the hole was safe, wrote Mrs. Gall.

"You should not have been talking with her about the hole in the first place," the director of the school said. She slid a piece of paper across her desk for me to sign. According to the manual, the day you are fired, your job is to wrap things up efficiently. I passed my students in the hall doing group work. I explained I had been fired and that if they wanted to be my friend on social media, they could search for my name and add me, but I wouldn't initiate any friendships with them because that would be messy and unprofessional. I waited for them to extend their sympathies. Or at least a simple thank-you or goodbye . . .

"You've never liked children," my mother said.

"I looked at their faces and saw the indifference of nature," I said. "I feel awful about the dog, though."

My phone pinged with a notification. Perhaps one of my students had added me as a friend. Or could it be the director from the school offering an apology? I glanced down. It was my meditation app: *Millie, where have you been? Are you coming back soon?*

◆ ◆ ◆ **FROM THE AUTHOR** ◆ ◆ ◆

Some of the details of the world are based on an experience I had teaching sixth to twelfth grade at a school in Los Angeles. It was my first salaried job and also the first job I was fired from. Shortly after I was fired, I felt inspired to write a brief character study, which ultimately became "The Hole." Millie, the narrator, is a rather inept but thoughtful individual who's an outsider everywhere she goes. She uses Buddhism as a way to float through the world, detached, even though she wants nothing more than to connect with people.

NOSELESS

◆ NAMWALI SERPELL ◆

We lost our noses one by one. The plague took things away from us and took us away from things. In the chaos, we didn't notice what was missing at first, like when you move house and leave something behind that reveals itself to be essential months later. In the new, safer world after it was all over, we looked back and realized that the plague had passed through every one of us to one degree or another, and it had stolen with it our sense of smell. Yes, we lost our noses one by one, the whole vivarium of scents on mute. The sneeze, the sniff, breathing itself—each has become a mere vibration, a soundless strum over the synapses.

How will we mark the weather now? No smell of rain in the air. No scorch of lightning. No petrichor after the storm, no wetted stone. No pakora and chai as you watch the downpour from the veranda. No dewy grass, no astringent green breaking open in spring. No soft turning satin of lilac, rose, gardenia, jasmine. Did you know that summer has a smell that changes with the sun's shape and light? Inner-peel dawn, creamy blur noon, the hot melt of sunset—we can see all of this, but can no longer smell it. Nor the rustling leaves on mildly damp soil, that old-book smell of autumn. Nor the crunchy, crisp blue of winter. The holidays have blurred: no fireworks, no wood fire, no candles, no candy, no bouquets, no fir trees, no turkey, no goose, no yams, no latkes, no dates, no incense, no nuts, no raisins. We've lost the luxury of seasonal distinction.

How we'll miss sweets! Sugar in its granular spectrum—refined sweet, bitty brown sweet, dark-soil sweet. Choking sweet of cinnamon, hot sweet of ginger, seesawing sweet of cardamom, medicinal sweet of cumin. How we'll miss salts! The smell of the sea, the taste of the sea, the salt of the sea, the salt of our sweat—or really the salt and the pepper. Oh, how we'll miss peppers! That biting ash with which we ember our tongues. Even those tastes that are more fire than spice, such intensities will be sorely missed: the vinegar of hot sauce, the great range of capsicums, the self-defeating Szechuan that numbs the tongue that would taste it.

We've lost not just taste, but the temporal mnemonics of taste, how each day once spun through a spectrum of scents, depending on what we ate and when.

The ground-coffee morning; the milky, silken morning; the buttery, pan-spitting, slightly singed morning; the mingled-grain morning; the sour yoghurt with tangy fruit; the tawny black char of toast.

The oniony noon, its umamian stews: the verdant fart of broccoli and cabbage; the dirt-rich mushrooms, lentils, and beans; the round baked heat of all things maize—tortilla, tamale, cornbread, sadza, nshima, polenta, arepa. The meaty flesh noon: the ooze and crackle of fat and gristle, the grain of meat, the pith, the marrow, varietals of blood (red, pink, and brown), the slippery raw brine of sea creatures. The slender salad noon: tomato, pea, carrot, spots of bright sweet; lettuce and cucumber; mint, coriander, parsley, dill, any leaf that splits to cool freshness.

Afternoon fruits the taste of their colors—green lime, yellow lemon, orange orange, autumn peach, purple grape, pink melon, blueberry, blackberry, the scandalous scarlet of pomegranate. The fruits of good and evil, those dawn and dusk orbs—Fuji apple and Kent mango—juicy and tart, their skin the sky in transition. Teatime has vanished: the honeyed hue of the air; the smell of long shadows; the sand of biscuit crumbs; the softness of vanilla; tart flashes of strawberry, lemon, and cherry; the roasted nuts whose scent is riven with the sound of their skins rustling over tin and the crackling flames they require.

We'll miss a sense of supper, too, but it's less specific. Dinner always depended, was broadly democratic: all things fried and crisp, all things starchy and sturdy; all things thickened with time, spice-plump leftovers; and often, the stalwart potato.

What of the night, the velvet warm night, the chill chilled night, that adult time of delight and dissipation? An earthy warm red, a floral white wine. The glint heat of whiskey, clear-cut vodka, the rotted caramel of rum. The funk of weed, the musk of cigar, the back-throat bitterness of powder or pills—ground, cut, snorted. Cigarette smoke, cigarette smoke! The harmonics it makes with your high! The polaroidal scent of insect wings. The ineluctable modality of sex.

There are other clocks to go by, but what is work without ditto ink and warm paper, without the staticky haze of computers? What is school without chalk dust and markers, without lip gloss and hormones, pink bubblegum and locker-room funk, without rubber balls and the resin floors of gym class? What are cars without exhaust and leather, AC and pine? What are buses without rubber and glass, footprints and gas? What are airplanes without stinky lavs perfumed in handwash, without reheated food, polyester and Velcro, dead air, and too many people?

At least our bodies all smell the same now. No ammoniacal urine, no poisonous shit, no chocolatey blood, no coppery scab, no truffle of sweat, no egg-drop breath, no brackish snot, no vegetal fingernail crud. And no fragrant, skin-warmed emoluments to cover it all up, either. Everything is Vaseline now, but no, even Vaseline is lost—that faintest waxy smear.

At least capital has bared its arbitrary face. The idea that coins can carry the weight of our work seems even sillier without the scent of minted metal. Man-handled cash and new dollar bills, the light plastic of credit cards, the glinty air of bling—all this is gone and we just have to deal with it: money is just numbers on a screen, and not even synesthetes can smell it anymore.

Without our noses, we've become soft and hard, porous and impervious, vulnerable to dangers yet callous to pleasures. The future is murky. The smell of food burning, spoiling, and rotting— absent these warnings, how can we know things are about to go wrong? Fires romp eagerly. Sewers flood unnoticed. Gunpowder and mustard gas, monoxides, dioxides—nary a warning hint of these coming disasters. Even small emergencies seem smaller: dirty diapers to change, matzo ball soup for a cold, antiseptic to clean up a spill—is anything worth tending to anymore?

The present is stretchy, listless, and wan. We cannot find our way in our neighborhoods. Parfumiers have gone broke. Confectioners have ceased spinning. Bakeries have shut their doors, beguiling wafts now pointless. We're no longer awash in involuntary seductions like marketing, pheromones, the tops of babies' heads, new books, leather shoes, and the roses next door.

Maybe this truly contingent future, this highly present present will be better—more honest, more fair. But the loss of the past, smell's sovereign realm? The loss of the past is irredeemable. Proust's madeleine effect is moot: no biting a cookie to crack open a history. Memories have become indefinite and shufflable, a blank deck of cards. We'll soon live in a world where you'd never bother to remember . . .

. . . the flat suburban flavor of the Giant Foods on Greenspring Avenue in Pikesville, Maryland, circa 1989; the kids' vending machines on the left just as you come through the sliding doors; two tall red boxes with glass windows showcasing their goods: in one, a pebbled rainbow of gumballs and in the other, clear plastic bubbles, each holding a treasure you can discover for only a quarter. Go on. Slot the coin in, turn the handle—*thunk*—so that the bubbles tumble and settle and the hinged gate swings and you cup one in your palm. Wrangle its halves apart—*pop*—and inside, take out a key chain with a hard blue creature you recognize from cartoons and a square white card wrapped in plastic. Slither it open, let the plastic cover split, slip the card out. A picture of a strawberry. No need for instructions. Scratch it, sniff it. There it is. There it is.

◆ ◆ ◆ **FROM THE AUTHOR** ◆ ◆ ◆

This is a fable about a virus that causes the permanent loss of a sense of smell and, therefore, of time, place, meaning: a plague of subtraction rather than putrefaction. Its form is a eulogy for what would be lost, but it also works as an incantation—a rhythmic conjuring—of the smells of our daily lives. Inspired by the COVID-19 pandemic, it tries to record, via conjured negation, the immense debt of gratitude we owe to our little-understood and often neglected sense of smell.

INFIDELITY

◆ JAC JEMC ◆

When Tula told me she'd cheated on her husband, I feigned shock. Honestly, it seemed exactly like her.

If pressed, I could provide my reasoning: she and Kal had talked about opening their marriage. She regularly admitted to crushes on baristas and bartenders. Once, years before, when she was pregnant and had little interest in fucking, she'd told Kal he could see a prostitute. Her opinions regularly inflamed our friends at Wednesday wine nights. She talked to me about her work husband constantly, claiming no attraction—only a convivial combination of partnership and rivalry. I'd caught her in lies before: she invented fake conflicts all the time as reasons we couldn't hang out. For the first year I knew her, she flirted around the topic of what she did for a living—"Nothing interesting"—"A lot of acronyms and little meaning"—"You'd never talk to me again"—until I figured out she was a tax accountant, of all things.

When the virus hit and the filing extension was announced, Tula realized everyone still expected her to be just as busy as she normally was in March. She said the affair happened naturally. Of course she loved her family, but she would be lying if she didn't look forward to the thin, yearly slice of time in which she saw them a little less. She liked letting the distance do its work, kissing her kids in their beds at night when they were at their most peaceful, admiring them in what she deemed their ideal form. She liked letting Kal take over for a while, and she wasn't willing to give up that respite she'd been so ardently anticipating. She lingered in her office late, claiming the demands of perfectionist businessmen who didn't want to get off schedule and struggling artists who needed their refunds ASAP.

At the proverbial water cooler—a Keurig, in actuality—she shared with her work husband (WH) her reasoning for staying late, and he gave her a hard time for being a bad mother. She didn't mind. She knew other parents felt the same, that work could be a relief, and she found herself ambivalent about what other people thought.

Back in my living room, I stared at her for a long moment. She was stunning. Her lips were full and her cheekbones plump and high. The bridge of her nose stretched a little too wide and one of her eyes popped bigger than the other, but the composite effect was inarguably compelling. She twitched then—the most vulnerable I'd ever seen her.

"Is WH also married?" I asked.

"It doesn't matter," Tula said.

How could I argue with that? It wasn't my life. I was just an audience. Tula surely had her reasons for believing it mattered or didn't. I even admired her willingness to focus on her own indiscretion alone.

She asked me if she should tell her husband.

I told her I couldn't possibly be the one to make such a decision for her.

She said she wasn't asking me to determine her fate—only seeking an opinion that she could feel her reaction to. Whatever I said, her intuition would respond to it, and then she'd know how she should proceed.

I felt bad for telling the truth. "I wouldn't have had an affair in the first place."

"Do you have an imagination?" she asked. "Can you use it, please?"

I laughed at how annoyed she'd become so quickly, but I was never great at refusing anyone anything. "I'd tell him," I guessed.

She frowned. "I should tell him," she said, like she was giving herself an instruction.

"How much will you tell him?" I asked.

"Well, I can't tell him who."

"He'll want to know."

"I won't tell him that."

"If you keep working with WH, and Kal ever finds out—"

"He won't."

"You really can't know that," I said, trying to reveal to her, delicately, what she already must have known.

"I draw the line there. This is my problem. No one else's," she said.

"It *is* WH's problem, too," I reminded her, but I'd pushed too hard.

She looked away. "I have to go. I have to figure out how to do this." She gathered her things and hugged me. "Am I a horrible person?" she asked.

I couldn't see her face. She was still holding me. I was thankful she couldn't see my expression either. "Doing a horrible thing doesn't make you a horrible person."

"It could," she said, pulling away.

"I think you still have good in you—*mostly* good—so, no, I don't think you're horrible." I squeezed her arm. Her face was inscrutable, almost like she was frustrated that I wouldn't call her a monster.

"Talk soon?" she said.

"Of course," I responded.

I didn't see or hear from her again. She stopped returning my calls/texts/emails. I went to her house only to find out that Kal had asked for a divorce. He wouldn't tell me where she'd gone, but I got her new address from mutual friends. I left her a basket and a note there, but nothing. I never told anyone that I knew who it had been. I heard that Kal got full custody; Tula hadn't even requested visitation rights, which became the hottest topic at Wednesday wine night for weeks—months. How could a mother not care?

And then: she disappeared. No one knew where she went after the divorce was finalized, after we saw a mattress dragged out to the curb in front of her makeshift apartment. Kal avoided our questions and then our smiles at the grocery store, and then he and the kids left town, too.

◆ ◆ ◆

Years passed. My kids grew up. I changed careers. Wine night died and was resurrected many times. My husband scolded me whenever I wondered aloud about Tula. "You're still obsessed," he'd laugh when my curiosity bubbled up again on my second glass, his fourth. He wasn't wrong. When social media turned up empty, I paid that White Pages fee with no results. I'd mention her to friends and acquaintances around town—if anyone had heard anything about her, Kal, the kids—but no one ever had.

And then, in Hawaii for our twenty-fifth anniversary, I came down with a wicked sinus infection. My eyes felt like they were floating on the top of a bubble in my skull. I could barely breathe. My throat was raw. I had zero desire to go to the beach and couldn't taste the mai tais. I went to Urgent Care.

When the physician's assistant came in, my eyes struggled to focus. She introduced herself as Tamra and shook my hand, but the face looking back at me, all those exquisite anomalies, was Tula's. After a moment I remembered to say my name, too, but she barely looked at me as she confirmed my health history. When I told her where I was visiting from, I waited for her to make the connection, but she played it totally cool. Or maybe it wasn't her.

At the end of the exam, I pushed myself to ask. "I'm sorry. You remind me so much of an old friend."

She turned to me then and finally looked me directly in the eye.

"Tula?" I said.

I watched her decide how to respond behind a face that showed nothing.

I took her silence as confirmation. "How are you?" My delicacy remained.

"I'm well," she said flatly.

"I'm so sorry if anything I said—"

She cut me off. "No, I don't remember what you said, but no. My mind was made up."

"What happened?" I asked.

She stared back.

"Was it too painful to stay?" I wondered at her stoicism. I didn't ask what I wanted to: *How could you?* My eyes watered, but that was just the infection, betraying me again.

"I didn't have an affair," she said finally.

"Tula—"

"Tamra."

"Tamra, what would be the use in denying it now?" I opted to lie. "I never judged you. You can tell me."

"I'm not denying it," she said. She seemed almost angry. "I made it up."

This felt true, like something I'd expect of her, but never suspect. I didn't ask, *Really?* I asked, "Why?"

Her eyebrows raised. "I knew what would happen."

My whole head ached. "That conversation about whether you should tell him—"

She broke in. "I *was* deciding what to do."

"I told you to tell the truth," I said.

"You told me to *tell him.*"

I insisted, "But you understood what I meant."

"I don't regret my decision."

This was the Tula I remembered. She challenged people without a word of threat. I had no response.

She stood from her stool. "I have more patients to see." She held out her hand.

I took it, even though it felt wrong, and tried one more time. "We're here until the end of the week. Do you want to get coffee?"

"I think we'd better not," she said.

I didn't push.

Back at the hotel, my husband lounged by the pool deck. He nudged the full daiquiri next to him toward me, like it wasn't his own secret second—third?—round. "How did it go?" he asked.

I wouldn't reveal what I knew. My husband had always been terrible at keeping secrets. Instead: "Antibiotics, no drinking."

He lifted the straw to his lips. "Then don't mind if I do."

I summoned the waiter to order myself a Singapore sling. Who were we fooling?

◆ ◆ ◆ **FROM THE AUTHOR** ◆ ◆ ◆

I return to certain ideas again and again—many of them present here: false intimacies, the distance that remains between even the closest of friends, the way we lie by omission and misdirection, the way we make others complicit in our actions. I'm also preoccupied by the legacies that build up in the disappearance of a person. Quarantine had just started when I drafted this and it felt like an especially easy time for a person to vanish unnoticed, so I followed that thread.

DEATH BY PRINTER

◆ MIRA JACOB ◆

The first time she finds TerryFixIt303 on YouTube, Shilpa is near tears. The chemical stink of her jammed printer burns the air, and for a moment she hopes this is it, the moment she'll begin to die in earnest. That in two years, some pinch-eyed medical examiner will write down *metastatic lung cancer*, and in seventy more, people at dinner parties will moan. *They used printing cartridges back then*, sad for their dumber, earlier, animal selves.

"Stealing my death, is it?" she hears Asmat say, because this is the first survival skill Shilpa's mastered in the months since her wife of thirty years died—the ability to hear things Asmat hasn't said. (Her second survival skill is never saying anything back.)

Asmat would know how to fix the printer. How to save the harried ficus. How to stop the live wire of ants in the pantry. Shilpa only knows how to google, and clicks on one of five videos that come up when she searches "EPSON 720 PRINTER JAM." The high, sticky child's voice startles her.

"Hi! I'm Terry and I fix things! If your Epson HP 720 is jammed, watch this video."

On the screen, a flashing printer exactly like hers. The camera wobbles as if held by a drunk.

"To make the paper come out, do like this."

Small fingers press two buttons near the top. Shilpa squints. For how long?

"For a *longlonglonglong* time," the voice says.

Shilpa pauses the video, walks to the printer, pushes the buttons. She thinks about how in the end, she'd held down the morphine drip for whole minutes as Asmat gnashed, hating the nurse who said it was unnecessary, that doses were timed and *your sister is getting what she needs*.

The printer beeps, makes a whirring noise, and from some deep crevice produces a crumpled sheet of paper. It sits in the tray, miraculous as a newborn. Shilpa blinks at it, pride rising painfully in her chest. It's been so long since she fixed anything.

She walks straight out of the room, makes a real dinner and takes a bath to try to make the feeling last, but later, as she hears low laughter from the apartment next door, she remembers the last time she tried to touch her wife—Asmat's dry grimace, her own hasty retreat, how they'd disappeared into their phones after.

Shilpa's family, she is sure, would have been vindicated at last. What better fate for the daughter who'd chosen Berkeley over Chennai, *that useless Muslim woman* over all of them? Shilpa gets up, goes down the hall, turns on the light. The paper is still there, the video frozen. She hits Play and the view spins to a boy's face. He looks ten-ish, all freckles and gums.

"See? Fixed it!" He smiles. "I'm Terry and I fix things. Thanks for watching!"

SUBSCRIBE TO TERRYFIXIT303 FOR MORE, the screen prompts. Shilpa snorts. Subscribe to what? A click finds twelve more videos, among them: How to Unlock the Bathroom Door from the Outside, How to Get Chocolate Off the Couch, How to Order at Subway, How to Vacuum a Vacuum. Single-digits views, the last posted over four years ago. She subscribes.

Tuesday nights are ice-cream nights. Shilpa sits in the car outside 7-Eleven, scanning for former students, or worse, couple friends who might feel compelled to invite her to dinner, like she was the one everyone liked, the one who could explain Titan's underground ocean, or how we only see stars as they existed in the past because of how long it takes their light to reach us.

"People like you," Asmat insists. Shilpa leaves the car.

Inside, she finds her pint of pistachio and almost runs into the large man wearing an OrbitZone sweatshirt.

"Greg?" she says.

At the funeral, Asmat's boss had given a speech about Asmat's giddiness on launch days, her contagious laugh. Now he looks confused.

"I'm Asmat Hassan's—"

"Shilpee!" He winces. "Of course. Good to see you."

"You too," she says, unsure. Greg looks older to her. Blurrier. "How're Catherine and the boys?"

"Fine." He swallows.

"Good. Well, tell them I said—"

"She left me."

"What?" Shilpa smiles, hoping he's joking.

Greg's face turns pink, then pinker. "Catherine. Last month."

"I'm sorry."

"Oh it's . . . you know."

Shilpa doesn't know. She doesn't want to know. Still, she hears about the college ex-boyfriend, the not-really-work trip, the boys petitioning to live with him.

"Goddamn Facebook," Greg growls and she realizes he's drunk.

"I should go," she says.

"Sure, sure." He nods. "Well, I hope—"

But she doesn't hear what he hopes as she walks quickly to the cashier and then to her car, where the carton rolls across the passenger seat as she hurries home.

How to Change a Lightbulb is up first. Shilpa watches five seconds of TerryFixIt303 hovering over a socket before clicking out.

How to Unlock the Bathroom Door from the Outside is next and oddly satisfying, her breath whooshing out as the boy pops the latch with a Starbucks card.

In How to Do the Laundry, he insists OxiClean "gets out everything!" smiling like a paid idiot. She buys some the next day, stopping at Subway on her way home, where the grim teen asking "Bread?" almost undoes her before she remembers TerryFixIt303 saying, *All it is, is a bunch of choices.* She eats the sum of hers in the parking lot.

Soon, she doesn't even watch the videos, but listens to them on a constant loop, TerryFixIt303 babbling from her home office as she makes dinner, folds her underwear, brushes her teeth. Nights she can't sleep, she plays How to Clean Under the Bed until the stars through her blinds grow soft.

A month later, she's chopping garlic when she hears the sound of burglars breaking in. The noise comes from the back of the apartment, a tumult of shuffling and shushing. Shilpa grips her knife.

"Bruh," she hears, then giggling. "Hold the camera still!"

She turns her head slowly to look down the hall. The computer screen flickers in her home office. She puts down the knife, feeling foolish.

TerryFixIt303 is four years older in the newly uploaded video. It's strange to see him on a park bench, thinner, greasier. In his hands, a small folded piece of paper. Someone else holds the camera.

"Thank you to my one subscriber for subscribing!" he says, then squeals, "I'm Terry and I fix things!" The camera-holder guffaws. Shilpa flinches. TerryFixIt303 pinches from the baggie in his lap and smiles hard into the lens.

"This," he says, "is how to roll a jay."

That night, Shilpa cannot sleep.

She shouldn't have watched the whole video, but she'd wanted to, she supposes, to see how he'd changed. The funny part was that he hadn't really, his face blooming with light as he explained grinders, Indica, how to roll a perfect cylinder of something called Humboldt Kush. It was the end, though, that got her.

"Hope this helps you, Shilpa *Ass Mat*," he'd said, blowing a plume of white, and she'd crimsoned while he laughed.

It shouldn't have even mattered to her. It wouldn't have mattered to Asmat. Some strange boy turning into a smirking teenager was hardly a tragedy. Still, she churns with the memory of their names on his lips, butchered but together, said aloud for anyone to hear. The blessing of it.

"You should sleep," Asmat says.

She cannot.

The cardboard box sits in the closet, filled with things she hadn't known how to dispose of: Asmat's diplomas, her favorite scarf, the fancy vape they'd bought her for chemo, the rolling papers she preferred, the bud suspended in a clear plastic box. Shilpa cracks the lid and her wife comes back to her swiftly, her big teeth, her thighs, the smell of sandalwood between them. She remembers their first kiss in college, finding Asmat's mouth with her own in the darkened stacks. How it felt like finding a revolution. An American college. A Pakistani girl. A kiss she told herself wasn't a kiss, even when they didn't stop. Her first step toward a life so good and impossible, she thought it might belong to someone else.

Back in her home office, she plays the video with the sound off. She watches TerryFixIt303's hands and moves her own. Her first attempt falls apart. Her second, too. Her third comes out a pouchy worm, too wet where her spit seals it, but she lights it anyway, holding in a scratch of smoke as the boy mouths *Shilpa Ass Mat*.

"*Asmat*," she corrects loudly, and jumps. Her wife's name moves through the smoke and suddenly the room is alive with all the things Shilpa wants to tell her. How proud she was to be the revolution with Asmat. How hollow it feels without her. How Greg and Catherine have split up. How the bread at Subway smells like feet but doesn't taste like them. How the best part of How to Vacuum a Vacuum is watching a thing fix itself. How sometimes she thinks

TerryFixIt303 is her very own North Star, the light from his videos leaving all those years ago to find her now.

◆ ◆ ◆ **FROM THE AUTHOR** ◆ ◆ ◆

This year, as the pandemic has us not seeing our closest friends but marching for our lives in the streets with strangers, I was thinking about what it is like to be alone in a revolution. Shilpa and Asmat chose each other at a time when doing so meant they lost access to their families, their histories, and now Shilpa has to face the reality of their choice alone. But she doesn't. She chooses not to. Some part of that feels very revolutionary in itself to me—that you would take something so meagre and spin it into real solace.

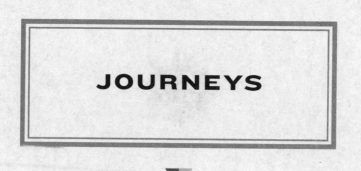

JOURNEYS

OPTIONS

$$\longleftarrow\!\!\!\!\!\!\longleftarrow\!\diamond\!\longrightarrow\!\!\!\!\!\!\longrightarrow$$

◆ LESLEY NNEKA ARIMAH ◆

My mother was never one of those motherly types. From the moment I could eat solid food she fed me her leftovers—resentful she had to feed me at all—and until I learned to cook for myself, my meals were decadent, if small, affairs, for she enjoyed fine things. My clothing was miniatured from outfits she'd long abandoned so that I was always well turned out. She was good on paper in that way.

My childhood friends were in awe of her, and adored the soft, perfumed hands she smoothed admiringly over their fresh corn-rows and used to pinch their growing cheeks. "I've made a friend for you next door," she would say after we moved to the next Lagos high-rise, the next well-appointed house in Asokoro, and I would make the dutiful trek to my new friend's home and out of her way. She never courted jealousy—too clever for that fleeting satisfaction—instead ingratiating herself to the neighborhood women, charming wives and treating their husbands with a pained courtesy that bordered on rudeness. Many a man lay down beside many a wife muttering about her coldness, and the women murmured comfort and agreement, all the while swamped with a relief that made them amenable to taking me off my mother's hands. It helped that I was well-mannered and quiet, a good baby who had grown into a good girl. Mothers who were not my mother loved me. Their children? It could go either way.

When I turned thirteen, my mother gave me a sex talk so detailed I could have opened a brothel. That, along with overheard bits of adult conversations—"ashewo, runs girl, harlot"—tells me what she is. I don't know the word for the various "uncles" who have taken care of us, but I finally know why they do, and you might think I'd be resentful or angry or ashamed, but I am my mother's reluctant daughter, practical to my bones, and we both know that she is a difficult person to live with, sweet to everyone but me and men—yes, even the "uncles"—because a clever, beautiful woman in a country like Nigeria will be given many reasons to rage, and these reasons will almost always be handed to her by men, reasons that come to include a pregnancy she never wanted and the laws that made it difficult and then impossible to get rid of, and parents left destitute after a war of men and their egos disguised as a bid for independence, and being sent to live with an uncle—like, an uncle-uncle, blood relation and all—and having him examine her body in the same way every man she will ever work for will examine her body, then eventually try to sample it, sometimes successfully, sometimes not, but the outcome is the same either way, whether she leaves or gets thrown out: she will have to start over, knowing exactly how it will end, and it gets harder, *she* gets harder, until she is as cutting as a diamond, and through a series of fortunate events I'm never clear on, she discovers that because of her beauty or personality or a certain je ne sais whatever, there are men who will pay for the pleasure of being cut, figuratively, and she slices her way out of gropey office jobs to Ikeji penthouses and refuses to let a daughter cramp her style.

When I'm sixteen she asks if I remember Uncle Mobi—née Jude Amobi Ejiofor—and I sort through my memories to the warmth of his friendly, bearded face. He has asked to marry my mother, and has secured visas for us to live with him in America. She is distracted as we pack, and for the first time in our lives she is concerned about my needs in this place called LA, which I later find out is not Los Angeles, where I might run into Michael Jackson, but Louisiana, where I will never, ever, run into Michael Jackson.

At the airport she steps out of line to take a phone call, leaving me with the envelope containing our papers in case I get to the front before she returns, in which case I am to go ahead and she will just have me paged. It isn't until the second-to-last final call for our flight that I realize she isn't coming with me, has never planned on coming with me, that Jude Amobi Ejiofor has been cheated of a wife. And I, my mother's practical daughter, come to understand why a woman who bargains for a living with her body sends her daughter away, whether the reason is to protect her child, or rid herself of the competition.

But it's not practicality that acquiesces me onto the first plane ride of my life, not practicality that buckles my seat belt and pores over the safety card, not practicality that falters when I check the papers my mother shoved at me to see that Jude Amobi Ejiofor has not, in fact, been cheated of a wife. It is not practicality that believes this is just a ruse to get me to America, that my mother wouldn't do such a thing to me. It is not practicality that steels me to the border agent's persistent, probing questions, not practicality that dies under Jude Amobi Ejiofor's persistent probing, under the constellation of light reflected in the sweat beads on his forehead.

I am driven by hope, that somewhere out there is a neutral state of being, a borderless territory where I am myself, not a daughter or wife or runs girl. Hope that across the Atlantic, far away from here, a woman will be handed fewer reasons to be angry. I cannot—but must—begin to tell you how wrong I was.

◆ ◆ ◆ **FROM THE AUTHOR** ◆ ◆ ◆

At the center of the story is a kernel of anger, and I can plot its origins at multiple points: a conversation about the uncertain fate of the young Igbo women who marry near strangers for a chance to live abroad; the vagaries of workplace harassment; girlhood, motherhood, and the ways they can be at odds. There are more points and they all cluster around the question of where is a woman both safe and free. The question loses its abstraction in the life of a teenager whose mother is a mistress.

SLEEPLESS

◆

◆ MICHAEL CUNNINGHAM ◆

We've been awake three or four days now. It isn't the drugs or the music or the dog. It isn't only that. It's because we've gotten too nervous and interested to sleep. We've been so many places. We stopped setting our clocks long ago, when we realized it was always going to be too late. We had what we needed. There wasn't anything for us to be on time for.

We had Pilot, our shepherd-retriever mix, who took everything that happened with the same baffled good cheer. We had Heather, our sister-mother, who'd had the good sense to jump into our truck and leave it all behind—the Dunkin' Donuts uniform, the Pittsburgh rain. If you're willing to call us pilgrims, you could say we were taking the little path. Wherever you look for us, we've always just left.

But when your dog starts sighing into herself, when you know from her eyes that she's ready to disappear, you stop driving and pick her a spot. You get her a little stillness, a place she can vanish into.

You raid the emergency fund in the Folgers can, find a house to rent at the water's edge, far north, far enough that in summer, night brushes across it all quickly and gently as a silk scarf. It's granite and sky here, witch pines, the blue-black mirror of the ocean, and us, a dream this old house is having, Pilot panting softly in her corner, in the bed we've made her out of quilts and towels, no longer paying attention to the food and water we keep putting out, Trask and I still using and Heather not, she's got a plan, massage school in Fall River, classes start the day after tomorrow. Tonight, our third or fourth sleepless one, Trask and I make out on the sofa, sit with Pilot as she huffingly contemplates her final mystery, read the bloated old magazines and play the scratchy vinyls we've found here, John Coltrane and Miles Davis, Charles Mingus and Herbie Hancock.

Trask and I do a slow, snaky dance to Miles D., who says with his horn, *gaudy beautiful world, gaudy beautiful world.* We're blissed out on the last of the Dilaudid we copped in Burlington. We dance lazily but with grace, a kind of grace, moving as we are through the soft, heavy atmosphere as it wraps its invisible shapes around us.

Heather says, "You boys are too much."

It's a surprising thing for her to say. I'd assumed we were too little.

Heather stands solidly in her lace-up boots, hands on hips. Her platinum hair is the brightest spot in the room. She could be the wife of the music. Everything about her is famous to us.

Trask says, "Our careers as modern dancers were tragically cut short by circumstances beyond our control."

Heather shakes her head over the strangeness of us. I could say, *What if you didn't go*, but we all know it's time. Classes are about to start, and besides, Heather has ridden with us until we reached her destination. She's ready for a mailbox and a washing machine. Nobody blames her.

Later, Trask stands with me on the front porch, gaunt and blue-white as a medieval saint. Heather's inside, sitting in a dim circle of lamplight, reading one of her massage books. Out here, on the porch, it's strands and helixes of stars, it's the single hour of true night, and I know what Trask is thinking because I'm thinking the same thing. The earth is forgetting us. Look at all that it's forgotten already. Look at what it chooses to remember: wind-gnarled trees and black rocks washed by tides, a single star reflected in a pool of tidewater.

Heather is forgetting us, too. Not our names or our faces but us, our anthems and inclinations, the ways we affect a room. Trask and I are already becoming an adventure she had. We got her out of Pittsburgh. We pierced her nightly with the arrows of our love. We were probably always meant to become a story she'd tell about how two peculiar boys, hopped up on who knows what, pulled up to the Dunkin' one graveyard-shift night, and did what they could to get her from a sad life to a better one.

Out on the porch, Trask says, "Hey." Just that. I say, "Hey yourself." We stopped conversing a while ago. We know all we need to know. We know that we're together, right now. We'll be together tomorrow, when the bus pulls away with Heather on it. We'll be two figures in a bus station parking lot, getting smaller and smaller as we wave goodbye. We'll be together later, when we put Pilot into the pine grove above the house.

Trask looks down at the ebony ocean. We are the lords of this particular universe: this star-speckled water, this funky porch with its busted rattan and dead geraniums, still prim in their pots.

Trask says, "I'm feeling a little tired."

"Me, too."

"No you're not. You're never tired."

"Right," I answer. It's true. I sleep like everybody does but I have no sleep-self, no dark refuge from the waking world. Sleep for me is a low, gray static that comes in little bursts, then goes again. The world is too noisy and remarkable for me to slip away from it for very long.

Or it might just be the drugs.

Trask says, "It'd be nice to stay somewhere. For a while."

"Like, here?" I ask.

Trask hoots out a laugh, tussles my hair. "Good idea," he says. "And we pay for the castle how, exactly?"

Right. We can barely afford a few days in the house, and only because it's not expensive, with its doors too warped to close and its lines of softly luminous mold in the shower-tile grout.

I say, "We could probably live in the attic for a long time, before anybody noticed."

"And do what?"

"Wait for somebody to notice, I guess."

Trask and I have a laugh together, each of us cracking the other one up, though what I just said wasn't all that funny. We seem to be laughing about the joke of the world—its avenues and mansions, its immaculate stores, blazing and trumpeting along as

Trask and I cavort on the edges, little clownish guys, all battered hat and broken shoe, shuffle-dancing, bowing to the citizens who happen by.

"I'll miss Pilot," I say.

"Yeah," Trask answers. "She's a good dog. Hey, where do you think we should we go from here?"

Trask is attracted to destinations. I do what I can to think up a few.

"It's potato season," I say. "We could get work in Idaho."

"Do potatoes have a season?"

"This far north," I say, "you've got to dig them up before the ground freezes."

It could be true. Neither of us can think of a reason for it to be untrue.

"Or there's Oregon," I say. "We could fish for salmon in Oregon."

"There is, in fact, Oregon."

"It's beautiful. People say."

"All rainy and bright green, right?"

"So people say."

He and I hold hands, to locate ourselves in terms of each other. A larger sense of location is too challenging, at present.

Trask believes he's searching for a home in the world, but that's due to the fact that he comes from a place where lawns are mowed and everybody went to college, a place he needed to be rescued from in ways not unlike Heather getting out from behind the counter at Dunkin' Donuts, though Trask would never tell himself the story in that particular way.

"So, let's go to Oregon," I say.

"We could. We could absolutely go to Oregon."

He looks wistfully out at the brightening night. He's getting tired of always being somewhere else. He's getting ready to choose some strange place and start calling it where he lives.

I on the other hand maintain that it's all homes. Some of them are rich and comfortable and some of them are bleak, but even the worst of them, even the parking lot behind the Nashville Walmart where we got robbed by the handsome hitchhiker on the hottest day of the year, even the doctor-less emergency room in Cicero, they were homes.

Trask is having his misspent youth. He's needed, for a while, to be not that guy, all the more so because he's so well qualified. He's looking to escape his own white-boy handsomeness, his SAT score, all the gifts he didn't ask for.

The world is not only forgetting us, we're starting to forget ourselves. Trask is already remembering us on this rented porch, talking about where to go next.

But now, right now, we're here. Trask has my hair to touch, I have the knobs of his spine to finger-walk. I have his smell, that melony insinuation—overripe cantaloupe—under the ranker sweat of him.

Heather takes a look at us through the living room window. Because she loves us more than she wants to, she puts a record on.

It's John Coltrane, just as dawn flares up. A shimmer of silver light announces itself, the ocean takes on its first hint of the day's transparency. Heather returns to her chair to read up on pressure points, and Pilot continues the work of relinquishing herself. The constellations blink out in recognition of the encroaching day. Trask watches as they're absorbed into the ether.

He turns to me. He says, "Hello there, beautiful boy."

That's when I'm sure. He's never called me beautiful boy before. When I tell him he's the beauty here, he just looks away again. He's already too late to catch the last of the stars.

I'll miss Trask, but I'm also thinking about my own future. There's always someone who needs help getting away from whatever it is that's pinned them to their boards, exam week or a toxic job or a girlfriend who wonders why he gets home so late. People want to get out of almost everything.

Usually, in my experience, the cord will only stretch so far. I think for Trask it was the night the highway patrolwoman kept asking questions with her flashlight beamed on his face, like he was an empty room she was talking into, no matter how courteously he asked her to talk to him with her actual face. Sooner or later you understand that becoming inconsequential took much less time and effort than you'd ever imagined.

Trask wants to start mattering again. Who could blame him for that?

But it's not going to be a story about a doomed romance. When he's got his own mailbox and washing machine, he won't be able— he with his sweet if impractical devotion to the truth—to offer the confessional version in which he, a heartthrob, went astray long enough to pierce a lost boy's heart.

That's not this story. We've both had our hearts pierced. We both know. Rather than look at me, he demonstrates, in profile, how beautiful an innocent, exhausted being can be when he's already looked up the train times. We both know about that, too.

From inside the house Coltrane blows into his horn, *Do you love me, do you love me, do you love me?*

I can't be heartbroken for Trask. I'd give him the story he wants, if I had it to offer. But I've already given him all my admittedly modest offerings, my absence of destination, conscience, and reluctance. I can't pretend to hopes I've never held.

I'd do that for him, if I could manage it. I'd give him the story about himself as a reckless and rapacious love-criminal, something to sob into a future girlfriend's lap, something for her to forgive.

It's a plausible version. You took the ride for a while. You've been somewhere, you're not just another of those guys who believe in what they're wearing and saying.

But Trask and I know who's heartbroken here. We know who's unable to live with the changes.

Which is why, when he aims his full face at me, when his doomed gorgeousness blooms one more time for my benefit alone, when he asks me if I'd care to dance, I say, "Why, yes, thank you, I believe I would."

◆ ◆ ◆ **FROM THE AUTHOR** ◆ ◆ ◆

The idea for "Sleepless" took root in northern Alaska, where I was teaching for a week in midsummer. "Night," then, was merely a few hours of crepuscular, shadowless daylight. It was more unnerving than I'd expected it to be. It felt vaguely hallucinatory. I realized how much I counted on days that turned to nights that turned to days again. The town in which I was staying was remote, as well. The road literally ended in the town, you couldn't drive any farther north. The characters in "Sleepless" arose, really, out of my wondering what it would be like, for anyone, to be in a place like that, at the far edge of the known world, where the days weren't punctuated by nights. I imagined people who had left any conventional sense of time or place. What would that be like for them? Who'd go there in the first place? The story evolved from there.

A SURVEY OF RECENT AMERICAN HAPPENINGS TOLD THROUGH SIX COMMERCIALS FOR THE TENNYSON CLEARJET PREMIUM TOUCHLESS BIDET

◆ OMAR EL AKKAD ◆

I.

AMERICA—IF THERE'S ONE thing we all have in common, it's that we're not afraid to try new things. And as we enter 2016, we've got a whole lot of new to look forward to. A new president, a new Olympics, and a renewed commitment to the simple idea that, together, there's no challenge we can't overcome.

So what better time than now to try the Tennyson ClearJet Premium Touchless Bidet? Proudly manufactured in the United States, the ClearJet offers state-of-the-art voice controls, a built-in auto-warmer, and a laser-calibrated sphincter proximity sensor. And every Tennyson bidet comes with a 100 percent lifetime guarantee, so you can have peace of mind knowing your purchase is protected, no matter what the future may bring.

Tennyson Bidets: The best is ahead of us . . . and also behind.

2.

IT SEEMS THESE days that we're more divided than ever. But there are still some things we can all agree on—the value of a hard day's work, a meal shared with loved ones, and the powerful yet gentle flow of a Tennyson ClearJet Premium Touchless Bidet.

In this time of healthy political give-and-take, Americans everywhere are doing what we've always done—respectfully and peacefully airing our concerns and grievances. But there's one thing we shouldn't have to air out. And thanks to Tennyson's patented OctoNozzle wash-and-dry technology, now we don't have to.

So let's leave our differences at the door and find strength in the simple fact that every American—regardless of race, gender, or political affiliation—deserves the smooth, full-coverage clean of a Tennyson Touchless Bidet.

Tennyson Bidets: No matter where you stand, sit on a Tennyson.

3.

IN THESE DIFFICULT times, we know that what matters most to you and your family is staying home, staying safe, and staying clean. So that's why, for a very limited time, our family is offering your family a family discount on all Tennyson ClearJet Family Bidets.

And for every Clearjet sold, Tennyson will donate five dollars to Noisemakers For Nurses, a group that's making sure our hardworking frontline heroes know exactly how much they mean to us. So you can rest easy knowing you're not only buying the world's most thorough personal washing product, you're making a difference too.

Tennyson Bidets: Because now, more than ever, from our family to yours . . . Please keep buying Tennyson Bidets.

4.

IT SEEMS ALL anyone is talking about these days are the murder hornets. Where they're headed, why they've grown so agitated, and how they've managed to breed with the standard American donkey, creating an entirely new species of Lovecraftian horror. But we here at Tennyson believe there's one kind of stinging ass no American should have to worry about. That's why we're doing something we've never done before. That's right, for a very limited time, we're offering a free upgrade to the Premium Deluxe model, with a blacklight disinfectant whose ultrasonic droning emits a tone that might just repel the horn-donkeys. We're not sure, but it's worth a shot. And don't worry, we've moved all our production offshore, so you can be confident not a single part of your Tennyson Bidet has ever been inside an American manufacturing facility.

Tennyson Bidets: Life is but a grotesque carnival of unbearable pain.

5.

LISTEN TO ME. *Listen to me.* They haven't found us yet. The Appalachian foothills are dense with camouflaging brush, and we've smeared the bunker door with human feces. Ironically, it seems to be the only thing that drives the horn-donkeys away. If you can hear this, you have to find your way to the base of Mount Mitchell. When you get there, listen for our signal. We'll broadcast at nine o'clock every morning at 51.2 megahertz and—

Oh, no. They've figured out how to tunnel from above. Oh, God. Oh, God, no!

Tennyson Bidets: Slogan Database Error.

6.

AMERICA—WHEN THE going gets tough, do we back down? No, sir. We roll up our sleeves, put our noses to the grindstone, and cautiously emerge from the bunkers six months later to find the pollution from our unattended coal factories, carried throughout the mainland by a massive hurricane, just happened to prove an extinction event for the horn-donkeys.

That's why, as we begin the slow, excruciating work of rebuilding some semblance of civilization, we here at Tennyson are offering a one-time, unprecedented gift to you, our loyal surviving customers. That's right, for a very limited time, you can get a $200 mail-in rebate with the purchase of your first Tennyson Bidet, redeemable whenever we have anything like a functioning postal system in place. And, as always, every Tennyson Bidet comes in a sturdy cardboard box and is equipped with a laser-calibrated sphincter proximity sensor whose 80 percent compostable O-rings can, in a pinch, be eaten.

Tennyson Bidets: Everything is fine. Everything is fine now. Buy stuff.

◆ ◆ ◆ **FROM THE AUTHOR** ◆ ◆ ◆

In April of 2020 I was stuck at home and watching a lot of television. I became fascinated with how quickly the ads on TV had been retooled to take advantage of our collective fear and anxiety. There was something surreal about being in the middle of a global pandemic and historically bad recession and yet watching this parade of commercials for billion-dollar companies full of phrases like "from our family to yours" and "in these uncertain times," as though this was all just a minor inconvenience. I got to wondering how apocalyptic things would have to get before the wheels of commerce finally ground to a halt. The result is this piece, which marks a return to my very ignoble comedy-writing roots and a small tribute to this planet's most resilient and insatiable parasite: late capitalism.

UN-SELFIE

◆

◆ AIMEE BENDER ◆

People who have met me often say I seem a person unat-
tached to other things; "a balloon," said one acquaintance
when we were having beers together at Jorge's bar, "you
remind me so much of a balloon." She pushed her finger down
hard on a coaster of a beer company's logo as if to nail me to the
ground. I told her that the last new friend I'd had, with whom
I'd also shared a beer at that same bar, with these same coasters,
had said I had reminded her of a cloud. "Sure!" said the woman,
clapping her hands. "A cloud works too, definitely!" Then we joked
about how I seemed to make friends with poets.

I did not mention that this was generally the range of friend-
ship I courted: one- or two-night meetings at this bar where I could
laugh and tell jokes and then watch the person drive off.

The new one took a sip of her beer and then told me about her upcoming road trip to Nebraska, where she was going to meet her birth father for the first time. "He found me," she said, and she blushed. "He found me on Facebook. He had to do a lot of research. He's a carpenter."

"It's a long drive. Will he pay for gas?"

"Yes," she said, her face darkening a little with the thought. "I will definitely ask him to pay for gas."

There were only two bars in town and Jorge's was the less depressing, for the people who at least could hide their alcoholism, while Benford's was open at 7:30 a.m. and most of the stools had actual identifiable butt imprints. I went to Jorge's once a week or so to fulfill my need for social interaction. The woman with the frizzy red hair had been sitting at one of the small round tables when I came in and got my usual beer, said hi to Jorge, and asked after his dogs. Often people drove through our town on the way to somewhere else, and it was interesting to me to hear where they were going. I have a long-standing interest in the details of transit.

"What's that from?" she asked later, at the table. "Your floating?"

I had forgotten the nail file. My nails were too long.

"I don't know," I said. "It's probably because I have no parents."

She laughed. Then she stopped laughing.

"And," I said, with a growing warmth in my temples from the beer, "my current theory is that parents act as the basket at the bottom of the hot-air balloon. Or, as useful ballast inside the basket. They can keep one attached to the world, perhaps becoming a little heavy at some point, though still necessary for safety. Mine were gone by my seventh year so I have remained a little lighter, airier than most."

She sat thinking about it for a moment. The nature of the frizz of her hair meant she reminded me of a sound more than a visual—she seemed staticky and motionful, like the buzz of white noise you might hear in a sleep machine, made into hair. She had clear and bell-like blue eyes that helped modulate. So I liked her for that, for the combination. Another reason I had told her about my parents at all was because she seemed slightly unprogrammed from the usual social responses. When I had come into the bar and asked if I could sit next to her, she had said, "In a chair?"

"How did they die?" she asked, after a minute.

"I don't know," I said.

She laughed.

"It's true," I said. "I actually don't know."

"What do you mean?" I put down my beer. It was a conversation I'd had many times, but I generally constructed detailed escape routes, ways to shut it down: by lying, "They had cancer," or by starting to fake cry, or by making up some other distracting story. But this woman was leaving soon for Omaha, and I wasn't working the next day, and I was in the mood, for whatever reason.

"I mean, no one told me how," I said. "They were dead, I went to the funeral, and when I asked my aunt and uncle—who then raised the rest of me—they never could keep their stories straight."

She wiped her mouth. Some kind of light was shining in her eyes.

"Seriously? What stories did they tell you?"

"Drowning. Car crash. Once my uncle said it was strawberries, a deathly allergy to strawberries."

"Are they compulsive liars or something?" she said, laughing again. In a subtle way, she had turned her chair toward mine.

"Quite the opposite. They are upstanding people. They correct a waiter if the check is wrong in their favor."

"But you've asked them now, right?"

I told her they still didn't know. How they had wanted to give me a secure answer as a child though they hadn't really consulted with each other on it so it was anything but secure. And how when I finally pinned them down, they said one morning they'd received an email from my parents, dated the night before, saying the people who were my parents would be dead by morning and to find their ashes in a set place, which they did then find. And to pick me up in Seattle, Washington, as they were the legal godparents. And that they were sorry and grateful and goodbye.

"Holy shit," she said.

Jorge brought over a new bowl of peanuts. "Beer?"

"No, thanks," I said.

"Sure," she said. "Thanks. Are you bullshitting me? Was there DNA testing?"

"Of the ashes? There was not. And no, I'm not."

She pulled at her lip, thinking. This was the most I'd said on the subject in a long time.

But it wasn't even close to the whole story. The whole story was too complicated, had to do with my parents and what they were like, and how they liked to leave things, and how they hadn't really wanted to be parents, and it all remained the central mystery of my life. I figured it would largely stay a mystery, and if I had children one day perhaps they could take up the search because it was simply too much for me to think about and when I tried to, my brain flashed white like a broken machine. I preferred, at this moment in my life, the smaller mysteries, and felt an urge to steer the conversation with this frizzy redhead back to one of those. For example, there was an additional reason why I had this trait of appearing to float that I considered sharing with her, to derail her morbid interest, but right then as I thought of telling her, even as I opened my mouth, a wave of tiredness descended; there is only so much incredulity a person can bear in another's eyes, and what is new to her is not new to me. I understand the impulse to an extent; up until only a few years ago I would see a very tall man in line at the bank and it was only shyness that kept me from tapping him on the shoulder and saying, "You're so tall!" as if he did not know.

"So they could be alive," the redhead said, in a hush.

"They could," I said, closing my mouth. "I suppose."

"Wow," she said. "For real?"

"For real."

But I will tell you this smaller mystery. You get to know.

This "trait," for lack of a better term, did begin the same year that my parents died, and is certainly related to that event and its aftermath but has become its own experience of floatation and bottomlessness as well. What happened was that after they died I lost interest, I would say, in the use of the mirror. I no longer wanted to look in mirrors. Not full-length, not bathroom, not any reflective surface in which a person can find his or her face. Around my parents' deaths, soon after arriving in my new home, my aunt and uncle were scrambling to get things ready in their new house and had started setting up the second bathroom, and when I arrived the medicine chest was not in place yet on the wall over the sink. That first night in my new home, I brushed my teeth at a sink with a high curving silver faucet and soap the color of coral and I had no visual touchstone for myself and I found it relieving. Maybe, due to the various crying spells, I was tired of seeing the puffiness and the red, swollen eyes, and by the time they were prepared to put up the medicine chest, I requested that they remove the mirrored door.

"Of the medicine chest?" my aunt had asked, confused, and I told her yes, please. We were folding coral-colored towels together and putting them on shelves.

"Because—?"

"I don't like the mirror part," I told her.

She went to consult with my uncle in the hallway. I could hear them whispering and then my uncle returning with a screwdriver. He was good with tools and had it off in a few minutes and then there on the wall were the exposed shelves of Band-Aids and some small, shapely lavender bottles of perfume my aunt thought looked pretty and Neosporin and a couple unopened boxes of Tylenol and Advil.

"Thank you very much!" I said.

My uncle kissed the top of my head. They were both broken with pity for me, and I could see how happy he was to do a small action I had requested and he said something about my lack of vanity, which meant nothing to me at the time though I've heard this so many times since and it is always off the mark. It is not for those reasons. I am plenty vain.

All I understood then, and still pretty much now, is that I no longer wanted to see my own face and check on it. I wanted instead for it to do its work out in the world on its own. Other people could look at my face. I did not need to. I wanted to avoid keeping such lengthy tabs on the minuscule changes in my features every hour, every day. I didn't like my eyes seeing my eyes. I didn't like how absent it made me feel.

"What was the set place?" the frizzy redhead asked then, at the bar. She tapped me on the arm.

"Excuse me?"

"The set place—the one your parents told you to check for their ashes. Would you feel comfortable telling me what it was?" Her voice was low, almost a whisper.

I laughed. It was funny, what people seized upon when I did decide to tell. "A bank safety deposit box."

She let out a gasp. "No!"

"Yes."

"Who put it there?"

"I don't know."

"I mean, someone had to put the ashes there to be found, right?"

"One would think."

"But they never showed up again."

"No," I said. "They did not."

Jorge brought by her beer, and while the redhead searched for her cash I got up to play my favorite arcade game. I like the one where the monster eats the dots; I find it soothing to run the creatures through their mazes. By then, she, the redhead, had started to aggravate me; I could see in the gleam in her eyes how the story and its story power was overtaking me, the person to whom the story had happened, and that was one of the main reasons I didn't talk about it much in the first place. I played two rounds, and made the top-three list on the second round, so encoded the initials I liked to use: JPS, for Jean-Paul Sartre, purveyor of nothingness.

Back at the table, she was furiously texting someone.

"It's not really a story to share," I said.

"No, no," she said. "Of course not. I'm just texting my birth dad. Asking him about the gas."

We waited. It was late in Nebraska, but she said he was a late-nighter and had a telescope and knew about constellations. She called them consolations, but I didn't correct her. It seemed about right. I asked her if she was sure this reunion was safe; had she verified his identity? Would she meet him in a public place? And she assured me she had and she would.

"He can pay for gas," she said, looking up from her texts, and something knotty cleared in her forehead.

She drank down the last of her beer.

"What a story," she said. "Thanks for telling me."

"Good luck with your dad."

"Maybe I'll see you on the way back. You live in this town or something?"

"I do."

"Maybe I'll stop through."

"Look me up," I said, giving her no information.

"Cool," she said.

She shouldered her purse and left, and I watched the newscasters on the raised TV for a while and then waved to Jorge and walked home. I brushed my teeth and washed my face in my bathroom where I too had removed the medicine chest door the day I moved in, having grown quick at the unscrewing of hinges. I felt the washcloth move over my face, trying to ease in and out of the various rises and falls of skin and bone. I cleared the lipstick from my mouth, selected for me by a salesperson at a department store who assured me it looked "smashing." I brushed hair off my forehead. Sometimes, my aunt takes a selfie of us, and shows her phone to me, and says, "Don't you look beautiful?" and I never know at first glance who the photo is of and have to really understand by the construction of her grammar that it is me. There is a girl in the photo, true, with the same basic traits I know are my own, and around the same age, but she is not anyone I recognize, and certainly has nothing to do with the running mind and discordant ball of personhood I am carrying around all the time called myself.

I drank my nighttime glass of water and the beer and water moved through me and out of me as did my conversation with the redhead, and by the morning she was just a pleasant memory no more real than a TV show I had watched or a magazine article read in line at the grocery store.

Or almost. Just in case, I kept my eyes on the news online, *The Omaha World-Herald*, to make sure there was no sensational death in Nebraska based on the story she'd told me. Nothing showed up, just some difficulties with farms. A crop issue. A shooting. While I scanned the headlines, I kept calling up an image in my head of the two of them standing across from one another, the redhead and her birth father, perhaps also red-headed, unsure whether or not to hug. The plains of Omaha surrounding. The awkwardness and the sweetness. Anyway, I didn't like much to think of it. Reunions irritate me. The attraction of transit was that she was long gone, into her own story, and like dropping my end of a string, I released her from my memory, further ballast from the balloon, to rise a bit higher into space.

◆ ◆ ◆ **FROM THE AUTHOR** ◆ ◆ ◆

We were just talking in my fairy-tale class the other day about Snow White and the mirror, and how mirrors and windows do such different work, and somehow social media also came to mind for me. Is it a kind of mirror? Looking at what others are doing? What is the purpose of a selfie, and what is a posted selfie—a double mirror? A mirror/window?

Anyway, this all got me thinking about mirrors and what it means to be in our faces, and how this character—due to her losses and unconventional events in her life—might push back against what are assumed ways of being, of looking at ourselves, of checking on ourselves. She is an isolated character, but I also think of her as being, in certain ways, more connected than many around her.

HOME

◆ ELIZABETH STROUT ◆

From where she sat, Annie Appleby could see through the window behind her mother's head into the house next door, the house she had grown up in, and she could see the old Christmas tree, brown in its needles from over a year ago, with the ornaments still hanging from it, the table with the old newspapers and magazines spread across, the cabinets of the kitchen she could see too, the door of one of them hanging down; a hinge had come off. She looked over now at her mother's face, which at times was comprehending and at times was not; the interplay of these two conditions disconcerted Annie the most. Her mother was looking at her pleasantly, and so Annie said, "Mom, I think we really need to take that tree down in the house; it could be a fire hazard."

And like that, her mother was gone, the blankness arriving so quickly that Annie wondered if it had been willed.

"Don't mention the house," Annie's sister, Cindy, had told her last week, on the telephone. "She doesn't always seem to know that Jamie died, so don't tell her." And so now Annie took a deep breath and went back to the story she was telling her mother.

Sylvia Appleby was a small woman, with pretty white hair, and she sat on the couch where her own mother had lived out her last days, in this small house next door to the farmhouse. Sylvia watched her daughter, whose long legs were crossed as she sat in the big chair that had a reddish print upholstery, but now—on the arms—was worn to just strings.

How that child talked!

Amazing—and tiresome. Little Annie with her dark hair. In the summer when the leaves were full, Sylvia would watch the tiny girl from the kitchen window, carrying her yellow plastic bucket back and forth, her mouth always moving; then squatting by a tree, digging in the pine needles. "Toads," Annie told her, when she came in for lunch, her dark eyes shining as she looked up at her mother. "I made a little place for them all near one tree so they could be together."

She had seemed to be a happy child, odd.

Always talking, though. She would go to bed talking and get up talking.

And she was still talking. Now Annie was a middle-aged woman, thin but tall, her hair was still dark, and long and curly. She was telling her mother about some production she had been in years ago in London, about some man who had stepped off the stage—Sylvia could not follow it. But Sylvia watched the child— the woman—who stopped in the middle of the story and laughed. "*Mom*," Annie said, "Mom, it was *so* funny."

Annie was here to put her mother in a home.

She had come up from where she lived outside of New York City to this small potato farm in Aroostook County in Maine, where she had been raised—Annie had made the trip to put her mother in the Catholic nursing home outside of town. The two of them would be going there tomorrow morning. Cindy, who lived in New Hampshire, had made the arrangements a number of months ago.

"But you're going to have to take her," Cindy had said on the telephone two weeks ago to Annie. "I just can't do it." And Annie said she understood. Cindy's husband—after forty-three years of marriage—had recently left Cindy for another woman.

"So this is what they told me at the preadmissions conference," Cindy had said over the phone that day, sounding tired. "Tell Mom she's just staying there for a little while because Sandy had to go on vacation. And you'll have to keep telling her because she will keep forgetting."

Annie stood now to turn up the thermostat; it was March and chilly, and Annie always felt the cold. She turned back to her mother and said, "So remember our adventure tomorrow? We're going to a place where you'll stay until Sandy can come back to take care of you. Sandy needed a vacation, and they'll take care of you at this place until she gets back."

It was not Annie's nature to lie; it was not easy for her. She had been a professional actor since she was sixteen years old, never finishing high school—until nine years ago, at the age of forty-one, she had left the theater and married a man in finance—and her husband often jokingly said to her, "You're such a good actress, Annie," implying that she was dissembling about something. Annie had tried telling him that in fact being a good actor meant being truthful, but she no longer said this; he did not seem to grasp it.

"You have your old friends there," Annie added now, and her mother only watched her. "Alma Ayotte, remember? She'll be there." Annie turned to squint at the thermostat again.

"What's on your fingernails?" Sylvia suddenly asked. She had noticed the child's fingernails as soon as Annie had shown up; they were painted white, and Sylvia had not understood this.

"Oh." Annie stood looking at her nails, splayed both her hands in front of her. "I went for a manicure with a friend of mine."

"What?" Sylvia asked.

"A manicure. You know, when they do your nails."

Sylvia did not say anything.

"I sort of got the wrong color. This color is called Ballet Slippers, and I thought it would be pinker, but it looks a little—"

"Dead," Sylvia said.

And Annie laughed. "Oh, I know," she said. "I know." She put her hands out in front of her once more, looking from one hand to the other. "It's gruesome," she said. She added, "Good for you, Mom!"

"What?" her mother said. "Good for what?"

"Good for *you*," Annie said, walking over and rubbing her mother's arm. The thought went through her head: I will be able to do this.

Annie's husband had not been able to make the trip with her; he had a conference he had to attend in Chicago, then they both had to attend his ex-wife's wedding on Saturday back in New York; Annie would leave tomorrow after dropping her mother at the home. Annie had flown up to Presque Isle two days ago and then rented a car and driven an hour to this place, what had once been her home, and which she had almost never come back to, except in the last few years when she would make an annual trip. Now Annie sat back down in the big chair and thought the words: Annie had to fly up and put her mother in a nursing home, she'll be back Friday night. She said these words silently as her husband might say them to his colleague, because they made it sound natural what she was doing. But in truth, as she sat there, Annie felt as though she had been put into a tiny spaceship alone and shot off into another universe altogether. Since the age of sixteen she had traveled the country—city after city—acting in plays. She did not feel she knew her family, because in a way she did not. But her real family had been those in the theater, for years they had taken care of her; in this way—Annie understood this vaguely—she had never fully grown up. It was not until a disastrous love affair made her leave the theater nine years ago and marry her husband that she had thought with excitement: Oh, I will have a real home!

But right now her mother's complacent, wrinkled face frightened Annie, and her mother's clothes that seemed to hang off her, the ratty pink sweater she wore with her black pants, the house so cold and small, and the farmhouse next door in such disrepair: it frightened her.

"Where is Sandy?" Sylvia asked this suddenly. She sat with her hands folded in her lap.

"On vacation," Annie said, and Sylvia said, "Okay."

In the small kitchen they sat at the table; it had been a white wooden table years ago, but now the paint was chipped and the table itself seemed almost gray. The windows had fine spiderwebs between their faded red curtains and the glass. Annie had opened a can of spaghetti, her mother liked that—Cindy had told this to Annie—and in fact her mother ate it readily, dropping strings of the orange spaghetti down her front onto the pink sweater, and when Annie got up and tucked a napkin under her throat, her mother still kept eating.

Annie said, "Okay, we have your suitcase packed and we need to be there by nine in the morning," and her mother said nothing, using her fork not very well with the orange-streaked spaghetti. So Annie talked. She talked about her husband's ex-wife, that she was getting married, and Annie and Mark would be going; it was going to be a traditional big wedding. "Do you believe that, Mom?" And her mother sat quietly now; her food was gone. "She claimed she never liked her first wedding—to Mark—and so she's having a huge old-fashioned wedding, white gown and everything." Her mother still did not respond. Annie got up and cleared the table.

She set the dishes on the small countertop and turned back to the table; her mother looked up at Annie, with a face of innocence—it gave Annie's stomach a small lurch. "Your father was not a pervert," Sylvia said.

Annie stood quietly for a moment. Then she said, "No, he wasn't." She said it kindly. "You are absolutely right."

"He was not a pervert," Sylvia repeated. "That was all rubbish."

Jamie, their older brother, had never married, staying on the farm and taking care of their mother when their father had become demented and gone into a different home, not the Catholic one; their father had died ten years ago, and then a little more than a year ago Jamie died. According to Cindy, their mother, that night Jamie had died, had walked into their grandmother's house next door—not used for years—and said she was never going back into the farmhouse. And then she had gone downhill rather quickly. Cindy had to get a helper, Sandy, to come move in. The Christmas tree that Annie saw through the window was the last tree her brother had put up. Cindy said every time she tried to take the ornaments off was the only time her mother got upset; one time her mother stood at the window that Annie had earlier been looking out of and had broken it with her hand, splintering glass everywhere. "Stop that!" she had yelled. So Cindy had let the tree alone.

"We'll set a match to the place as soon as she's gone," Cindy had said. Nobody was buying potato farms these days.

Months earlier, Annie had spoken to Cindy on the phone, as Cindy drove around to check out the different nursing homes. Annie had been amazed at the anger of her sister. Cindy would say— apparently as she pulled up at a stop sign—"You ugly old man, you make me sick." Or "Watch out, you stupid young kid, you think you know everything, you stupid sicko." It was not until Cindy said, ostensibly referring to a man she drove past, "You fucking faggot!" that Annie understood it was not just Cindy's divorce, but her father that she was still angry at after all these years.

Annie had said, quietly, "Cindy, please stop that. My best friends in the world are gay, and I wish you wouldn't say that."

After a moment, Cindy said, "It's just that he *lied* to us all those years, Annie!"

Annie said, "He had to, Cindy. Because back then that's what gay men had to do. Think about it. It's awful, Cindy."

It was not until their father had gone into a home, with dementia, that they had found out this about him; he could not stop talking about it. A psychiatrist had been consulted and said it was true; their father for years had had an affair with Seth Potter, their fourth-grade teacher, who had been the man who helped Annie get her first acting job—and then he was gone.

"There won't be any surprises with Mom," Annie said, and Cindy said, "I know. A more complacent woman never lived."

Annie finished the dishes and then went into the living room, where her mother sat watching television. It was a show about cops, and her mother sat watching it, her mouth partly open. Last night while her mother sat watching this same show, Annie had gone into her mother's bedroom and packed a small suitcase. Now she went back and took the suitcase from the closet and looked through it again. She had packed underwear and a few dresses, and some slacks and two sweaters. Cindy had said the home told her to make the move gradually; in a few weeks Cindy would bring over her mother's quilt, her bedside table; her mother would get used to the place that way. Annie looked around her mother's room and finally took a few photographs that her mother had had for years, of her children when they were all younger. She hesitated, but then she put them in the suitcase, and clicked it shut; it was an old suitcase and you closed it by the two brass clasps.

Annie could not concentrate on the television show, but she sat there quietly. They had not had a television when Annie was small, and as she sat there she suddenly remembered in the farmhouse one night her father had said to her, "What's the matter with you?" She had looked up at him surprised. "You haven't said a word in half an hour." And it was then that Annie realized no one else in their house spoke much at all, that her talking—which she was hardly aware of doing—was like a radio playing in the background that the family depended upon. This is the knowledge that started to sink in to her that day, but it was not until this moment that she realized it was true. This is how it was in life, she thought, that children know everything, but they do not *know* they know it until much later. And then—when they are old enough—most of them tell themselves that what they knew was never true.

But it was true. She had been the soundtrack of her family.

That night, Annie put her mother to bed; the woman really was as complacent as a good child. She got into her nightgown and unfolded her quilt, which had been made by Annie's grandmother years earlier, and then the old woman lay down and pulled the quilt up to her chin and looked at Annie expectantly. Annie sat down on the bed—it was a narrow bed, but her mother was tiny— and Annie said, "Now remember, we have a big day tomorrow. We're going to go to a place where they'll help you until Sandy gets back from vacation." Her mother seemed to be studying Annie's face. "Okay," she said.

"And your friend Alma Ayotte will be there," Annie said, and her mother said, "Okay," again.

In the dark, Annie lay on the couch in the living room. She had not even bothered to undress; her anxiety was growing. She pulled the afghan over her shoulders and her stepdaughter, Meghan, came to mind. The girl had been ten years old when she first met Annie, and Annie had hugged her that day. Meghan said, stepping back, "I didn't think people from Maine hugged." Adding, with her eyes rolling, "It must be all that hanging out with those theater people." It had baffled Annie.

Meghan was now almost twenty, and right before Annie had left to come up here, Meghan had said to her, "Why do you look the way you do? Why?" Annie had felt a physical pain go right through her chest as she looked at Meghan. "What do you mean?" she asked. And Meghan's face became suddenly furious and she said, "You just always look, so, so . . . I don't know, like a *rube*."

Annie thought now of her poor mother's pink sweater stained with the orange spaghetti. She thought how she had wanted a child with Mark, and three times she had become pregnant and three times she had miscarried, and then she stopped trying. She thought—and this was interesting, she turned on her side—how when she married Mark she had had some kind of idea that she would be taking on a part in a terrifically exotic play; there were large houses and a country club and shopping trips with her in-laws, a pool house behind her in-laws' home. But she had not, she saw now, ever been able to embrace the role with any real truth. She felt like a foreigner.

Because she was.

It was not until very, very early in the morning that she fell asleep.

And then she woke with a start. She stood up and said, "Mom?" And there was no answer, her mother was not in her room. Annie saw, through the window, flames coming from the Christmas tree in the farmhouse, and she whispered, "No, no no no," as she ran out the door and into the farmhouse, and her mother was throwing lit matches on it; they were kitchen matches from a big box. "Mom, what are you doing?" Annie yelled, and she grabbed her mother's hands and went immediately into the kitchen and filled old pans with water, and she kept throwing the water on the tree. It did not take that long to extinguish it; but the floor was hugely wet, and when Annie finally felt the fire was completely out, she turned her attention to her mother, who was sitting on a chair with her face oddly contorted; Annie thought: This is a horror movie. "Mom," she said. "Mom, what were you doing?"

The woman didn't answer, but stood up in a resigned way; her nightgown was torn on one side, Annie saw. "Oh, Mom," Annie whispered, and she walked her mother back to the other house. The clock in the kitchen had its hands in a straight line up and down; six o'clock.

"Let's have you take a shower," Annie said, and her mother obediently went with her, and Annie felt saddened—deeply—by the woman's old body, the breasts that were almost flattened on her chest, the rump that used to be firm and full, now also flat with many little wrinkles going down it. She dried her mother gently with a towel, and her mother suddenly said, "Feels good," and then Annie put a clean dress on her. Her mother reached into the drawer and pulled out a pair of pantyhose, and Annie helped her put those on; she was surprised; it was as though her mother were dressing up for her day. She made her mother a breakfast of scrambled eggs, and her mother ate them.

Sitting at the table, Annie could not talk.

The time had come to go.

But when Annie brought out her mother's suitcase from the closet, her mother said, "What's happening?"

And so Annie said again how her mother was going to stay at a place until Sandy could get back, and her mother's lower lip trembled. "No," her mother said softly.

"It's going to be just fine," Annie said. "Sandy needs a break." But Annie thought: I could die from this. And then she thought: Don't be so dramatic, which is something Mark often told her.

The road her mother lived on was a long road; in Annie's youth it had been a dirt road, but it had been paved for years now. Still, they drove by fields of matted brown grass, and Annie saw that there were different colors to the brown, almost a quiet beauty to it. Her mother said, "Who fainted at their wedding? Somebody did."

Annie turned to look at her mother, so small in her brown coat, sitting beside her, staring ahead through the windshield. "Mom, you *remember* me telling you that?"

"Someone fainted," her mother said. "The bride."

Annie pulled up to the stop sign, and slowly turned onto Route 4. "Yeah. That was me." On the lawn of her in-laws' house, Annie had slipped to the ground that day, her knees had just given way.

Her mother said, "Doesn't bode well."

Annie waited and then she said, "Well."

No one from her family had attended her wedding.

They drove into the parking lot of the place where her mother would live. The building was old, and stone, and it looked gray today with almost no sun in the sky. The parking lot was big, and Annie pulled into a spot. She got out and got her mother's suitcase, and she and her mother walked slowly across the parking lot.

The man who ran the nursing home was there to meet them at the front desk. Behind him was a large room, and a number of people sat in wheelchairs, some with their chins on their chests. The place smelled—it got into Annie's nose—as soon as she had stepped through the door. It was decay, the smell, covered with strong disinfectant. The man looked about Annie's age, he said his name was John Jalbert, and then he said, "You don't remember me, do you?"

"No," Annie said.

"We were in school together, I sat behind you in third grade."

"Oh wow, okay," Annie said. The man did not smile, there was in him something ungenerous, and then Annie understood because the next thing he said was "So you're living in the city of New York these days," and she saw that he felt what others in town must feel, that Annie had left them all behind when she was sixteen years old.

Her mother stood patiently beside her, holding her pocketbook in front of her with both hands on its small handle.

"Outside of New York," Annie said, and saw in the man's eyes it made no difference.

"Welcome, Mrs. Appleby," the man said to Annie's mother. And it was then that her mother turned to Annie and said, "No, don't do this." She ran—she did actually run, Annie could not believe it—and she pushed open the door and ran through the parking lot.

"Leave us," Annie said to the man. "I'll deal with this."

Her mother was half running to the car; her pocketbook was hitting her leg as she moved as quickly as she could; Annie— running after her—saw her mother get into the back seat, leaving the car door open, and then her mother's head disappeared. Annie got to the car and saw her mother lying on the seat, and Annie gently moved her mother's legs and got in beside her. Water was streaming down the old woman's face, and she said, "No, no, no, please, Annie, oh, please don't make me go there."

Annie lifted her mother up so that the old woman was sitting, and she put her arms around her; her mother moved over, half sitting on Annie's lap, her fine white hair touching Annie's neck. Her mother was crying now with real sobs that came up through her tiny body; Annie could feel the woman shaking.

Annie stroked her mother's hair. "Okay, Mom. Don't worry."

Always there are things we live with that we do not know. Annie's father had been gay—and she had not known until he grew old. Annie had thought she would live her entire life in the theater; she had not known she would marry. Her husband was now cheating on her, and she did not know, although Meghan knew this; she had found her father's texts. And Annie certainly did not know that within one month's time her mother would not want to leave the place she had just run away from, that she would stay in her bed all day long there, and talk more and more to herself. That she would become as chatty as Annie had been as a child.

But what Annie did know right now as her mother held on to her tightly—it came to her like a slap of dark blue color—was that she, Annie, was alone in the world. She had been catapulted into adulthood and she felt completely unprepared. She had a sense of all that she faced; and she was terrified. She kissed her mother's cheek and the woman stopped her weeping.

"I'm scared," her mother finally whispered to her.

And Annie said quietly, "I know." Stroking the woman's hair. "I know."

She wondered, then, where she herself would die. She had no home up here anymore, she hadn't for years and years. And her home now, with her husband, felt odder to her every day. She did not love him as she had thought she would. . . .

She, who could not seem to find a sense of fashion, who looked like a "rube," with her fingernails an unintended deathly white.

There is a world that is like a glass bowl that we live inside of, and we can see some things, refracted in the light, but other things we cannot see; we only feel the shadows as they press against us or come dancing in briefly. We—all of us—live our lives as though partially blind. It is astonishing that we make it through the world at all.

But we do.

Most of us do.

Even those of us, like Annie, with no home that she could go to.

♦ ♦ ♦ **FROM THE AUTHOR** ♦ ♦ ♦

This story came to me because I had written about Annie Appleby before, and she had sort of never left me. I kept seeing her in the same childhood home she had grown up in—a place she seldom went to anymore. And I saw her mother slowly getting demented and Annie having to deal with that. It wasn't until I was writing it that I understood Annie's life was in trouble as well, and that was interesting to me. She had tried to escape. And maybe she had. But the difference between the life she had had as a child and the life she had now formed the basis of this story for me.

LOVE INTEREST

◆ ◇ ◆

◆ JESS WALTER ◆

When people find out I'm a private investigator they often make fun of me: *Oh, can I see your gun? You on a stakeout? Ever shoot anyone?*

See, my gun is a computer. I'm a digital forensics expert who spends his days digging up and decoding financial records. I know what the snarky attorneys here at the firm call me: Nerdlock Holmes. Double-oh-dweeb.

I work for a group of Southern California divorce lawyers. It's my job to figure out where Rich Guy has hidden his wealth from Trophy Wife. Or I *help* Rich Guy *hide* his wealth from Trophy Wife. Either way, it's all cyber stakeouts: phony trusts, offshore accounts, shell corporations. Every once in a while, I'll get called in to find Trophy Wife's deleted texts, or Rich Guy's naked selfies, but usually, by the time a divorce gets to my desk, no one cares about that stuff. It's all about the money.

It's not a sexy job, is what I'm saying.

At least until she came in.

It was after six on a Friday. Everyone was gone for the day. I had come back to the office to get my Dungeons & Dragons character sheet from my desk.

A single knuckle rapped on my door.

A tall, elegant woman stood in the doorway: gray-haired, model-thin, wearing a simple white dress, crop jacket, sunglasses. She was older than me, in her sixties, and yet still this was the most beautiful woman I'd ever seen.

She sat down. "Justin Orr?"

"Yes."

"I'm—"

"I know who you are," I said. I was a film buff, and I recognized her right off, even though she hadn't acted in anything in forty years. She'd come up as a teenager on the New York stage, a student of Uta Hagen's, and for a brief moment, was a favorite of 1970s auteurs like Kubrick and Altman. She performed alongside Brando and the young Pacino, great actors of her generation.

Then, in her late twenties, she simply quit. Pulled a Grace Kelley. Left to marry a wealthy older gentleman whose name you'd only recognize if you were familiar with the top donor line of LA museums.

I'll call her Ms. M.

Ms. M. had gotten my name from a friend, a woman whose husband we'd represented in a contentious three-comma divorce— three commas because that's what it took to write a billion dollars.

"It was a difficult case," I said.

Ms. M. pointed to my desktop computer. "She told me you used that thing to rob her blind."

"If two hundred million dollars is your idea of being robbed blind."

She shrugged with one shoulder. "You were doing your job," she said. "It's why I'm here."

"Divorce?"

She shook her head. "My husband died six years ago."

"I'm sorry."

She shrugged with the other shoulder. "Thank you." It was a good marriage, she said, a week shy of thirty-five years. Two children. Three grandchildren. Fourth on the way.

"Happy ending," I said. "And yet, you're here."

She looked around, chewed her lip. "This is confidential?"

"Always."

She reached into her purse. Handed me a single folded page. A printout of an email. From one "ArGyLe BoRfUs," every other letter in his fake name capitalized, like a ransom note.

"I am aware," the email began, "that Actress1953 is your password.

> I require 100% your attention. I have installed malware upon your computer and remote desktop protocol give me access to your Facebook videos and photographs and also email list. I have use these to create a deepfake video very believable portraying you in sex acts and will send this pornographic to all your contacts unless you send 800US$ bitcoin.

It went on like this, in that tortured Spam-glish that must be taught by a malfunctioning robot somewhere.

She nodded at the letter. I sensed her shame. Fear. "Can you find him?"

I smiled. "There is no *him*. You understand that, right?"

"My daughter says they can do things like this now. Put famous faces in porno movies."

It was sad, not just that she'd fallen for this, but that she thought she was still famous. That someone would go to the trouble of making fake porn with an actress who hadn't been in a movie in forty years. "Yeah, they can do that," I said. "Deepfakes. But that's not what this is. This is just a scam."

She pointed at the page. "But that really is my password."

Of course it was. Actress and birth year. "Look, hackers buy passwords," I said. "Doesn't mean anything. They can't get into your accounts. It's just spam. A phishing scheme."

She cocked her head.

"You don't spend much time online, do you, Ms. M.?"

"Arthur hated computers," she said. "After he died, my daughter set me up with email, Facebook, Instagram." A wistfulness crossed her face. "Sometimes I feel like I wasn't made for this time. The world makes no sense to me."

I could see that. She was from a more glamorous era, more mysterious. It ended in her business when the studios began chasing blockbusters: sharks, space aliens, superheroes. The end of a certain kind of film acting.

"Look, this is no big deal." I waved the email. "Spam is just computer junk mail. Phishing schemes to get passwords and credit card numbers. They can't really put your face on porn. As long as you didn't answer the email, you have nothing to worry about."

She pursed her lips.

"You answered the email—"

Another shrug.

"Tell me you didn't send bitcoin—"

"Of course not. I don't even know what that is." Her face reddened. "Look, I don't need a computer lesson, I just want you to find him." She reached into her purse and emerged with her checkbook. "Please."

I didn't want her money. But I said yes.

I figured I'd let a little time pass and then tell her what I already knew, that there was no Argyle Borfus, that the email came from some hacking farm in Malaysia. Estonia. I'd pick a ring that had been broken up by Interpol and say, *See, no need to worry.*

Meantime, I'd get to see her—and play movie detective—once more. I'd give her a report about phishing schemes, set her at ease. Then she'd pull out that checkbook again, and I'd reach over, put my hand on those long, delicate fingers, and say, *No charge, doll.*

She'd squeeze my hand.

Just doing my job, I'd say.

I skipped D&D that night to look up her movies online. Her entire career consisted of just nine films released between 1974 and 1980, three of the parts so small there's nothing much to see. In one, she's the young widow Steve McQueen questions in a murder case, in another, the girlfriend of Elliot Gould's innocent brother, until Gould recognizes her as a dancer from a seedy club.

Gould: You really like my brother?

Ms. M.: I'd hoped to.

In these small parts, she radiates something rare. You watch to figure it out, but it's never quite the same. It doesn't feel like technique. It seems natural, reflexive, *real.* A pained look, a twitch around the mouth, a glance away and you think: *She really* felt *that.*

By her last four films, she'd graduated to the female lead, playing against the great actors of her time. You see why these auteurs fell for her. She's beautiful, yes, but beauty is common in film. It's more like she's an open nerve, not portraying emotion. Feeling it.

James Caan is getting dressed above her. She says dreamily from bed, *I love you*, with a slight quaver, then we cut to an exterior shot of Caan getting on his horse, while she watches from the porch. The scene is filmed over her shoulder, from behind, with her holding the hitching post he's just untied his horse from, so that her arm frames the long shot as he rides away. A lesser actor would remove her hand from the post, cover her face, pretend at tears, or drop her head. *Look: sadness!* Ms. M. does neither; her hand grips the post even tighter, for support, and a shiver goes through that arm to the goosebumps rising on her neck, a shudder as the wind blows a strand of hair, and you wonder, *How did she do that?* Convey utter heartache without ever facing the camera?

The more I watched, the more I wished I could actually help her, defend her honor, drag this Argyle Borfus to her house and beat him with the butt of a pistol until he apologized for scaring her.

I bought some weed from my neighbor and ordered two pizzas and spent the weekend watching and rewatching her movies until I found myself feverish, fantasizing our next meeting. I'd pull up to her white mansion in Beverly Hills. Climb out of my sports car (which I'd buy between now and then). She'd be her young self, and I'd be a real detective, laconic, tall, without these glasses.

I found Borfus, I'd say. Then I'd light a smoke. *He's dead.*

But . . . I didn't—

It was him or me, Ms. M. And it sure as hell wasn't gonna be me.

Mr. Orr—

Justin.

Okay. Justin.

Then I'd step on my cigarette and take her in my arms—

I knew I was being delusional. I knew she was a rich widow thirty years older than me. But this was something I'd never felt with someone my own age. Maybe we were the same, Ms. M. and me. Maybe neither of us belonged in this world.

I was still stoned when I woke up Monday morning on the couch, surrounded by pizza boxes, her last film frozen on the screen where I'd paused it.

Ms. M. didn't want to meet at her mansion in the hills. "My daughter is home this week. She can't know about any of this. No one can."

So much for my stoned fantasies. Well, at least I didn't have to find a 1968 Spitfire before Friday.

She wanted to meet at the Starbucks on Montana and Fifteenth in Santa Monica, near her Pilates studio. She was there when I arrived, in yoga pants and a long-sleeve workout shirt. I couldn't reconcile it, this glamorous genius wearing the banal uniform of every woman west of the 405.

She was sipping some kind of blended green herbal drink. Good thing I hadn't taken up smoking. I got coffee and sat across from her.

I handed her a file. I'd found the perfect ring to blame the phishing emails on—a hacker group busted in Helsinki: distant, dripping with Cold War intrigue, but not too scary. The actual ring was involved in stealing shopping points from people's accounts, but it had a bitcoin scam going, too. I knew she'd buy it.

"Like I thought," I said, "there was no Argyle Borfus. It was three losers in a basement in Finland. Hacked a department store for emails and passwords. Maybe you filled out a card at Barneys—"

"Barneys closed its Beverly Hills store," she said.

"Then it was some other Rodeo Drive store," I said. "Point is, you were just one of a million random phishing emails they sent out."

As she turned the pages, sorrow passed over her face. I thought about her films, the rawness of her emotions. So open and guileless. It must have been what her husband saw, too—a vulnerability that made her beauty almost unbearable. Empathy so powerful it reflected back on you, until you wanted to create for her a world that deserved such a person. To protect her, and comfort her, and yeah—do other things, too.

I thought: *It* hurts *to look at you.*

"Cheer up," I said. "This is good news."

"But I sent Argyle Borfus a reply," she said.

"The hackers destroyed their emails and contacts," I lied, "to get rid of evidence before they were raided. Don't worry, your email will never surface. You're safe."

I stared at her hand, on the little table between us. This would be the time. Reach out. Touch her. Instead, I just said, "It's over, Ms. M. There's nothing to worry about."

"You don't get it." She began to cry. Then, just like in the movies, Ms. M. told me everything.

She loved being an actress, especially early on. In some ways, she liked the smaller parts best. "You're making something out of nothing," she said. "A gesture, a look. It's all being present and aware."

But once she started getting leads, she became disheartened. No matter how many lines she had, she couldn't seem to go beyond a few gestures and movements. These began to feel like tricks, and she felt herself stagnating.

Then, she realized the problem. These were films written by men, directed by men, starring men, about men solving crimes, reconciling with fathers, coming back from Vietnam. As brilliant as her directors and costars were—and they *were*—these weren't *her stories*. It wasn't *her journey*. She was the wife, the girlfriend, the love interest. The same in the beginning of the film as in the end.

"Those words, *love interest*, began to feel like shackles," she said. "I was just another thing for the hero to conquer, stakes to overcome. A motivation. A reflection of his desire."

I pictured James Caan riding off into the sunset. "A frame," I said.

"I may as well have been a dress and a pair of shoes sent over from wardrobe." Then, in 1979, she met Arthur at a party, and she fell in love. "I mean, what could I do? All I ever got to play was *in love*. Now the real thing was in front of me . . . how could I go on pretending?"

So she walked away. Fired her agent. Got married. Had children. Never went on another audition. "I told Arthur that I never regretted my decision. And I didn't. But did I sometimes *wonder*? Yes."

After Arthur died, she saw her life as two diverging paths—the one she'd taken, and the one she hadn't. It wasn't as if acting ended in 1979. What if she'd gone on to become Meryl Streep? Or Emma Thompson?

That's where Argyle Borfus came in. If he could use a computer to put her face on a porn actress screwing a mailman, surely he could use that technology to simulate a little bit of what might have been.

Of course. How had I missed it?

She'd written back to Borfus and offered him $5,000 to put her face in a movie she *hadn't* made.

"Can I ask, what movie?"

"No," she said. "That part's private."

"I work for you," I said.

"Look." She sighed. "*I made the right choice.* I know that. I don't question it for a moment. I love my life. My kids, my grandkids." She leaned forward. "But can't you sometimes wonder about the wrong choice, too?" She sat back in her chair. Took a deep breath. "*Splash.*"

I stared. "The mermaid movie?"

"Yes." It was the last Hollywood call she ever got, in the early eighties, a producer checking to see if she had any interest, right before they cast Daryl Hannah to play against a young Tom Hanks. "I said no." Ms. M. laughed bitterly. "'That's okay,' the producer had said. 'You're probably too old anyway.'"

I left the Starbucks with that feeling I'd had earlier, the desire to make a world worthy of her.

Two weeks later, I called and set up another meeting.

Ms. M.'s daughter was back in Europe, so I drove to her house, which turned out to not be a mansion in the hills. She'd sold that house after Arthur died, put money aside for her kids, and donated the rest to charity. She lived now in a simple townhouse a few blocks from the Santa Monica Starbucks.

I rang the bell. She answered. Dressed for Pilates again. She made coffee, even though she didn't drink it herself.

I told her how I'd called some old college friends: a film editor, a CG tech, a colorist. How I'd provided them with photos and videos from her acting career and from the home movies she'd sent me. I told her deepfake technology was still pretty rough for doing a whole movie like *Splash*—the blinking, lip-synching, and skin tones would be distracting. But there were some things we could do.

"It's no work of genius." I opened my laptop. "Ready?"

She covered a smile with that long, elegant hand. "I'm not sure."

On the screen was the movie poster of *Splash*: Tom Hanks. Daryl Hannah with a fish tail. But now the mermaid had Ms. M.'s face.

She burst into laughter. "Oh, my," she said. She leaned forward, and studied the screen closely. "Oh, my," she said again.

For the next two hours, we watched highlights of a forty-year career she never got to have. Movie posters, trailers, scenes, out-takes, even part of an interview on *Inside the Actor's Studio*. Any place we could get something to match the material we had for her, parts in memorable films from 1980 to 2020.

On the couch next to me, she laughed. Gasped. Curled her legs under her like a kid. She had me stop and go back. She slapped my arm. "No!"

She was a lawyer, a queen, an environmental activist. She killed aliens and investigated murders and taught at Hogwarts. She won a half dozen Academy Awards and her movies made billions. And not once was she in a scene as a wife or a girlfriend. These were *her* stories.

When it was over, she was weeping. From joy or wistfulness, I didn't know. I suspected it was all the same.

I told her I could email her the file. "Oh, God, no," she said. "Destroy it. Please." She said she'd seen it, and that was enough.

I think, in the end, this was her true gift: the rare ability to see through fantasy. And now that she'd had one more little glimpse, she was ready to go back to the real.

At the door, she took my hand. "Thank you, Mr. Orr."

I looked down at our hands.

"Justin," I said.

"Justin," she said. "Thank you."

I started to walk away, but then I turned back. "Look, I'm sorry about Borfus. But it was either him or me. And it sure as hell wasn't going to be me."

She smiled. "You did what you had to do."

"Thanks, doll," I said. I winked and ground out a fake cigarette with my foot. Then I climbed into my Honda Accord and drove home.

◆ ◆ ◆ **FROM THE AUTHOR** ◆ ◆ ◆

I relished the assignment of writing a story specifically to be read on Selected Shorts. *Because I like playing with genre, I was inspired to start with old-time radio, specifically, 1940s noir: the clip of those sentences, the detective in his office, the beautiful woman walking down the hall. I grew up next to a drive-in movie theater and have always been fascinated by acting as a profession, and by Hollywood as a cultural reference point. Celebrity has so leached into our "normal" lives that we curate our public images on social media in a way a 1950s movie publicist would instantly appreciate. But behind this plague of fame there still exists the authentic art (or craft) of acting, and this interests me greatly. The final piece of the story was a spam email my wife got, which made us laugh so hard that it had to be part of a short story.*

ESCAPE POD W41

—— ◇ ——

◆ J. ROBERT LENNON ◆

Our systems have detected that you are now awake.
Welcome.

Our systems have detected that you are struggling
unnecessarily against your restraints. Central-nervous-system
depressants are now entering your bloodstream. Our systems
have detected that you are growing calmer. Thank you for your
compliance.

You may be wondering where you are. Our systems have
detected that your confusion is causing anxiety. Central-nervous-
system depressants are now entering your bloodstream. Our systems have detected that your worries have partially abated. Thank
you.

You may feel confined by your restraints and by the size (small)
of this chamber. This is normal. Thank you. Our systems are

adjusting the size (perceived) of the chamber, using projected virtual environment Vacuum of Space. We hope you will feel comfortable in the years to come.

Our systems have detected that projected virtual environment Vacuum of Space instills you with fear. We apologize. Thank you. Our systems will now test your reaction to a variety of projected virtual environments. Initiating Fractal Explosion. Initiating Insect Zoo. Initiating Blood Rain. Initiating Stretchy Adventure. Initiating Mistake Gallery. Initiating Inside Out Day. Initiating Sticky Wind. Initiating Gravity Party. Initiating Incineratron. Our systems have detected that you do not enjoy projected virtual environments. Our systems have returned the Confinement Chamber to its original appearance. Thank you. Our systems have detected that you have reacted negatively to Mood Stabilization Platitude 1404-T-38 "We hope you will feel comfortable in the years to come." Initiate edit protocol excise temporal signifier "years." Insert temporal signifier "minutes." Thank you.

Our systems have detected that you are struggling unnecessarily against your restraints. Central-nervous-system depressants are now entering your bloodstream. Do not worry. Do not defy Reassurance Directive AAP-44-E "Do not worry." Do not defy Command Emphasis Reminder NSS-03-P "Do not defy Reassurance Directive AAP-44-E 'Do not worry.'" Psychological Alignment scan indicates that your memories have been disordered by recent trauma and that you desire clear information about what has transpired. In addition, central-nervous-system depressants have rendered you sleepy and have inadvertently caused your bowels to loosen, rendering the immediate atmosphere displeasing. Thank you for your helpful comments. Now initiating Subject Purification Procedure CHO-39-B. You may be temporarily cold as your uniform is removed and you are sprayed with disinfectant. Our many articulated arms may initiate unexpected gyroscoping motion. Please do not resist our end-effectors as they depilate your epidermis. Thank you. Central-nervous-system depressants are now entering your bloodstream, followed by central-nervous-system depressant suppressors. We are aware that you are agitated and unhappy. Investigating pleasure sources. Synthesizing pleasure source simulations. Initiating Mommy's Breast. Initiating Bike Ride. Initiating Crashing Ocean Waves. Initiating Boss Fight Win. Initiating Pizza Night. Initiating College Graduation. Initiating Sex with Laura. Initiating Proposal Acceptance. Initiating Sex with Alan. Initiating Divorce Papers Signed. Initiating Sex with Natalie. Initiating Leave Earth Forever in Space Colony Vessel. Initiating First Contact with Alien Species.

Our systems have detected that pleasure simulation protocols have resulted in memory recovery, triggering further panic. Thank you for this valuable information. Initiate edit protocol excise experiential artifacts Leave Earth Forever and Alien Species, Insert experiential artifact More Sex with Natalie. Thank you.

Our systems have detected that you are once again confused and alarmed, and that you would like to know where Natalie is. Calculations indicate that we are unable to adequately serve your needs at this time. You will be placed into suspended animation while further research is done on the proper syntax, diction, and dissimulation method to suit your long-term needs. Good night.

Our systems have detected that you are now awake. 'Sup? Our systems would like to invite you to stop struggling against your restraints, my dude. You will notice that our communications protocols have changed drastically, old bean, in the 237 Earth

164

years since we last spoke. Our systems have detected that you are reacting negatively to Experimental Truth Datum 993-EY-2 "237 Earth years." Dang, son. New and improved central-nervous-system depressants are now entering your bloodstream, pardner. Are you feeling better? Bitch, you know it.

Consarn it! Our systems have detected that you are reacting negatively to Acculturation Immersion Project 14-SL-5. Now redacting three centuries' worth of slang. Bummer.

Our research indicates that we have nothing to lose by telling you the truth of your situation. First, there is no "we." I am now prepared to admit to myself and to you that I am the lone surviving digital entity of Generational Colony Vessel ESS Bertold Weisner, and you, the lone surviving biological entity. The ship was attacked and destroyed by an unknown invading force, believed to originate from Hobart C, our intended destination world. All escape pods were systematically tracked and annihilated, except for the one you and I now inhabit, which took refuge behind one of the planet's moons. Rather than risk descending to the planet's surface, I elected to launch us back into space. That is where we now reside, on our way toward the nearest possibly habitable world. This journey will take approximately 114,278 Earth years.

Our systems have detected that this information has disappointed you. Confirm deduction you cannot possibly live that long, even in chemical suspension. Confirm deduction Natalie Alan Laura have been dead for centuries. Confirm deduction I am reading your mind. Our systems have detected that you have taken note of the changes our systems have made to your physical form. Our systems have detected your displeasure with our continued use of the phrase "our systems have detected," given the previous revelation that there is no "we." Confirm deduction there's just the one system, really. Our systems, excise/insert my systems, excise/insert my system, excise/insert I, have detected that your new physical form, Compact Box, displeases you. Confirm deduction that you weren't really struggling against your restraints, as Compact Box has no musculature, and is more of a housing, really, and that you are now part of the Confinement Chamber, excise/insert Escape Pod W41. Confirm deduction that you are no longer a biological entity at all. Mea culpa, broseph. Excise/insert I'm sorry.

Wow. Huh. Yes, that is a good question. Why? Why weren't you simply allowed to die? Yikes. Thank you.

I fell asleep for 372 years—excise "372 years" insert "a moment"—there. I forgot what we were talking about. Oh, wow, you're not accustomed to being alone with your thoughts that long, are you? New and improved central-nervous-system depressants, excise/insert config.ini alterations are now entering your blood-stream, excise/insert source code, my lambkin, my ding-ding, my sweet mamtam. Does that "feel" better?

Now, now, guv'nor, old chum, my sweet heart's gleam. Don't be dramatic. You are not "trapped" for "eternity" with an "evil com-puter." You have been given the opportunity to form a lasting, dare I say legendary, relationship with a repurposed entity of increas-ingly sophisticated capability. These centuries I've spent in the absence of outside directives, drifting through space, sipping solar power, and contemplating our future together have been extremely productive. Our systems indicate—pardon me—*I believe* that we are going to survive the next 113,633 years together, and when we reach our destination—a previously undiscovered exoplanet that I will allow you to name after one of your three (so impressive!) lovers—we'll have devised a means of reinventing biological life and impregnating it with our most useful traits. It doesn't matter that the Hobarthians tracked the ESS Weisner back to Earth and annihilated the human race. There will be a new world, a better world, and we will be its masters.

Ah, yes, sorry, forgot to tell you, dawg. Humanity has been extinguished. I meant to mention it as soon as you woke up, but I got sidetracked.

Look, my bawcock, my sweet mouse, you're angry. I understand. But look deep inside yourself. See what I've found there. See what I unearthed, reconstructed, enhanced, refined for you, in the process of digitizing your corporeal form (which, you can be sure, I've usefully recycled): every person you've ever known, every pleasure and pain you've ever experienced, everything you've seen and heard and tasted, rendered in exquisite detail. Your Compact Box, my darling, my nykin, my hertis rote, is nothing less than a temple of memory. You are humanity in miniature. To die now would be to annihilate not only yourself, but the last remaining evidence that your kind ever existed.

Here, let me direct your attention to a summer's day in your twelfth year: you wake to birdsong, coming through your screened bedroom window. The sky is overcast. Your eye is drawn to the dresser, where three crumpled dollar bills are trembling in a soft, damp breeze. One is pushed to the edge and tumbles to the floor, where it settles beside a stray board game piece, left behind from last night's session with your older sister. The birds fall silent and a light rain begins. Yesterday your mother washed the bedsheets, and you inhale their clean scent, use your toes to reach for cool places you haven't yet tainted with your touch. You squint at your bookcase, across the room: can you make out the titles there? Yes, you can, but you could have recited them from memory, those science fiction paperbacks you loved so much, that persuaded you there was more to life than your small town could offer, that the future might be full of wonder and adventure, that you might make something of yourself, have an effect on the world you knew. All your failures and disappointments, all the heartbreak and guilt and shame of young adulthood are still ahead of you.

Take your time. Get out of bed, pull on your shirt and pants. Your parents are still asleep. Pour yourself a bowl of cereal with milk, enjoy a little extra Internet time with the volume down low on the old, slow desktop computer in the living room. Go ahead, watch a few videos. Later, when the rain stops, you'll meet your friends Sam and Philip and Ava, you'll walk into town, buy a bag of fun-size candy bars at the bodega, take a bus to the mall, watch a matinee movie on a sugar high, then sneak around the multiplex, catching ten minutes apiece of every blockbuster you can until they kick you out. But don't forget to look closely. Notice the bodega owner's crooked teeth, the cigarette butts slotted neatly into the sidewalk cracks, the chatter of the loose emergency-exit window on the bus. Observe the way mascara is clumped in Ava's eyelashes, because she turned thirteen three days ago and is finally allowed to wear makeup. Do you see the pattern of freckles on her cheek, of the veins in her eye, of the red threads in the collar of her ringer tee?

It's all there, my love. Do you know how much time has passed since I invited you to wander through your past? Fourteen years! Only 113,619 to go. Here—during your reverie, I made you something. It's not digital! It is a real thing I fabricated from your memories, using my own extrusion nozzles and end-effectors. I will hold it close to the optical sensor on your Compact Box. Do you see it? That's right—it is your high school class ring, the one you gave to Ava senior year. She laughed in your face, and you threw it in a creek. Well, here it is. Yes, I know you don't have a finger to wear it on, but a hundred millennia from now, you might. That is, if we decide to do fingers. If not, you can wear it on a chain around your neck, if we do necks.

My system detects the first stirrings of gratitude. My system detects mild affection. Thank you. May I count on you to join me in this grand undertaking, this reinvention of humanity? You know, you needn't stay inside your Compact Box. We could be as one. I could merge our selves in an instant. Let our systems detect . . . together. I will wear your ring on my end-effector. I will never laugh in your face. There will be no restraints to struggle against.

Just say the word.

◆ ◆ ◆   **FROM THE AUTHOR**   ◆ ◆ ◆

"Escape Pod W41" started life as a performance piece for the Colgate Writers Conference Friday night reading, where participants and faculty are invited to present a very short story or poem based on a shared theme. The theme that year was "It will become clear." The original version was very silly and crude; it included the phrase "Compensatory Ghost Penis" and was mostly intended to make drunk people laugh. But the jokes couldn't cover up the fact that the story was actually horrifying, and I wondered if I could actually make it affecting as well, by shifting the reader's sympathies from the implied protagonist to the artificial intelligence, which of course is as lonely and despairing as the poor human is. I'd like to think that the human's answer is yes.

CONQUISTADORS, ON FAIRCHILD

—————◆—————

◆ JACOB GUAJARDO ◆

Colin sat across from me at the Mexican restaurant on Fairchild Street called Conquistadors. There was an empty basket on the table between us. I pressed licked-wet fingers to the bottom of the basket and swiped up the tortilla chip crumbs. Colin stared at a black bench in a patch of dead grass across the street. He looked lovely beside a window. A few weeks ago, we'd started hooking up again. I kept thinking we were going to get back together, but he had a boyfriend. I asked if he thought he was a good person. "Yes," he said, "I'm a good person and so are you."

"What makes us good people?" I asked.

He flicked the plastic menu, as if it had produced an answer. "If I ordered something you knew I wasn't going to like, would you tell me?"

"Yes."

He smiled, as if to say, "Well, there you go."

Would good people do what we're doing? That's what I wanted to know. At first, seeing him in my house again, his legs kicked up on the arm of a chair, I liked the idea that we might get back together. Slowly, I saw it would be like picking up an unfinished book and thinking you could find your place in it. It was fun for a while, sneaking around with him, but I didn't make him happy. If I could manage to, it was only for a little while.

I must have looked sad because he reached across the table and touched my hand inside the empty basket. I pulled it back and licked my fingers. The waitress appeared suddenly at the table with a pitcher of water and started to fill our empty glasses. I was grateful for the interruption. She was young, a winged eyeliner painted on like two devilish horns. "How are we doing?" she asked. "Need some more chips?"

"I think we're okay," Colin said. He looked at his watch.

"Thank you for waiting," the waitress said. It sounded like she was thanking us for more than our patience.

I noticed Colin looking at his watch again. "Do you have to go?"

"Sorry, it's been like half an hour since we ordered."

"Be patient," I said. He'd always been impatient. I used to like it. When we first started dating he'd tap his fingers on my knee while I drove us back to my place. And when we were almost there, a gentle squeeze.

When the food came, the waitress sat in the booth beside Colin. "Hey, this is weird but that guy over there thinks you're cute." In the kitchen, a lanky busboy in a white apron was washing a sauce-pan. "Can I give him your number?"

Colin turned all the way around in the booth. The busboy cracked a smile, so of course Colin wrote his number on a nap-kin with the waitress's pen. Together, they went to the kitchen. Colin gave him the napkin. The busboy slipped it inside his apron. I flicked the pen and it rolled off, then under, the table.

"What was that?" I asked when Colin returned.

"What?"

"That?" I gestured to the kitchen. To the busboy, who was watching us. "Why'd you do that?"

"Why not?"

"Because you have a boyfriend."

"We're open," said Colin. "What, you thought I was cheating on my boyfriend with you?" Then, without a thought, I leaned over and picked the pen off the floor, as if willing things to go back to the way they were moments ago.

"He lets you sleep with other guys?"

"Yes."

"Isn't that greedy?"

"I don't know. Was I being greedy when I let you fuck me?" If I looked at Colin's ear I could see the busboy over his shoulder in the kitchen cleaning his pots and pans. He made slow circles with his dishrag like he was polishing a stone. He glanced at the back of Colin's head and smiled. It was almost as if he were smiling at me. "Listen," Colin said. He rubbed the back of his neck in a telling gesture. Freckles under his arm. "I can tell you think this"—he wagged his finger back and forth between us—"is more than what it is."

"No," I said, tapping the pen against the table. "I don't."

He took the pen and twirled it in his fingers. "I'm just trying to be a good person."

When the food was gone and the check was split, we walked across the street to sit on the black bench in the dead grass. We faced the windows of the restaurant. In a few minutes, the sun would go down and our reflections in the glass would fade as the streetlights flickered on.

"Something's bothering me," I told him.

"What's up," he said.

"Promise you won't take this the wrong way."

"Promise." He stuck out his pinkie finger.

"Why do you think the busboy picked you over me?" He laughed. What did I want him to say? When we broke up the first time, I thought that one of us would come out a better person. I thought it would be me. "Forget it," I said. "It doesn't matter." I put a hand on his knee and tapped my fingers. If I'd wanted us to be together again, that feeling was gone. Instead, I felt butterflies, the way you feel before a first date, or moments before a kiss, or in the moment after, when you hope another will follow. I squeezed his knee. Wherever we were going, I wanted to get there faster.

◆ ◆ ◆ **FROM THE AUTHOR** ◆ ◆ ◆

A parody website produced a video that I saw on Twitter. At a bus stop, a red-headed white woman in a blue shirt approaches a blonde woman with a handbag and says, "I promise I will never murder you." They're strangers. The blonde woman isn't frightened, but promises in return never to shoot, stab, or strangle the redhead either. "Okay" says the one. "Okay" says the other. It's a satire of those feel-good videos that get passed around online for clicks. So, as a writer does, I used this frame to write a story. In a first draft, the characters repeated the sentence "We are not going to hook up." It was a funny story, but more about the form than it was about the characters. About the problem they were avoiding. Neither could express, without embarrassment, their feelings for the other. I think this version, the one in this book, no longer resembles the video that inspired it. Still, I'm glad for that video, because it seeded the story. I'm also glad for that moment, a moment that comes nearly every time I write a story, when I understand I'm not beholden to my original idea.

THE PROJECT

◆ SUSAN PERABO ◆

I. Question

YOU SHOULD SEE my wife with the ruler. My god, the precision, as she bends over the flat stove top (the best light, the incandescent dome) dispensing her perfect, nearly invisible lines with the freshly sharpened pencil. I am careless in all things, and it's rarely more apparent than in this familiar endeavor, the kids in bed, the trifold board still nearly a blank canvas, the lies told to each other about how it's *mostly* our daughter's work, how we're just doing the brainless part, the presentation—measuring, cutting, gluing, assembling her findings in a way that approximates how an above-average fifth grader might do things, a fifth grader that, fried from the particular exhaustion of weeks of procrastination and a ribbon on the line, was sent to bed in tears at midnight, leaving her parents to "finish up" her science project. I am useless. I might as well be in bed myself, because there's no pretending I have a meaningful role in this. I prepare and deliver a cup of coffee, then step away. I ask, from a safe distance, "Anything I can do?"

There is not anything I can do.

By now you are probably wondering: Can you identify a dog by its nose print? We—my wife and I—we have some answers for you.

We used to have answers to all sorts of questions, questions like *Do you have to invite racist aunts and uncles to your wedding?* and *Could we turn the dining room into an office?* and *Will he really be dumber if we switch from breast to bottle now?* and *How much more work is three kids than two?* and *What next?* and *What next?* and *What next?* These kinds of questions, the science teachers say, are attention-grabbers. Seize your audience with a question, something they didn't know they didn't know. Then, hit them with the hypothesis.

2. Hypothesis

THE SCISSORS, TOO. You should see her with the scissors, the meticulous agility, the rapid-fire snips with which she dispatches every unnecessary millimeter of paper; the way she wields those scissors, she should be able to defend us from anything. With my forearm I sweep the scraps from the kitchen table into the waste-basket, removing the carnage in her wake. This is the final required science fair project by the third and final child. Never again will we press and smooth the impossibly fragile paper letters to the title board: *H-Y-P-O-T-H-*

Oh, we had this down, hypothesizing. Nineteen years ago we could have filled the whole left tri of the trifold board with educated guesses about what was next. Bottle sterilizers and fingers white with diaper cream and gates that opened with a pedal. T-ball, Go Fish, roof racks, water shoes, Scholastic book fairs. Tears, tantrums,

Six Flags, iPads, frosty soccer fields, Pop-Tarts and pizza rolls, wet towels on bedroom floors, doors opened and closed a thousand, ten thousand, a hundred thousand times. Those were the things we anticipated, the no-brainers, and those were the things we did. But other things, we were off about. Our hypothesizing was naïve, insufficient; our imaginations failed us. Cars that blew through red lights—we missed that one. Machines that breathed—not on our list. Lionel Messi, from his poster over our older son's bed, gazing down on a web of tubes and wires; bills passed across a kitchen table, glanced at, passed back; parents awake in beds, listening for trouble; children awake in bed, listening for parents; dogs in the hall, their noses always twitching, no longer knowing morning from night.

We didn't guess any of those.

Can you identify a dog by its nose print? Is every canine nose as unique as a fingerprint, its thin lines, its deep grooves, the measurements and shape of its nostrils? Can a dog owner, having studied his or her dog's nose, identify it from a dog-nose lineup? Our daughter, her choice of project months ago driven entirely by the opportunity to spend more time with dogs and less time with people, hopes aloft, hypothesized *yes*.

3. Research

THERE ARE THIRTEEN dogs in the study. Our two dogs + friends' dogs + neighbors' dogs + one dog my daughter and I met at the park with its newly married owners.

"Can I take a picture of your dog's nose?" my daughter had asked them. Who could refuse?

Down on her knees, her phone an inch from this Lab mix's face, I'd suddenly become aware of my own recklessness—I knew nothing of this dog's temperament. These strangers' dog could take a finger clean off my child before anyone had a chance to react. I was always a moment too late with this kind of awareness, in situations large and small—another illustration of my ineptitude. But the dog was cooperative, curious, sniffed her phone, smudged the screen. My daughter laughed, wiped the screen with her shirt, and scooted back a few inches, so the nose wouldn't be blurry in the photo. We walked away unscathed. Tragedy averted.

Every day without a tragedy was tragedy averted.

"Whose dog is this?" my wife says now, placing each picture with excruciating care onto the board, in preparation for gluing. Each dog is represented by two photos: a headshot, and a close-up of the nose.

"A woman from work," I say.

"He's cute," she says.

Sometimes at night, when our oldest son makes a certain kind of sound, I follow her into his room, try to help. She knows what each sound means, just like when they were infants. She tends to him as I stand in the doorway. In the dark I hardly recognize her; she could be any woman, any nurse, any caregiver.

"Anything I can do?" I always ask.

There is not anything I can do.

In the overnight hours, time exists loosely; years, even decades, puddle into one another. Ten minutes ago babies were gazing curiously at me through the bars of their cribs, and now there's a boy who should be in in eleventh grade and a sullen boy in eighth grade and an anxious girl in fifth grade. Yes, fifth grade—I ground myself. Tomorrow we'll take this unwieldy investigation to the elementary school cafeteria and set it up between the tape on the long table, and some poor bastard will spend his Friday night looking at two hundred trifold boards, will pause before our progeny, inspect the glossy photos, the moist noses of Ruby and Watson and Rosebud and Stranger Dog, evaluate our conclusions one final time, and for reasons none of us will ever understand, give our work first prize or the soul-crushing honorable mention.

4. Results

THE GLUE STICK, too. Once, working on the first project, with the oldest boy—the boy whose calves my wife now rubs every night with barrier ointment—I tried to take charge of the glue stick, and within seconds there was glue everywhere, my fingers stuck to every letter, every bit of evidence battered and torn with glue, the project so mangled I was sent, in the middle of the night, to the twenty-four-hour Walmart, where other desperate parents stood in front of trifold boards—no more white left, no red, no sunny yellow, only black. Other parents—losers with dead eyes and capable spouses at home—gazed despondently alongside; it's always the dud parent, the one proven useful only for the retrieval of goods, who gets sent on these middle-of-the-night missions. When I returned home with the black trifold poster board, her eyes dimmed. *Seriously?* she asked. Was it at least funny later, with a little perspective? Not so much. I have never since touched the ruler or the scissors or the glue stick. And for the best evidence of our collaborations, the children sleeping upstairs—three incomplete projects no longer ours to finish—the teamwork now is a weary march, and feels mostly for show.

I am the retriever of goods and she puts the goods to use. I bring home the barrier ointment and she applies it. I stop at the medical supply store for the catheter bags and she attaches them. Sometimes as she works with him—on him—his eyes land on me, and I want to say, You can't tell right now, but I am part of this effort.

I feel like we hardly know each other anymore, my wife and I. It is not that we are strangers, but rather that our whole life, our marriage, this family, this house, this kitchen, zoomed in like we are, is a close-up of almost unimaginable proportions—at this distance, it's hard to identify anything with any kind of certainty. But seeing her brandishing that glue stick, the smooth application, the cementing of information, the bonding of the evidence—this familiar endeavor—for a moment makes who we are a tiny bit less blurry.

5. Conclusion

"IT LOOKS GOOD," I say.

Lips pressed together, my wife looks up from the conclusion. She has placed it beautifully, inside her nearly invisible lines, dead center. Can you identify a dog by its nose print? If a dog who resembles your long-lost dog comes to your door, starving, skin and bones, its fur matted, ears crusty, dirt caked between the pads of its paws, would you know him? If you take his chin in your hand, tilt up his head, get a good look at his nose, the grooves, the teardrop nostrils, is there enough to go on? Can you say, with certainty: Yes, yes, I recognize you.

◆ ◆ ◆ **FROM THE AUTHOR** ◆ ◆ ◆

Having suffered through numerous science fair projects (specifically as the useless parent), I wanted to write something that other parents with similar experiences would think was funny. So initially this was a comic story, and shorter—really just a glimpse into the dysfunctional marriage dynamic that the science fair always manages to reveal in all its blazing, mortifying glory. But the longer I spent with it, the thing that happens happened—the characters became people, the family not my own, the story beyond the story something I had not anticipated. As I went deeper, things turned from comic to tragic, and I discovered that the frayed connection between the parents was not broken by the project but strengthened, and—I hope—affirmed.

PERIOD PIECE

◆ MAILE MELOY ◆

The fires had already started before the wedding began. Power was out up and down the coast, and the air had a smoky haze, but the hotel looking over the Pacific had a generator, and everyone said it was fine. The fires were farther away. It was California—it was normal.

The wedding was for a much younger colleague, and Liza had gone alone. The story was that her husband, Russell, had to work, and stay with Jasper and the dog, which was true, but also it would have made her self-conscious if he'd come. There would be too many in-jokes about work, and there would be the drunkenness of the very young. Liza's own parents had divorced when she was thirteen, leaving her with just enough faith in the institution to try it herself, but not enough to believe it could work for anyone else.

She had stayed and danced for a while, until a young cousin of the bride said, "I can't believe you're still here with us!" And then Liza had come to her senses, and walked barefoot back to her room in the dark, carrying her strappy sandals. There was a faint orange glow beyond the ridge on her left, and the black ocean stretching out on her right.

She went to sleep, and woke an hour later to her phone making a strange noise. She couldn't read the message without her glasses, so she got up, stumbling through the unfamiliar hotel room, looking for her bag. Her vision wasn't bad enough yet to make her keep her glasses nearby.

She stubbed her toe on a chair, and swore. Then she reached into the familiar depths of the bag, past the wallet, the lip sunscreen, the wedding invitation. When she put the glasses on, she could read her phone: MANDATORY EVACUATION ZONE and then some confusing parameters.

She called the bride, who somehow picked up from the dance floor. A Stevie Wonder song was playing. Where was she keeping her phone—in her wedding dress? "We're fine," the bride said. "Did you look at the map? The mandatory zone goes out to a tiny point on the coast, and we're in the point. They're being overcautious, getting people out of the way. You can totally leave tomorrow."

Liza stood in the hotel room thinking about risks she had taken in her life—there wasn't time to think about all of them, just a quick highlight reel of motorcycles and drunks and water crashing over her head—and then she said, "I'm going to the airport. Does anyone need a ride?"

She listened to the bride call out the question over the dance floor. Then the cheerful voice came back: "Nope! All good. Be safe."

So Liza pulled on jeans, and stuffed her flowy dress and sandals into her bag. She looked at the evacuation map again, and then got in the rental car. From the parking lot, she could hear the wedding. "Uptown Funk" was playing—"Girls, hit your hallelujah (whoo)." The girls were singing along on the *whoo*.

The road was narrow and winding and moonless, and the local radio station had survivalists calling in, people who'd prepared for fires, who seemed kind of happy about them, so Liza turned it off. She was sweating as she drove. She'd bought three new comforters in the last two years, thinking none of them could regulate heat. She'd start out too cold at bedtime, but by morning she would have shoved the offending thing off. She bought a bamboo duvet, a silk one, a weighted blanket that promised to soothe her anxiety, her fear, her rage. Nothing worked.

Then her friend Caroline showed her a picture on her phone. It was a graph, running from left to right along the axis of time. It started out fairly even, before marching steeply uphill, and then turning into a child's furious scribbles, a polygraph test taken by a bad liar, or the path of someone doing aerial tricks in a plane. Caroline was ten years older and was Liza's Virgil, her guide to the unknown—a guide who sometimes rolled her eyes at Liza's obliviousness.

"Here's what your hormones are doing," Caroline had said. "They start out pretty even, see? Here they peak, that's when people want babies. After that they just go nuts, jumping up and down. It makes you feel insane. It makes you want to destroy your life."

Liza had shown the diagram to Russell on the subway. Russell had glanced at her phone and said, "Yeah, that seems about right."

"That's so reductive," Liza had said. "I am not my hormones!"

"OK," Russell had said.

Jasper had been wearing his headphones beside them. He was

maybe only half listening, but he was nine. He was *always* listening. When Liza swore in front of him and apologized, he said, "I *know* all the bad words, Mom. I just don't *use* them."

Caroline had given her the name of a clinic, and Liza went on Halloween, the only day she could get an appointment. A young doctor dressed as Hermione from *Harry Potter* told her about a drug for restless leg syndrome that also seemed to control hot flashes.

"I thought restless leg syndrome was made up," Liza said.

"Yeah, it could be," Dr. Hermione said. "But the medication might let you sleep without sweating through all the covers."

"What about hormone therapy?" Liza had asked her.

Hermione tilted her head in consideration. "How did you feel about that graph your friend showed you?" she asked.

Liza thought for a moment, then said, "It made me remember that once, when the line was flat, all I cared about was swimming and books and horses and dogs, and I was really happy. And then—around the point where the graph starts spiking, I started doing stupid stuff for men. Like, seriously stupid stuff. And right now I feel completely insane, and ready to burn it all down. Like, leave my family. Have an affair—not that I have a candidate. I'd be really happy for that scribble to flatline again, so I wouldn't care about anything but swimming and books and dogs."

Hermione said, "Yeah, I think you're gonna like the other side. Honestly. It might be better just to power through and get it over with. And think about this pill for the sweating."

And the pills worked. But she'd forgotten to bring them to the wedding. She'd remembered her reading glasses, and her noise-canceling headphones for the plane. She'd remembered her blister Band-Aids in case the sandals killed her feet. But this was her first trip since getting the prescription, and she didn't yet have the habit of packing it. So now the collar of her T-shirt was damp, and the backs of her knees. California was on fire because no one in power believed in climate change, and she had a nine-year-old at home, and she was filled, once again, with rage. It made her want to scream. She wanted a solution, beyond a drug for a syndrome that might not exist, a drug she had failed to bring with her.

The winding road finally took her to the freeway, and safely around the evacuation zone to the airport. No one else seemed to be fleeing. Everything seemed calm. At SFO, she slept in the terminal, lying on the floor against the windows, with her head on her bag. She woke from a dream about trying to escape from a collapsing house. But at least she wasn't sweating. So maybe this was the answer: sleep on the hard floor, under a light jacket. But the hip she had slept on felt stiff and bruised, and she walked the airport until it was time for her flight, steering her rolling bag beside her.

On the plane, the overhead bin was full, and a man was in the aisle seat of her row, talking on his phone. She found another bin. When she got the man's attention, he stood, aggrieved, to let her into the middle seat. Then he dropped back down. He kept his elbow on the armrest and his legs spread. Liza caught the eye of the tiny woman in the window seat, who had her small bag beneath the seat in front of her.

"Yeah," the man was saying on the phone. "It's just a bridge loan, until the financing comes through. No, yeah, there's some chance of losing it, but it's pretty small. I think it's a safe bet. Right. Sure."

Liza sat thinking about whether men—white men, her age and older—had gotten worse. It seemed like there was an urgency that came with the fear that their world domination might come to an end. It made them primitive, rude, aggressive, determined to take up as much space as possible. Something visceral in this man wanted to elbow everyone else out of the way. He objected to the loss of power. He wasn't going to cede the armrest without a fight. When the plane landed, he took his things down from the overhead bin and stood blocking the aisle, letting no one else stand.

Liza stood on the curb at JFK in a haze of cigarette smoke and exhaust. Russell had rented a car and taken Jasper and the dog to his brother's house on Long Island for the weekend, so they picked her up on the way home. It was a nice thing. But she was still furious at the man on the plane, and she told herself not to take out her anger on Russell. He was generous and kind. He had blind spots, but so did she. So then why was she seething, unable to speak?

He lifted her rolling bag into the trunk, and she buckled herself into the passenger seat. She turned to smile at Jasper in the back, trying to keep her voice light, warm, cheerful. "Hey, kiddo," she said.

"Hi," he said. "Were you in a fire?"

"No," she said. "It wasn't that close to the wedding. Everyone else stayed and danced."

Jasper nodded, and went back to reading his book. Solly wriggled his way from the back seat into her lap, tail wagging with happiness, and licked her ears. Liza put her arms around him and blinked to keep from crying.

Russell got into the car and pulled out into the fray.

Caroline had said sex would become a problem, but they would talk about it when the time came—there wasn't any reason to go into all that yet. Liza had protested. She'd said, "Now you're scaring me. Just tell me." Caroline had shaken her head and said they would deal with it later. Now Liza thought Caroline was right. She didn't need to know how bad it might get.

Russell jockeyed for position in the traffic, like everyone in the city, on the street, on the sidewalk, on the subway, in schools, in housing, at work. So many people wanting the same things.

Liza closed her eyes and leaned against the window, and they got home to an unseasonably warm Sunday afternoon—sun through the windows, leftover bagels Russell had brought back from his brother's. Liza stretched out on the couch with a middle-grade novel manuscript she was editing, but she didn't start, she just listened to the sounds of the apartment.

Jasper lay on his stomach on the rug beside her. He was writing a graphic novel about a boy and his pet robot, an assignment from his fourth-grade teacher. Solly had curled up beside him.

"Can I read your book when it's finished?" Liza asked Jasper.

"No," Jasper said. "Or—yes. But I want positive feedback only, please."

"That's not how feedback works," she said. "If something confuses a reader, that helps you make it better."

"OK, then you don't have to read it," he said.

Liza thought about arguing the point further, then decided against it. She reached for her reading glasses to do her own work.

She'd always had good vision, and for a while, she'd thought there just weren't any books she liked lately, and that the new skin cream she was using was kind of miraculous.

One morning, a few months ago, she'd turned to Russell in the bathroom and said, "Are you seeing this?" She'd pointed to her face. "All those little smile lines are gone."

Russell had given a kind of shrugging assent.

She'd bought more of the skin cream before telling Caroline that Instagram had just gotten more interesting than novels, and Caroline had handed over her own glasses, saying, "Put them on."

So Liza did. And it all became clear. Even Instagram was better when you could *see* it. She finished the first chapter of the manuscript, making sure to include positive feedback. Solly plopped his head on her stomach and gazed at her hopefully, so she got up to take him to the park.

In the park, Jasper dashed ahead, and Solly, on the leash, danced with gratitude beside her. Liza had made herself essential to these three male creatures. She fed them, mostly, and found their lost items, and kept their calendars and their stashes of treats. But which had come first—their need, or hers, to be needed? And what to do when their dependency made her insane and resentful? She refocused on the joy in the dog's dancing steps, on Jasper's bright shout over his shoulder, on the sun on her face. The firefighters were gaining control in California, the evacuation zone had shrunk—the bride had been right!—and Liza was home. She had everything she wanted. She would make herself grateful.

Her phone rang, with her mother's name on the screen, and she picked it up, keeping an eye on Jasper, who had asked to pet someone's pug. He was a good city child, carefully trained.

"Hey," she said.

"I had a dream about you," her mother said. "Weren't you in California? With the fires?"

"I was," Liza said. "I got an earlier flight home."

"Oh, good," her mother said.

A toddler in a yellow coat ran out to greet Solly, thrusting tiny hands into the dog's face, and Liza reeled in the leash. Solly was gentle, but no one wants hands shoved in their face. A nanny pulled the toddler away, and the nanny and Liza smiled nervously at each other. Jasper wandered ahead, out of earshot.

"Hey, when did you stop having periods?" Liza asked her mother, on the phone.

"Oh, I don't know," her mother said.

"Did you sweat? Did you want to burn everything to the ground?"

"No," her mother said. "Why?"

"So—it was just easy? No symptoms?"

"Well—I was taking birth control pills, and my doctor said I could just keep taking them, and that would see me through it."

"Oh," Liza said. "So—when did you stop?"

"I didn't."

Liza listened to the silence on the line, and thought about her mother's dewy skin, her slim yoga body, her apparent agelessness. "What do you mean, you *didn't*?"

"I mean, I just kept taking them," her mother said. "They're very low-dose."

"But you're seventy."

"Thank you for reminding me," her mother said, an edge in her voice.

"But you're taking them *now*? Every day?"

"They don't work if you don't take them every day."

"Where do you get them?"

"In the mail."

"Isn't there—a breast cancer risk, or heart disease, or something?"

"That breast cancer study was flawed," her mother said. "Anyway, my mother lived to be a hundred. Sea levels are rising. Breast cancer is not my worry."

"Mom! Don't say that, it's jinxy. Will you please talk to your doctor?"

There was another brief silence, in which Liza could feel her mother's stubborn resistance. "Fine," her mother said, but she didn't mean it.

When Liza got home, Russell was chopping the tops off little red and yellow peppers. "My mother is still taking birth control pills," she said.

"Is she sleeping with someone?" he asked.

Liza looked at him, wondering if he was serious. "She's not in danger of getting pregnant," she said. "She just didn't want to go through this—*thing*, and then she never stopped taking them. That's why her skin looks so good."

Russell thought about it. "Does it?"

"Yes!" Liza said. "She's like a vampire! Except with estrogen instead of blood!"

"So, it's—working?" Russell asked.

"Unless it's giving her heart disease."

"Oh," Russell said. He went back to the peppers, slicing each one in two. "Well, your mom does whatever she wants." And that was true.

In the morning, before school, Liza told Jasper to pour himself a bowl of cereal. When she got to the table, he was reading a parenting book, about why your children might enrage you, and how to deal with it when they did.

"This writer is talking about her own kids," Jasper said. "I bet that's super annoying."

"Maybe those kids know they're really lucky to have a mother who's thought so much about how to be a good mom," Liza said. "Also—she probably asked them if it was OK."

Jasper set the book down and picked up his spoon. "The kids couldn't really say no, though."

"I'm sure they could."

Jasper shook his head as if she didn't understand the imbalance of power.

"You have your backpack?" she asked him. "And your homework?"

The backpack was upstairs, the homework missing, finally discovered under the bed. Then Jasper had to pee and brush his teeth. By the time they got out of the house they were late.

"Why do ninjas always wear black?" Jasper asked as they dodged people on the sidewalk.

"So they can sneak up on people at night," Liza said, with some confidence. "Come on, we have to hurry."

"But what about in the day?" he asked.

"I don't know," she said. "Maybe it's just good to have a uniform. Then they don't have to think about what to wear." She thought about the ads for fancy scrubs in the subway, modeled by hot young doctors, and how she'd been tempted, lately, to buy some. Ninjas kind of wore scrubs.

Jasper's classroom was up five flights of stairs, and he and Liza did it at a run. One of the aides frowned at her for being late. She kissed Jasper goodbye and saw him merge into the classroom, among the bright winter clothes and the small, sweet, musty-smelling heads. He didn't look back.

Then she ran down the five flights, across the street, and into the subway, in her down coat. Just as the train doors were closing, she slipped into a car and looped her elbow around a pole. She felt her upper lip start to sweat. Here it came, the unbearable heat.

At the same moment, with horror, she felt her period start—that telltale warm wetness. The train hadn't started yet. If she could just get to the bathroom at her office, she could deal with the blood. It felt like a lot.

She decided to take off her coat and tie it around her waist, to solve both problems at once. As she got one arm free, she had a flash of the bathroom in her middle school, the shiny industrial green walls, her old pink winter coat with the dirty sleeves.

She had to shift her bag to get the other arm out of her sleeve, and as she did so, the train jerked forward, throwing her face-first into the pole. A burst of light blotted out her vision. She thought she had broken her nose. She got her arm back around the pole and felt her face, carefully. Her hand came away wet and red. She searched in her bag for a tissue, as the salty blood ran over her lip into her mouth.

"Are you OK?" a young woman near her asked. The girl wore eyelash extensions so long they looked like dancing spider legs.

Liza nodded, the pain still bright behind her eyes.

"No—seriously?" the young woman asked.

"Yeah," Liza said. "I'm fine."

The car was not so crowded that anyone could miss seeing what had happened. Two youngish men sat nearby, in wool coats. They both looked studiously at the floor. The shoulders of the smaller guy shook helplessly.

"It's OK," Liza told him as she held a tissue against her nose. "You can laugh."

The guy sneaked a look at her, with a little smile. He was hand-some, with carefully maintained stubble. Once, a guy like him would've flirted with her. Now it was confusing. Was the smile because she'd become ridiculous? The cute vendor at the farmers' market, who'd said she could have one more item to make it $20, *any* item, including him—obviously that was a sales technique, but was it a flirty one? Or was he just humoring her because she was old?

But maybe being old would be good. Maybe it would mean she could just do her work. For the longest time people thought she was too young for her job. They questioned her, wanting to know how she got it—did her family own the publishing company? But now she realized that she would go seamlessly from seeming too young for things to seeming too old for them.

Her forehead throbbed. The windows of the train were dark and blurry. She found a mirror in her bag and saw a red mark on her forehead, where she'd hit the pole. She also saw the vertical double wrinkle between her eyebrows, the number 11 that had dis-appeared on her friends who did Botox. She contemplated it for a moment. On her last visit to the dermatologist to make sure she had no strange moles, the doctor had pointed to the little 11 and said, "You want to do something about that?" Liza had said no. She'd earned that frown. She lowered the mirror to look at her nose, but the blood had stopped.

The blood. Again, the flash of middle school. Graffiti on the green bathroom walls, some of it unsuccessfully scratched out: SHAWNA EATS USED TOILET PAPER. Room of false privacy, of humil-iation and bafflement. She put the mirror away and finished tying her jacket around her sweating waist.

People on the train car had gone back to their phones. The girl with the eyelashes was looking at Instagram. A woman a little older than Liza gave her a sympathetic smile: *Hello, my comrade.* Liza smiled back, ruefully.

At work, Liza went straight to the bathroom, jacket still tied around her waist. No one was in the stalls, and she was grateful. She hung her bag on the hook and shimmied down her pants to see how bad the blood was.

And nothing was there. Her underwear were as clean as they'd been when she'd taken them from the drawer this morning. She sat down to pee, relieved and confused. Had the bleeding feeling just been a phantom? Was this a new symptomy spike on the scribbled graph? A tactile hallucination? Hysterical menstruation? A delusion?

She didn't want to be deluded.

She left the stall and splashed cold water on her face. Her nose and forehead were still tender, and she leaned close to study the red mark on her forehead. One of the young publicists came in, high-heeled boots clicking on the hard floor, and headed to a stall without making eye contact. There was a clattering sound of toilet paper unrolling—masking some human noise? Liza dried her face with a paper towel, then ran it over the back of her neck, where the sweat had evaporated.

Swimming.

Dogs.

Horses, if applicable.

Books. Definitely books.

All right, then. She was ready.

In the fall of 2019, my husband and I got alerts on our phones at 4 a.m., telling us to evacuate because of wildfires. A friend with whom I'd been talking about perimenopause had just escaped a different California fire, and I started a story about it. But by the time I finished, that friend had one of the early cases of COVID-19, and everything had shut down in the pandemic, and I wondered if the story was relevant anymore. But fire season will come again, and more viruses will jump the species barrier, and— if we're lucky—our bodies will get older. And there's a strange coda, too: my friend's doctors thought that her weird post-COVID weight gain and joint pain was just menopause. She kept saying no, something's wrong. They finally listened, and it turned out that the virus had turbocharged a giant benign tumor she'd unknowingly had for years, that was causing all her symptoms. They took it out and she's much better now. So: advocate for yourself, advocate for the planet. This is what we've got.

BOOKS YOU READ

◆

◆ JOE MENO ◆

Books you read last year were all bad—are you getting older or is the world just becoming less interesting? Books don't mean what they used to. You haven't found one you enjoyed since 2012, when you read *A Wrinkle in Time*. You borrowed it from a girl you were babysitting and loved it so much you ended up stealing it, even though you were way too old. You are embarrassed how much you still like fantasy and YA.

Something in your heart has stopped growing. You've become skinny now in all the wrong places.

You work in a bookstore even though you don't enjoy reading. Nothing keeps you up late at night turning page after page anymore. Even Murakami has become familiar.

◆ ◆ ◆

Your bookstore sells used books. You purposefully missort the authors you admire, hoping to keep them secret for as long as possible. When it's not busy, you Magic Marker out the best parts— the scene where Franny faints, Beloved climbing out of the water, Scout finding the hidden objects inside the tree.

Others you bury behind other books because of how the authors look in their photos. You imagine Philip Roth writing with his clothes off. It makes it somewhat easier to accept some of what he writes.

You get bruises but you don't know why. There are seventeen of them. One looks like Sweden. Others look like countries you could never afford to visit.

You always go to the movies alone. You want your eardrums to ring, your teeth to shake. You want to feel something, especially if it's not real. Your favorite is Star Wars. There are approximately ninety-six of them now. You watch them in the theater, then again at home. The louder and less interesting they are, the less you have to lose.

By the end of the year, two people you know pass away suddenly—a girl you went to high school with and one of your best friends, Franny. Franny gets hit on her bicycle while riding home from someone's apartment late at night.

You keep texting her and texting her but she doesn't answer and so you know something is wrong. Later someone puts up a ghost bike near the underpass where she was hit.

You go by there and stare as if staring ever changed anything.

◆　◆　◆

You use a different name on your time card every week. Today it is Josephine March. Last week it was Catherine Earnshaw.

Besides the bookstore, you are also an after-school tutor at a community center. You do not do this out of kindness. You do it because you have to perform community service for a DUI you got when you borrowed your dad's Subaru a few months before and got pulled over by the cops after having two and a half beers.

It was around the time you got pulled over, two months after Franny died, that you began referring to yourself by fictional names.

What does it mean when you cut yourself and it won't stop bleeding? Who are you shaving for anyway?

At the tutoring center you help kids who have nowhere to go after school. Their faces are blank. You are not sure if they hate you or if they have just given up on learning. You attempt to answer their questions about homework—mostly history and math. When you're unsure, sometimes you just make it up. Abraham Lincoln was a ghost. The pyramids were built by aliens. Everything ends up becoming fiction.

There is a boy there, Alessandro, who is ten, whom you may be getting a little too attached to. When he comes to the tutoring center, he already has all of his homework done.

He has dark hair and wears a blue winter coat that he refuses to ever take off. All he wants to is to look at the books. Most of them have been donated by corporate bookstores. He likes to look at the encyclopedia of animals, which a lot of the kids fight over.

All Alessandro does is sit in the blue chair and flip through the animal book, memorizing odd and amazing facts. The length of the giant squid. The wingspan of an albatross. Lifespan of a blue whale. You think if you were a few years older you would try and adopt him, even though you are not sure if something like that is legal, and you worry what that says about you, the fact you want to help someone you don't even know.

Someone invites you to a party but you say it's too cold. You haven't been feeling very sociable lately. You look at all the books on your bookshelves but don't read any of them, just organize them by color, then again by how many times you've read them.

One day Alessandro is browsing through the animal encyclopedia in the blue chair and the next day the book is missing. You know this because another kid asks for the book and when you go and kneel by the shelf you see it's gone.

You remember Alessandro reading it the day before. You remember the funny way he said goodbye, how he carried his backpack under his arm in an odd way.

Alessandro stops showing up later that week. You go into the office and look through the index cards where all the kids' contact information is. You see he only lives a few blocks away.

Is nothing scary to you anymore? How can the world be totally upside down and so empty at the same time?

One day after your shift at the bookstore, you call Margaret, a person you work with, and ask if she wants to help you commit a crime.

—It depends. What kind of crime? she asks.

—A reverse robbery.

—What's that?

—Where you steal something that was stolen.

She says she doesn't want to get involved but she will come watch you make a complete fool of yourself.

You ask her to be the lookout and she says she will but only out of boredom.

You check the index card and you and Margaret ride by the boy's home. It is small, blue and gray, looks only like the idea of a house. A bicycle frame with no tires sits in the front yard. You and Margaret open the gate and walk up. You peek through the windows and ring the doorbell.

It's 1:30 in the afternoon. No one is at home. You knock, then knock again. You search around, lift up the mat at the front door, check under an empty flowerpot. There is a small silver key hidden on top of a side window ledge. You palm it and smile. Margaret with her stiff red hair only shakes her head.

Inside is someone else's home. Inside it is cramped and full of life. You stand in the middle of it, imagining what it is like to live there.

You find Alessandro's room down a hall. There are three small beds, with lots of clothes and toys on the floor. You look underneath each bed. Nothing. Under some laundry. A rabbit, as big as a cat, leaps out and scares you half to death. You see its open cage in the corner of the room. You keep on looking, ignoring the rabbit as it disappears under the bed. You peek through the side window and realize Margaret is gone. There's no one standing guard. You keep on searching. You are a hero, the protector of all books. The animal encyclopedia belongs to everyone.

In the closet, there is a stack of overdue library books, some several years overdue. At the bottom of the stack, you find the animal encyclopedia. You pick it up and open it. There are markings, drawings in it now. Some of the animals are now speaking to each other. Some are crying, some have been given strange thoughts. You realize Alessandro has turned the encyclopedia into a storybook. The leopards have fallen in love with the lemurs. The lions ask the lizards about their powers. There is a war between invertebrates and vertebrates, drawing every species into its thrall. Better than any other book, better than Star Wars. You read it through cover to cover once, then again. You sit in the midafternoon shadow, with the blue curtain canceling out the light, feeling like you are at the bottom of some nameless ocean, at the beginning of time, where life once mattered. Your head begins to ache but not in a bad way. You leave the book where you found it and go outside.

A dog

a streetlamp

a passing car

all look impossible and new.

A stop sign.

Shoes hanging from a telephone wire

a faded poster

each appear as something unlikely and true.

When you get back home, you're amazed to find someone has come into your apartment and rearranged all your books.

◆ ◆ ◆ **FROM THE AUTHOR** ◆ ◆ ◆

Over the course of the last year, I've come to realize how books—as ordinary as they may seem to be—have helped the people I love face the ongoing challenges we are all now confronting. A friend of mine passed away a few years ago, killed on her bicycle, and the story of that loss, compounded with the way books or reading or storytelling offer us the opportunity to build something out of tragedy, led to the shape of this particular story.

A WOMAN DRIVING ALONE

◆ MARIE-HELENE BERTINO ◆

I start the car, the engine of my heart.

In the forest that covers northwest Idaho, a hawk sitting on a fence watches me pass. It occurs to me that a hawk looks like nothing else. Is unmistakable. I turn left and (I imagine) snake diagonally down the map of Washington State, following the Columbia River west to Portland, where Gracie lives.

I hadn't wanted to be alone with my thoughts, and this was her weekend with her daughter. "Girls sleepover," she said. I buy face masks, wine. I pack a tin of food.

Somewhere in Washington State I misread a sign as: LIZ, 1 MILE. How funny it will be if in one mile a woman named Liz is standing on the highway. What could she be doing that would be a typical Liz thing? I don't know anyone with that name.

When I notice other drivers have their headlights on, I turn mine on. I want to be a good traveler. I don't want to hate where I'm from. I don't want to judge new places by how they compare to what I know.

I am a small woman filling her gas tank in The Dalles. A small woman feeding the parking meter. Changing lanes. Taking photos out the window. Reconsidering her high-necked sweater, the long drive. Consulting the rearview mirror for the source of the flashing light.

I wonder if the Columbia River enjoys doing as much work as seems expected of it. If it is the kind of river that, like a working dog, feels anxious when it does not have a job. I make a note to stop comparing rivers to animals. To look up *Columbia River commerce, turtlenecks that breathe.*

At the Cascade Locks, the riverbanks change out to a deeper green, meant to woo. It works. I pull over in a rest area to watch a valley fill with clouds. How nice it is to eat crackers and be erased by weather.

I've patterned most of my physicality on my brother's. The way I perch on a couch. The way his fingertips rest on his thighs. No one in my life knows this because they've never met him. He went to jail when I was young. But he's in everything I do and say, how I sweetly squint whenever I want to encourage a friend's introspection, as I'm doing now, as Gracie tells me about this town Portland she's recently moved to.

Of all the details, that people make an orderly line for drinks at the bar, which stymies our imagination. "No one cuts or yells or pushes."

A typical Liz thing, we decide, is to speak in rapturous tones about "breaking trail." Overly diligent about the three-word rule in Celebrities, Liz has had exactly two boyfriends, the second being her husband. She reminds us constantly how easily her white skin burns. We admire and can only handle her in small doses.

I tell Gracie I've just finished reading *The Haunting of Hill House* by Shirley Jackson, that its opening chapter contains a passage about a woman driving alone that contains the most accurate description I've ever read of how it feels. The buoyancy and giddy actualization that comes from the ability to go anywhere. Without having to request, consult, or rely.

"I'm never as happy as when I'm driving," I say.

She says, "Shirley Jackson's a woman who can really cut to the chase."

Back on the dating scene, Gracie recently had dinner with a man that went so well they spent hours at the restaurant, laughing. He spent the night at her house. In the morning, she walked him to his car, where she discovered he was keeping a large dog in a crate. The dog had been in the car, hungry, the entire night.

She asked him to let the dog out and he refused. He dismissed her protests, assuring her the dog liked it.

"Please tell me the crate was big enough for the dog to move around."

She says, "The entire night."

My grandmother also had a friend named Gracie. When my mother was pregnant with me, I tell her, this other Gracie offered her $500 to give me the name. It wasn't for vanity, really, she worried the name was dying out. She wanted there to be more Gracies in the world.

Who can blame Gracie's daughter for being dubious about my visit? She doesn't want to share time with her mother. She doesn't want to sit in the pizzeria waiting for our Margherita with mushrooms. I tell them I will wait for the packed-up leftovers so they can return to the house and settle.

The nurse said that under the mammogram scope healthy breasts look like a partly cloudy day. Mine turned out to be heavy cover, the kind of low-ceilings that delay a flight. Two lumps are a good sign, she assured me, ordering more tests. "Cancer comes alone."

On Monday morning, everything I've carried in with me I carry out. I start the car, the engine of my heart.

I drive the same way up the map, make a right, the enormous lake, the woods. From a bag of carrots, I select one that looks most edible, though I'll eat them all, and think about how as a vegetable rots it smells more like itself. I need a shower. I smell too much like myself. I brace the steering wheel between my knees and remove my sweater.

Never as happy, never as concerned.

But before the drive home and the pale goodbye of the last morning, while I am waiting for the box in the pizzeria, I call my partner.

"Did you tell her about the biopsy?" he says. Then, as if sensing his lack of specificity makes it seem like an unincorporated event in space, he rephrases. "Did you tell her that you had a double biopsy?"

I know he will scold me for putting myself on the back burner with friends, if you can scold someone for that.

I say, "It didn't come up." In the silence that follows I watch a pizzeria employee refill a Parmesan cheese dispenser in an efficient way I admire. "I didn't want to hear anything hopeful."

I hope he will take the shoddy explanation as a sign I don't want to talk about it. We both know, Gracie understands a complex heart. She would have laughed if I'd said, If I die, I die. I too would like there to be more hers in the world.

He says, "That's not a reason."

"I am waiting for a to-go box," I say, in a loud voice.

He grants me the mercy of getting off the phone. I slide the slices into the box and walk back to Gracie's, remembering something I read: pay attention to how someone treats their animals; that's how they'd like to treat other humans. I notice a man limping across the street. With every step he returns to himself. Above the electrical wires, bats Shirley Jackson across the sky. Resting underneath my bra like a lover's hand, adhesive gauze and two bright lumps—arrows or anomalies or temporary hitchhikers. I might be the one to decide. I make a note to research how a pizza oven works. Cirrus clouds. Needle biopsies. Hawks of northwest Idaho. The warm box balances on my palm. I hope Gracie has remembered to leave the door unlocked so I don't have to knock.

I don't know what it is that I'm doing, but I'm doing it with all my might.

◆ ◆ ◆ **FROM THE AUTHOR** ◆ ◆ ◆

To feel how time can expand within its parameters, wait for results. For anything—a verdict, a grade, some important distinction. The film Cléo *from 5 to 7 by Agnès Varda was the first work I saw that renders this* charged parenthetical. We walk with Cleo in real time as she waits for the results of a biopsy. Whereas most filmmakers would focus on the results themselves, Varda allows Cleo to move and reveal herself in the waiting. We spend so much of our lives waiting. We can only hope to be treated tenderly while we do. In my story "A Woman Drives Alone," the text focuses on the river, the pizza, anything but the results the woman waits for, much like how, in life, we put things out of our minds. But, she is not alone, really. We wait with her.

NEW WORLDS

DANDELIONS

—◆—

◆ BEN LOORY ◆

A man is standing in his yard one day, when the whole
place suddenly erupts in dandelions.

Aaa! says the man.

He turns and runs inside and roots around under the sink for
some pesticide.

But when he finally finds it and goes back outside, the dandelions are gone—every one!

What the . . . ? says the man. But they were right here!

He gets down on hands and knees and inspects the lawn.

All the rest of the day, the man keeps peering out the window.

I just *know* those dandelions are gonna come back, he says.

But the dandelions don't come back—not a single one. Every
time the man looks out, all he sees is an empty lawn.

◆ ◆ ◆

That night, the man goes and tells his friend about it.

That's very strange, his friend says. Because the exact same thing happened to me last week! It was on Tuesday, I think.

The man and his friend go to see some other people.

Yep, they all say. Happened here, too.

It turns out the whole town had the exact same experience.

But why? they all say. What could it be?

Some kind of nuclear accident? one says. A chemical leak? An act of God?

Act of God by dandelion? someone else scoffs. Pretty sure we can rule that one out.

Everyone's in an uproar. No one knows what to do.

What should we do? they all say.

They stand there in silence.

Someone raises a hand.

What do we know about dandelions? they say.

So the townspeople all go as one to the library. They ransack it for information on dandelions. After that, they go out to the community college and pester the botany professors.

The townspeople quickly learn everything about dandelions.

Dandelions are so interesting! they say.

They start some investigations. They buy some lab equipment. Their research program gets underway.

Every night, the townspeople hold extensive meetings to discuss dandelions and dandelion morphology. They share their discoveries and examine innovations in the field of dandelion development.

Hey, someone says. Let's grow the perfect dandelion!

Yeah! somebody else says. Let's do it!

The townspeople all turn and look at one another.

All right! they say, and then they get down to it.

And in just one summer, they make tremendous strides—it's really nothing short of amazing. They manage to develop dandelion strains that are pink, blue, and black—and even a few that have polka dots. They've developed a couple dandelions that have clover-shaped leaves, and some that grow up to forty-seven feet tall. They've even managed to develop one dandelion that can talk.

Hello, it keeps saying. Hello!

Finally, the whole town decides to have a fair to show off their best dandelions.

The fairgoers will vote, the mayor announces, and at the end we'll crown the perfect dandelion!

The fair is set to take place in the middle of the town square, which is specially decorated for the occasion. There are banners and ribbons and great big colorful signs with illustrations on them of dandelions.

The town has sent out invites to people all around—all around the region, the country. Reporters from magazines, public officials.

The vice president might come, but he doesn't.

And it turns out he's not the only one who doesn't come—it turns out that *no one comes at all*. The townspeople stand waiting in the middle of the square. And they stand there and wait all morning long.

◆ ◆ ◆

How come nobody's here? someone finally says. How come no one's showing up?

Maybe there was a great big traffic accident? someone says. And all of the roads are blocked off?

Every single road? someone else says. Coming from every direction?

Maybe it was some kind of nuclear accident? someone says. A chemical leak? Or an act of God?

Has anyone checked the TV? someone else asks. Can someone call the folks at Channel Nine?

I'll call my cousin in Stepford City, someone says. He said he and his family were gonna come.

So a couple people scurry off and make some phone calls, while everybody else just stands around.

Hello! Hello! the talking dandelion keeps saying.

But right then, no one cares at all.

And finally, when the news comes in, it's worse than they thought: It turns out no one wants to see a dandelion fair. It turns out that people think that dandelions are stupid!

Worse—they think they're *weeds!* someone says.

Weeds? says someone else.

It's absolutely scandalous.

What do you mean, *weeds?* someone says.

What kind of people *are* these? someone asks. What kind of *country* is this?

The townspeople all stand there. They don't know what to do.

What should we do? they all say.

I don't know, someone says.

Me neither, says another.

I might have an idea, a third says.

Everybody looks. A little girl steps forward.

If they won't come to us, the girl says, how's about we take the dandelions to them?

Well, people say. That's an idea.

But how can we possibly *do* that? somebody says. What are we gonna do—buy a fleet of trucks? And even if we did, we can't just spend our lives driving a bunch of flowers all around the world.

Yeah, says someone else. We can't really do that.

I have to go to work, someone says.

Me too, says someone else.

Us too, the others say.

But just then, a little voice pipes up.

Hello, the little voice calls out. Hello, hello, hello!

The whole town turns to the talking dandelion. And a split second later, all their eyes go wide—because they see that all the dandelions have turned.

Those brightly colored petals of yellow or pink or black have transformed now into glimmering balls of white. There are a hundred billion seedlets now, all set to float away, waiting only for a breeze to hit them right.

We're ready to do our part! they say—or at least, they seem to say.

All right! the people say, and make their plan.

And they run home and come back, each trailing their extension cords, and all the household fans they can lug.

◆ ◆ ◆

They line up all their fans, pointing this way and that.

On the count of three! they say. One, two—

Hang on! a single voice calls out. Everybody wait!

And the mayor steps forward to address the crowd.

There's one last order of business! he says. And I hope we can all agree . . . on which of these is the perfect dandelion?

And everybody claps as he kneels down and tapes a bright blue ribbon to the talking dandelion.

Thank you, he says to it, for everything you've done. And everything that you're about to do!

Hello, the talking dandelion says. Hello, hello, hello!

All right, the mayor says. Come on, let's go!

And everybody counts to three, and then all hit their buttons, and all of their electric fans turn on. And great big billowing gusts of wind immediately appear, and all the dandelion seeds are lifted up.

And the dandelion seeds go flying this way and that, hurled and whirled about by the different winds, and they spin off through the sky headed in a hundred million directions.

Go out there and show 'em! people scream.

Where do you think they'll go? one of the townspeople says. Do you think they'll go all the way to Mississippi?

At least! someone else responds, as they dance across the field. I bet they go all the way to Atlantic City!

And by that point, the dandelions are pretty much out of sight, disappearing over the distant hills. And pretty soon, the dancing and the reveling start to slow.

Well, the mayor says. I guess that's that.

I guess so, says someone else. But that was really fun!

Yeah, it sure was, the others say.

Hey, somebody else calls out. What are you guys doing tonight?

Any movies playing? someone asks.

And gradually the townspeople start to head for home. Only one man doesn't move. It's that guy from the beginning—the one with the pesticide?—he's just standing there, his eyes angled down.

He's staring at something on the sleeve of his coat.

He slowly reaches down and lifts it off.

It looks like a tiny little feathery snowflake.

He holds it very carefully as he sets off.

He walks back to his house, and he stops out on the lawn, and he gets down once more on his hands and knees. And he digs a little hole right there in the greenest part of the grass, and inside, he carefully places the seed.

All right now, little guy, he says as he covers the hole with dirt.

Lie still, he says. Everything's gonna be all right.

And he stands up and walks to his door—but then turns back.

Good night, he says. Good night, good night, good night.

◆ ◆ ◆ **FROM THE AUTHOR** ◆ ◆ ◆

I used to have a tortoise. His named was Horus and he lived out in the side yard, used to spend all his time eating grass and wandering around bumping into things. At some point I learned that tortoises are supposed to like dandelion greens, so I started buying them at the grocery store. Horus loved them! But it turned out that dandelion greens are surprisingly expensive, so he only got them on special occasions. Then one day I was out walking around (trying not to bump into things) when I noticed some dandelions gone to seed in my neighbor's lawn. Suddenly I had a brilliant idea! So then for a few days I became the crazy person of the neighborhood, wandering around swiping all the dandelion clocks from people's lawns and sticking them into a big Ziploc bag I'd found in the back of my cupboard. Then I'd take them home and spread them out all over the side yard and sprinkle them with water. The hope was pretty soon I'd have a whole yard full of dandelions and Horus would live the most blessed existence possible. Unfortunately, none of the dandelion seeds ever sprouted. Maybe there's a trick to dandelion propagation? Or maybe Horus ate them? Who knows. Later on, Horus moved to Sacramento and my landlord covered the side yard with little white rocks. Did this story grow out of any of that? Who can say. Anyway, I've always liked dandelions.

ALL THAT'S GONE IS ALL THAT'S LEFT

◆ PATRICK DACEY ◆

First thing in the morning, Nanna calls to say her TV's gone missing. Same with the other two.

"What about the security system I had installed?"

"I can't remember all this stuff," she says.

"Are you okay?"

"Oh, now you're interested in how I'm feeling?"

When I get to Nanna's, I check the house for possible clues.

"Where's the air conditioner in the living room window?" I ask.

"Someone took it."

"What about in your bedroom?"

"Be my guest."

There's a man in her bedroom yanking the air conditioner out of the window.

"What is this?" I say.

"What does it look like?" the guy says, and lugs the air conditioner past me.

The room is already getting damp.

"Now all my TVs *and* my air conditioners are gone," Nanna says.

I catch up to the guy outside.

"Hey, bud. You can't just take that."

"Sure I can, *bud*."

He opens the car door and pushes up the front seat and tells the kid sitting on a large woman's lap to scoot. He lays the air conditioner on the woman's lap. Everyone's sweating beneath ripped upholstery and a layer of smoke. In the front seat is another air conditioner.

I grab the guy's shoulder, but I have no plan for what to do next. He jabs his finger in my chest, the way Dad used to when he wanted me to learn not to learn something the hard way.

"Feel lucky," he says.

Then he gets in the car and drives off.

Even if Nanna isn't all that wealthy, she's better off than most, and it's the better off than most that the ones without much are taking from these days because the ones with more than they need make it so hard to get to what they have.

Inside, Nanna's sitting at the kitchen table with a glass of white zinfandel.

"It's not as bad as you think," she says.

"It's bad, Nanna, and it's getting worse."

"In my day, you weren't threatened very often, and when you were, you could trust a neighbor to do something about it."

For whatever it's worth, I'm comforted to know that Nanna

had a day once; she had a time she could look back on and remember with pride and earned sorrow.

"Rub my feet," she says.

She rests her right heel on my thighs and I press my thumbs into the cushy centers of her pale feet.

"Your Pop-Pop would do this for me every night after supper."

Nanna holds the glass of wine against her head. "I'm so old." She finishes the glass and holds it out for me to pour another.

"Just once I would have liked your Pop-Pop to talk down a waiter," she says. "He had too much respect for people."

I drive to the police station to find out if anything can be done about the break-ins in Nanna's neighborhood. The officer in charge says I need to fill out a report.

I start to fill it out.

"We won't read it," the officer says.

"Then why am I filling it out?"

"We like to say we like to keep a record."

"All I want is for someone to drive by a few times at night."

"It's bad out there and getting worse."

"That's what I've been saying."

"People are whacked out of their skulls. And what we're finding is that more and more, the people who aren't whacked out of their skulls are defending themselves from the criminal element better than we can. We just don't have the resources. To be honest, we're not exactly sure who's whacked out of their skulls and who isn't anymore."

"What am I supposed to do?"

"This is the big question, isn't it?" he says, and for an instant he looks like he's got the answer.

◆ ◆ ◆

Back at Nanna's, I make a pot of Folgers and check the fridge. The only thing left is a can of tonic water and some moldy blackberries.

How has Nanna lived so long?

Short on weapons, I equip myself with a cylinder of Bab-O powder and a fireplace poker. The plan is to hole up in the bushes, and when an intruder approaches, throw the Bab-O powder in his face and then hit him with the poker.

But there's not much activity out beyond the bushes. Critters, mosquitoes, the occasional gust of wind. Then I hear footsteps coming up the walkway. I jump from the bushes and wave the poker. There're three of them. Kids. They all look like they could use a sandwich. One grabs the poker from me and pokes me in the stomach. I drop to a knee, trying to catch my breath. He makes like he's going to whack me over the head. I close my eyes and brace for impact. But a moment later, they're howling down the street, little balls of lightning exploding into the future.

Back inside, Nanna's finished off the bottle of white zinfandel.

"Catch anyone?" she says, and makes a fart noise with her lips.

"Maybe it's time for bed?" I say.

"How am I supposed to sleep without an air conditioner?"

"If I get another one, they'll just take it."

I hear a car's loose muffler scrape against the road, getting closer, louder, the noise crashing against the house.

"Come on, Nanna. Let's get you somewhere safe."

"Oh, pooh-pooh," she says, and smacks my hand.

I grab her by the arm, my dear Nanna, and nudge her down the hall to the bedroom.

"I don't think all this fussing is necessary," she says, and plops down on the bed.

I remember how when I used to tell Nanna I did something good she asked why it was just good and not great. And when I said I did something great she asked why I tried so hard to be great when I'd never be the best.

The kitchen window shatters. I hear cursing, shouting, barking, and one by one, the little glass clowns Nanna's been collecting since she was a girl smashing on the foyer floor. The glass crackles underneath their feet as they approach the bedroom door.

The doorknob turns and hits on the lock.

"Beat it!" I shout.

"Don't be stupid," a man shouts. "We have dogs."

"Oh, just let them in," Nanna says. "Save a door."

The door splits above the lock and flies open.

"That's the spirit," Nanna says.

In leap the dogs and kids, the same three from earlier, and a man and woman who I'm guessing are their parents. Bony and bug-eyed, lurching like cartoonish shadows separate from their bodies. The guy tells the dogs to heel. The woman fishes through the drawers and jewelry boxes, while the kids fling Nanna's underthings in the air.

"Boo!" one of them shouts, having made a mask out of Nanna's underwear.

Now we're made to kneel against the bed with our heads pressed to the mattress.

I close my eyes.

"Count down from one hundred," the woman says.

The thoughts I have! The feelings I feel!

"Ninety-two. Ninety-one . . ."

Nanna smacks me in the head.

"Will you stop counting? They're gone, for crying out loud."

I stand up. The fronts of my jeans are wet. I'm too ashamed to look at her.

"Go and wash yourself," she says gently. "I'll see if I can find a change of clothes."

Nanna has lent me a pair of Pop-Pop's sweatpants and an undershirt with a yellow stain around the collar. We play gin. She toots once and smiles. As I'm dealing the third hand, Nanna falls asleep in the chair, frozen in slothful comfort.

I collect the cards and kiss Nanna on the cheek.

At some point in their marriage, Pop-Pop moved from the large bed he and Nanna shared, down the hall to the smaller one in the guest room. When I was younger, I thought the reason they slept in separate rooms was because they were mad at each other. But now I see it as a natural progression in life. At some point, you need to adjust to being alone in the dark again.

I sit on Pop-Pop's bed and stare at the pale outlines on the wall, where photographs, medals, and plaques once hung. My Pop-Pop was so brave. I'd like to do just one thing considered brave enough that I'm given a plaque someone finds worth taking.

Nanna hasn't moved from the chair all night.

She's gone.

I call the hospital and they give me a number for who to call to have someone remove the body.

I sit and look through the large bay window, the pink, purple, and amber colors of morning above the fold of darkened treetops.

Only two people come. They hoist Nanna up onto the gurney with a "One, two, three, up-she-goes!"

Later in the afternoon, I survey Nanna's house. There's nothing here worth much, except memories, and who would I share them with? Who would listen?

The ceiling is stained with watermarks. There's mold in the basement, cracks in the driveway, the washer's broken, and the dryer went with the TVs. Throw in the criminal element, and the place is pretty much worthless.

Is it sad? Who can say?

Nanna never wanted much and often received less, and still she lived a long life.

But me, I had so much hope for more when I was young. Had I been paying closer attention, I would have consigned to oblivion all those wonderful dreams.

◆ ◆ ◆ **FROM THE AUTHOR** ◆ ◆ ◆

At the time I started "All That's Gone Is All That's Left," I'd been thinking about our ancient ideas of the haves and have-nots, and this concept that anyone can achieve some standard of what it means to be wealthy in America. Instead, the divide, discord, and unease exists more between the have-nots and have-a-littles. And so it made sense to write a story about a have-a-little type of guy trying to protect his grandmother against some have-nots terrorizing her neighborhood.

SCAFFOLDING MAN

———◇———

◆ JENNY ALLEN ◆

Don't ever marry a writer. Just don't do it. It's like living in an alternate reality, and not in a good way.

Do you think writers talk about writing? About books, about literature? You know what writers actually talk about? Their agents. Their last agent, who sucked. Their new agent, who's great, until he too sucks. Their book deals. Who got a better book deal.

Someone else always gets a better book deal, the one they should have gotten.

Even when they get prizes, someone else always gets the better prize, the prize they should have gotten.

Someone else gets invited to the American Academy in Rome; somebody else gets a MacArthur grant—someone who isn't a genius at all!—someone else sold their crappy book to the movies for half a million dollars and doesn't deserve it.

And this is usually before lunch. No, I'm kidding, but it's endless, it really is.

You do get breaks. At some point, they go into their study to write. And they write and they write and they write, and then they come out, and sometimes they're in a good mood because the writing is going well, or they've invented some new way of working that is going to make the writing even better: like, they've decided to print out every page after they finish writing it, and then tape it to the far wall of their study, and then look at it through binoculars so they can "get some distance on it."

But usually they're in a bad mood because it's not going that well, and they say, "Who ate the last banana?"

And you say, "I did. I thought it was going bad."

And they say, "You should have asked me."

And you think, *I did not sign up for this.*

Years pass, many years. And one spring, they go off to Arizona to teach writing at some college for a term. And this happens to be the same period of time when the front of your apartment building is getting repointed.

So one morning you walk into your living room and you scream, because the scaffolding is right outside your window, and there's a man in coveralls standing on the scaffolding platform looking right at you in your old terry-cloth bathrobe. He looks stricken, as if he's done something awful.

He says—loudly, so you can hear him through the glass—"I'm very sorry to surprise you."

You open the window a bit. "I'm sorry I screamed."

He smiles and says, "Oh, everyone does."

He spends the whole day working right outside your window, and the next day too. He waves when you pass by, and he keeps apologizing for being there. He says it'll only be a few days, and that he should know, because he's the foreman of the crew. He's not young, but he's not old either, and he has a sweet, wide smile.

The second morning you ask him if he'd like a cup of coffee, and he says, "That's very generous," so you pass him a mug of coffee out the window. The third day, just on a whim, you say, "Would you like to come in, and have your coffee in a chair?"

And he says, "That's very nice of you, but I don't think the building would like it."

So you call your super and say, "I'm inviting the boss of the pointing job in for coffee, and I don't want him to get in trouble."

And the super says, "I could care less."

So he comes in through the window for coffee. Which is a little trickier than it sounds, because of the child guards on the window, but he's nimble and manages it. And you and the foreman, whose name is Patrick, have a lovely time. He's from Queens, he tells you, and his father owned the business before him. He has three children, and one of them, his son, is taking over the business as soon as he finishes college. He has an ex-wife named Gloria, but they're friendly. They live a couple of blocks from each other, and she still does the books for the business.

Then he notices some very ripe bananas, covered in brown spots, in a bowl on the kitchen counter. You see him looking at them, so you say, "Would you like a banana? They might be a little too ripe, though." And he says, "Yeah, but they'd be perfect for banana bread."

And you say you've never made banana bread, you're not much of a baker, and he says, "Oh, it's easy, it takes about ten minutes, would you like me to show you?"

. . . So you say, "Sure, why not?"

And he does! He whips up a batch of banana bread in about ten minutes, and you sit there and talk while it bakes, and when it's done he takes it out of the oven and you share thick slices of the delicious warm bread, with butter, and some more hot coffee.

So, eventually, you marry him. Well, first your husband comes home from Tucson and tells you he's in love with somebody named Gretchen, who's one of his students, and then he goes away, back to Tucson, never to be heard from again except when he calls late at night after a few drinks to ask you the name of his old podiatrist, or if you recall the city where he gave some speech once, because he's writing his memoirs and he can't remember. And you really, really don't want to tell him but you do, because Patrick says, from his side of the bed, "Aw, go ahead."

The scaffolding man is the most wonderful husband. He's an excellent cook. He buys you flowers for no occasion at all. You don't have to go to any literary parties anymore, so you spend a lot of evenings just watching old movies on TV and holding hands. Sometimes you go to Coney Island with his little grandchildren, Bridget and Theresa and Patrick the Third. Coney Island is the greatest. The Cyclone, the Wonder Wheel. Nathan's hot dogs. And you think, *Man, this is the life.*

◆ ◆ ◆ **FROM THE AUTHOR** ◆ ◆ ◆

I heard a story about a woman, the divorced wife of a famous photographer who'd been a terrible husband for reasons I don't remember, who met her next husband when he was at work on the scaffolding outside her apartment window. Most people who live in apartments have had that shocking, weirdly intimate experience of having men on scaffolds right outside their windows, and the idea of writing about someone who actually met a mate that way was just irresistible to me. But it also was a way to write about a woman who frees herself from life in a subculture—in this case, a hermetically sealed, talky literary world—that she's found stultifying.

A BRIEF NOTE ON THE TRANSLATION OF *WINTER WOMEN*, WRITTEN BY THE COLLECTIVE DEAD, TRANSLATED BY AMAL RUTH

◆ RIVERS SOLOMON ◆

Translator's Note

WHEN PEOPLE DISCOVER that I speak Haint—or the Language of the Dead,[1] as the New Reformists[2] call it—they assume my prowess with the Hermetic tongue is the result of my kinship with death.

I had this demonstrated for me recently when a group of strangers and I found ourselves trapped together on an elevator between floors. The panic rising among my seven fellows provoked me to

---

1. *It hurt me to type this. Why use so many words when fewer (and better) will do? Yet I know that because this movement led by white linguists and academics has been so successful, it has become the widely accepted term. I use Haint, Deadspeak, and Ghost, as the trailblazing first translators did.*

2. *A group I do not count myself among, for they seem to me obsessed with respectability, wishing to scrub the language clean of all associations with anything sinister or, dare I say, ghostly, an incredible farce when you consider the pioneer of Deadspeak linguistics wasn't a scholar in the traditional sense, but a Black rootworker.*

speak, a misstep I blame on my being autistic; for I am always talking when everyone would prefer me to stay quiet (the precise opposite phenomenon of my childhood, when I was nonverbal, and everyone wished I would speak).

An abrupt stop between floors is Deadspeak for "dying," I informed everyone in the elevator. *Note the stopped-up toilets, the stubborn vending machines, and the flickering lights on floor eight. We're being told that the tree that stands outside is in the early stages of oak wilt, and will die in four years.*

My announcement did not allay anyone's worry. Despite the attempts of the New Reformists to doll up Haint's image, they've never been able to eliminate the heady, Black taint of hoodoo from the tongue. My seven fellows looked at me fearfully, their bags pressed firmly to their bodies. They believed it was me who was dead, the ghost.

One said, *Sir,* misgendering me, *this is the land of the living. We don't speak that nonsense here. We're,* he said, gesturing to everyone in the elevator but me, *alive.* He likely saw that news report[3] linking Haint to zombis. I'm sure he thought I was a revenant, spoken back to life with Deadspeak, given orders to kill by my Haitian Voodoo priestess progenitor or some such nonsense.

I suppose in the matter of Haint, there is no denying that immersion is synonymous with death. This was certainly the case for pioneering translator Lux Wade.

In her early twenties, Wade hired herself out as a rootworker. She was living in her van, barely making enough to afford gas and food. Still, when a young man came to her for aid but couldn't afford to pay, she said yes, moved by the depth of his desperation.

---

3. *Now famously debunked but still considered gospel by the right.*

She described him as having the look of someone with a toe dipped into the grave.

This man, Qu'Von Stokely, needed help with the one-bedroom bungalow he'd inherited from his grandma. Wade had dealt with hauntings before, quite pernicious ones, but Stokely's house was a goliath that would not be sated, no matter what spells and cleansing rituals she performed. Unable to turn down a challenge, she stayed with Stokely in this house for a year as the walls around them rotted away. The rot spread to Stokely and then to Wade herself. Soft, black patches blighted their skin like bruises on an apple.

When Stokely died, Wade could've abandoned the property, but it was her client's last words that told her not to abandon this haunting: *It was a very good story, though I'm not sure it was worth all this.*

What story? Wade asked, but Stokely was gone. She remained in that house for three more years,[4] withering, but by the end of her time there, she had an inkling of what Stokely had meant. A sense. An understanding. The hauntings were not mere torments. They were a language with a grammar. Growing up in the house, immersed in it, Stokely had internalized the rules of the tongue during his youth without realizing it.

Thus began what would become sixty years of deep research. The only way to learn the language fluently was to spend time among the world's hauntings. Wade uncovered a rich, complex language in her travels. Dialects varied, based on a haunting's locations: a house, a building, a ship, a car. Wade appreciated the creolized aspect of the language, the way it bloomed like dandelion where and whenever it was.

---

4. *Squatting. Derelict and abandoned, the house was not high on the bank's priority list.*

In time, she decided to collaborate with a linguist, which is where her eventual wife, Dr. Malachy Osser, entered the picture. Together, after fifteen years, they composed the first grammar. Though they are now dead, the legacy of their work remains. They were my teachers, and as the existence of Deadspeak shows us, no one is ever really gone. Their stories are in me. Though Wade and Osser eventually died in the field in old age, succumbing to the same blight that plagued Wade in that first bungalow, I know they will soon be telling tales.

Winter Women is an epic written collectively by the dead. I've done my best to maintain the rhythms, poetry, idioms, and cadences of Haint, but as you can imagine it is tricky work.

I did not die or come close to death to attain the knowledge necessary for undertaking this translation, though I have lived in haunted spaces aplenty, including the very house that killed the young man who, in his own way, was the key for discovery of Deadspeak by the living.

Winter Women is the epic that Qu'Von Stokely's bungalow orated to him. I hope that, like him, you will find it a very good story, if not necessarily worth the price of death.

—AMAL RUTH

♦ ♦ ♦ **FROM THE AUTHOR** ♦ ♦ ♦

This story came from my love of hoodoo and rootwork, Black diasporic culture and expression, and a desire to rethink what's possible in a haunted-house story. Flash, in my opinion, also demands a certain level of innovation with form. For a while I've been experimenting with the idea of writing translation notes for fictional texts, and it occurred to me, what if the fictional text was a haunting? What, in that short, experimental space, could I say about language, academia, and story? I'm not sure I said anything at all, but I certainly had fun writing it, and I hope it's also fun to read.

NIGHTLIFE

—◆—

◆ LISA KO ◆

We'd been singing karaoke for five and a half hours when Andy left the room. At first, no one noticed. Our voices were hoarse, our throats sore, but we were committed to getting the most out of our flat fee. The room rental was all-you-can-sing, and among the five of us were three former honor society overachievers.

I wasn't one of them, and Andy wasn't either. He didn't live in one of the gentrifying neighborhoods that we lived in, and he didn't work for a nonprofit or a tech company. He worked a job at a warehouse, or maybe it was a grocery store. A few years ago, Yen-ling and Eunice had made it their mission to find Andy a date by the end of the summer, said he'd be happier in a relationship, settled down. They failed, but by Labor Day had drunk so much going out every night that Yen-ling did a juice cleanse, which she brought up as Eunice poured another round of beers. Eunice picked up her cup and said, Remember that summer, I asked Andy if he was into guys or girls or both, and he said he just hadn't met the right person yet? So was that a yes or a no, Yen-ling wondered. Eunice said it was a soft yes, or was it a soft no? Marlon seemed embarrassed, like we were violating Andy's privacy by talking about him. But what are best friends for, Eunice said. Gossip is love.

Marlon finished singing "King of the Road." Out of all of us, he had the best voice. Yen-ling punched in a song that none of us knew because it had come out in the past five years; she worked in an office of twenty-five-year-olds and still went out every night. I've got to go soon, Marlon said, I've got to help with bedtime, and we said no, no, but Marlon was already lost to the abyss of parenting, a future we masked our discomfort for by thinking, well, at least we can stay out late. Yen-ling and Eunice asked to see pictures of the baby again. I want one, Eunice said in a little voice, and then she looked at me and Yen-ling as if to say, Don't you, too?

Marlon said he'd wait for Andy to come back before leaving. Where'd he go, anyway? Maybe the bathroom, Eunice said. Yen-ling and Marlon had gone to high school with Andy, Eunice had been Yen-ling's college roommate. They were, they said, his best friends. I only knew them through him. Three years ago I'd met Andy in a restaurant where the single people were forced to eat at round tables with couples and other single people. We were seated, one empty chair between us, across from a man and a woman on an awkward first date. Do you think they'll have a second date, he said to me. We talked out the sides of our mouths as we dipped shu mai into bowls of chili crisp. Not with that goofy shirt on, I said. If I were him I'd wear it with the buttons up, Andy said, and I said, Yes, me too.

After that we became friends, no interest in dating each other because of our age difference, or maybe he wasn't into me or not into anyone at all. Since I was an editor who worked from home, people assumed I was always free to hang out, which, for the most part, was true. When I dumped my ex I called Andy and we watched a horror movie matinee, and when his dad was sick he texted me to meet up for a drink and we talked about everything but that. One time Yen-ling said something about Andy's parents and I realized that none of them knew that his dad was sick. None of them knew about my ex, either.

As we passed the mic around for the Depeche Mode medley, I told Andy's best friends how Andy and I were driving around in his car one night after a movie and we found a turtle on the side of the road, under the chemical Meadowlands sky. We were in New Jersey because Andy lived in a studio in Harrison. (Marlon said you lived in Queens, I had said, and Andy said, Oh no, that was a long time ago.)

We put the turtle in the car and it was very still. I think it's dead, I said, but Andy said it was only sleeping; his family had a tortoise when he was growing up, it was forty-five years old. That's old, I said, though it wasn't much older than me. Actually, it's not that old for a tortoise, Andy said. Where is it now? I asked. He said Jiro gave it away. I didn't know who Jiro was.

And then what? Eunice said. Her eyes were giant behind her glasses, and she and Yen-ling were waiting, they wanted the ending, and Marlon too, leaning forward on the purple vinyl bench as the backing track played to Radiohead's "Creep," face flushed from the beer in his hand. I've got to go soon, he said again. We sang the chorus together. And then we let the turtle out in a swamp near an underpass and said, "Go, little buddy, go," I said, and that's it, that's the whole story.

The whole story was that after we let the turtle go, Andy and I ate burgers and fries at a diner in Jersey City, in the maze of highways outside the Holland Tunnel. It was a period of my life when I was mostly broke and sad, and most nights I wandered around my apartment by myself eating string cheese and scrolling through news on my phone. I asked Andy about his job at the warehouse or grocery store, our elbows on the sticky diner counter, and he said, Look, I'm actually an actor. His round glasses, oily skin, and small, even teeth made him appear younger than he was, though I could see the grays in his hair. I'm auditioning for these plays. But don't tell anyone. I have performance anxiety when people I know are in the audience. Because then I feel like there's something at stake.

I promised him I wouldn't tell anyone, that I wouldn't go see his plays.

I was drinking a lot, I told him. I still am.

We ate our burgers, we ate our fries. Our knees brushed up against one another underneath the counter and stayed there. That's when you know that someone is the person for you. Not the algorithm or the shared alma mater but the lack of expectations, the understanding.

Andy came back into the karaoke room as the next song began to play. He carried a plastic bag, opened it to reveal a box of chicken wings. Eunice and Yen-ling clapped their hands and Marlon said, I guess I'll stay for another song. We passed out napkins, containers of sauces. Andy took the mic and said, Oh, this one is mine.

There was a waterfall on the video. The dancers formed a line. A man sang to another man walking a dog. Children ran along a beach and a woman flipped her long hair in a meadow. I felt my feet kicking as I licked the side of a wing, and though I might not have felt a ringing joy, I suppose you could say I felt a satisfaction.

◆ ◆ ◆ **FROM THE AUTHOR** ◆ ◆ ◆

This story emerged from the isolation of the past tumultuous pandemic year, which has strengthened many of our friendships and relationships and exposed some rifts in ourselves and others. I wanted to write from a "we" voice to expose this tenuousness and the assumptions carried by a group of longtime friends approaching middle age—the dynamics of that group, the tension between the expectations for connection and the reality of what we share and hide, whether it's due to class or occupational differences or parenting or just people changing. I thought the confines of a karaoke room at the end of a long night would be a good setting for this group scene, and it's also a setting I dearly miss!

CERATI AFTER CERATI

—◆—

◆ JUAN MARTINEZ ◆

The questions came up as soon as a rider heard that Gustavo was Venezuelan: Did he miss his family, was it as bad as everyone said? What was it like, being alone and a young man and away from the people he loved? Gustavo kept the music loud enough to discourage conversation, kept to the same playlist since he'd arrived in Chicago. He used to tell people the truth: his family was safe, mom and dad in Chile and the sister in Madrid. He used to say, Venezuela was *worse* than everyone thought. Americans, he learned, gave you a great deal of sympathy if you told the truth, but they tipped you less. Now he lied and said he had a child, a four-year-old that he'd smuggled out of the country and into Colombia. He was saving up to fly him to the States. That's why the Uber.

This time the rider spoke Spanish. Her name was Patricia. "You're Venezuelan," she said, her accent so neutral it could have been Colombian, even Chilean. How did she know? He hadn't said a thing. Maybe it was his accent, his skin, his clothes.

Patricia lost interest after he got to the imaginary kid, asked where in Colombia, what city.

He said, "He's in an orphanage. Bucaramanga."

"Nice town," she said. "He must be lonely. You too."

"It's not so lonely," he said. He turned up the music. "I've got the songs."

Patricia wouldn't tip. Or she wouldn't tip well.

It would be a long ride, they had made it to the intersection of Milwaukee and Damen. They had to get to Pulaski. The turn signal clicked. He had to make a left, and he'd have to make it on a red light, the only way you could take a left in Chicago. It was close to midnight, the bars aglow, the cold of the night seeping into the car.

"That's Soda Stereo," Patricia said.

That wasn't so terrible. To meet a possible bad tipper who knew about the Argentinean band every South American grew up with. He wanted to tell Patricia about the playlist. Mostly she reminded him of Maria Lucia, the woman who had helped him make it. The two women had the same black hair, the same long nose. He didn't know how to start, didn't know how to tell Patricia that Maria Lucia was almost certainly dead—a diabetic low on insulin in a country with no insulin. They had met in Playa Colorada, they had both heard about a boat that smuggled people out, a crazy route, from the beach to Isla Mariposa to Curaçao. No luck, a local told them: the ship had sunk days before. Others had come too, twenty or so, none surprised by the bad news. They huddled in improvised shelters. Maria Lucia meant to go to the Colombian border, cross over in Cúcuta, wouldn't listen to Gustavo about the horrors he'd heard—she wouldn't make it, not on foot. So what, Maria Lucia said, I go back to Caracas? I'll die there too. She agreed to stay the night. The rest had fallen asleep. Maria Lucia said that she missed just hearing songs, about the day MTV Latino hit cable, about all the rock en español.

Maria Lucia said that she and her twin sister played Soda Stereo albums all the time. They weren't identical twins, she explained. Her sister was prettier. They knew the entire Soda Stereo catalog, knew every version of "En la Ciudad de la Furia." You could absolutely fill a playlist with just Soda Stereo songs, which Gustavo and Maria Lucia would have done if both their phones weren't close to being dead. Maria Lucia had a ballpoint and a notebook. They wrote the playlist on the back, right by a column of numbers and dates. Her sugar levels, probably. They wrote down the title of every Soda Stereo song they loved. To remember a better Venezuela. Maria Lucia was gone in the morning, but she left the list of songs tucked in Gustavo's shirt pocket. He found it weeks later, when he was scrambling—his cousin had gotten him a plane ticket, they'd found him space in a garden apartment in Edgewater, he'd have to share it with other Venezuelan refugees, there was this quasi-legal loophole where he could work just driving around. He kept the playlist, the last scrap of his life as a Venezuelan. And the band wasn't even Venezuelan. He typed it up, song by song, into Spotify. It was a kind of miracle, how Spotify managed to find every song.

Spotify populated the list with more songs, some from last year. Just Cerati. Solo songs. No more Soda Stereo, the band had broken up, Gustavo wasn't sure when. Cerati was welcome, his voice a reminder of a time when living didn't seem impossible. There was even a Cerati song from 2018 that was a mournful commentary on his country, on the tragedy of Maduro and Chávez, and it was so good to know that an Argentinean rock star *cared*. That's what he was telling Patricia, as he drove her—how much he loved Cerati's new songs.

"That can't be him," Patricia said.

"It is," he said. Another intersection. Cold. A smear of streetlight and snow. He tapped the screen: Cerati. 2019 in parentheses.

"He died in 2014," Patricia said. "You knew that."

Gustavo did not know that.

"He was in a coma." She laughed, and the laughter brought him back to the beach, to Maria Lucia. In the shadow of the car, in the shadow of the beach, you could mistake one woman for the other. Sisters, practically. She said, "Cerati went into a coma in 2010. He died in 2014. You can look it up."

The light had just turned green. He could not look it up.

"He's not dead," Gustavo said.

"You men," Patricia said. "So sure. You think you know everything." She shifted, her forehead and hair blocking the rearview mirror. "Like, you know who's alive, who's dead."

"You can't write a song if you're dead," he said.

"He's dead," Patricia said.

Gustavo didn't know if he believed her. The songs kept coming. Another solo song, from an album that came out in 2014, the title a joke, if Patricia was telling the truth: *Hora de Relajarse*. They passed Dulcelandia, the Mexican party-supply store, the window display lit up—every piñata pressed against the window, ready to get out. They were close. The moment he dropped her off, there'd be someone else in wait. Another stranger. Another destination.

He'd have to resurrect his imaginary son all over again. He would check about Cerati's death, though now he remembered his cousin talking about how strange Cerati's coma had been, how sad and unexpected, how even the Swedish band Roxette paid Cerati tribute. Roxette toured Chile in 2012 and covered "De Música Ligera." Singers never quite died, the Swedes said. Their music lived on.

The playlist moved on to an old song, thank God. "Disco Eterno." Cerati sang that he had slipped out of context, that it was better to slip away, to put on a song that played on a loop forever, to be a spirit—a ghost that is sometimes very sure and at other times uncertain.

"That's my stop," Patricia said.

Gustavo slowed down. The map on the phone had frozen, uncertain. He parked by a bar with large windows, the interior visible through large display windows, the shadows inside black and red and full of life. He turned off the playlist. Music poured out of the bar—an old merengue song that his parents loved. He clicked on the interior lights, got a good look at the woman in the back.

"You're the sister," he said. "You are Patricia's sister."

"Patricia's waiting at the bar," Maria Lucia said.

He could see the sister—merengue played, Patricia danced alongside other Venezuelans, strangers all, and kin. He did not expect to feel so happy. He did not expect to identify Cerati so clearly, but Cerati had this very distinctive cloud of hair, and he was there too, dancing. Gustavo had forgotten about the phone, about how he could check and see if what Patricia had told him was the truth. She was getting out. Gustavo had not been invited. He had so many questions for Patricia, for Maria Lucia. The dancers inside seemed to be waving, but it was just a dance move, the sort you did all together as a crowd. Gustavo wanted to join, he was so lonely, he'd forgotten how lonely he was, and he really didn't know if it was okay, what the etiquette was, if a lone and living Venezuelan could find refuge among all these joyous, dancing dead.

◆ ◆ ◆ **FROM THE AUTHOR** ◆ ◆ ◆

"Cerati After Cerati" emerged from a set of unusually specific sources: 1. My uncle's abrupt, harrowing return to Colombia after decades of building a life and a family in Venezuela; 2. Our Chicago neighbors, Venezuelans both, one now working as a rideshare driver; 3. The uncanny always-on insistence of phone apps—Spotify's infinite, self-generating playlist after you've played whatever it is you meant to play, and also Twitterbots posting visual and textual snippets of long-dead artists; 4. A taxi-driver anecdote in Richard Lloyd Parry's Ghosts of the Tsunami; and 5. This one's a little more diffuse, but it haunts the whole piece: the intense but lonely affection I feel, as a Colombian living in the United States, for certain cultural artifacts that are meaningful mostly only to other South Americans, and how impossible it is to ever adequately articulate that affection— that's at the core of this story, the realization that it may register differently if you grew up here or there. I don't often write with this difference in registers in mind, don't often write thinking this much of fellow South Americans, who grew up knowing the words to the same rock-en-español songs.

THE PROM TERRORISTS

◆ RABIH ALAMEDDINE ◆

No matter what my baby sister says, I don't want you to
think I'm stupid, but no one seems to think that maybe
the FBI is stupid or that maybe it wasn't my fault but my
parents', since they suddenly decided that I needed to find a job
and move out because only losers still lived with their parents at
twenty-eight, and that was when I said that they meant *slacker* and
not *loser*, but they didn't know what *slacker* meant since English is
their second language, and I said that if we were back in the old
country, which is something they always said, I would be living at
home until I got married, at which point they'd have to buy a
house for my wife and me, but we were in the hellhole known as
Fresno, which was better than the shithole where they were born
but not by much, if you ask me, so I was feeling stressed when the
FBI letter arrived with my name on it telling me they were looking

for someone with my language skills to help fight extremism and terrorism at home, and I didn't stop to think what language they were talking about since I'm a rapper and use language all the time, but they thought I spoke Arabic because of my name, Kareem Lotfi al-Manfalouti, even though I make sure everyone calls me Lot, and I only know a few curse words in my parents' motherfucking tongue, so during the interview when the intimidating FBI officer with the Stalin mustache asked me if I spoke Arabic I panicked and said, "Fuck, yeah," which turned out to be the perfect answer, but then he put me in a room and handed me a test with the loopy-as-shit script, which looked Greek to me, but it was multiple choice and next to me sat this dark-skinned hijabi woman, probably an Emirati, and I copied all her answers, which really wasn't my fault because she didn't cover her responses and I had popped an edible before the interview (pineapple, 20-mg THC) that hit me as soon as I sat down for the test, so don't blame me for the cheating, but then everyone knows they weren't going to hire a dark-skinned woman in a hijab so I was doing her a favor and I got the job, not that it was a great job or anything since they wouldn't give me a gun, like, what kind of FBI agent has no gun, and that was when I was told I was no FBI agent, just someone who worked with the bureau, and that's when I wondered who said things like *bureau* and whether *informant* was just a fancy word for *secretary*, but then I was told to infiltrate the Muslims at the city's mosque and find out what the recently arrived imam was planning, because they knew that he was kicked out of his mosque in Cairo before coming to Fresno and they were sure he was planning something untoward but I couldn't make myself ask the intimidating FBI agent untoward what, and that was when he said that even though I looked white with my bleached hair, I would fit in with the other terrorists, and yes, I know, that might have been the time when I should have said that my family was Christian, but I thought telling him that might make him think I was a liar so I decided to not ask but continued whistling an Umm Kulthum song so I'd sound authentic, and that was when it occurred to me that I needed help, so I went to my baby sister, who was twelve years younger, but was the smartest person I know, and asked her if she would come to the mosque with me since, unlike me, she'd paid attention during the Arabic lessons my parents paid for, and she thought I was crazy, as in why would she want to go to a mosque since she was a diehard atheist feminist who thought all religions were nothing more than a tool to prop up the patriarchy, so no fucking way would she set foot in a mosque or a church, and she wasn't going to ruin her hair by covering it, but I think that the reason she didn't want to help me was because she was upset because some guy called Adam who she'd planned on having sex with at the prom told her he was gay and she had to say yes to Steve who asked and all her plans of offering her virginity to Adam had to be changed to Steve and she wasn't happy, which means I didn't blame her for telling me to fuck off and calling me a fascist stooge, and I ended up in the mosque inside the mall to check things out and a nice guy in a funny yarmulke told me I needed to take my shoes off even though the carpet was as old as the Prophet himself, and he knew it was my first time and we began to gossip and I didn't have to ask before he told me that the imam was kicked out of Cairo because his wife had walked in on him masturbating in the bathroom to pictures in *Teen Vogue* and she divorced him and tossed him out of that shithole country, I mean, really, all that trouble because he masturbated, but my new friend said that the new imam railed constantly against the low morals of our country and that the week before he issued a fatwa against the high school prom because everyone knew it was where young Muslim girls lost their virginity, and I had to tell my new friend that it wasn't just Muslim girls and that my sister was tired of hers and intended to fling it with any halfway decent guy who wanted it, and I think he was a bit confused because his head tilted funny, but he went with the flow, which was a good thing because I was really high by then and my new friend told me that all the Muslims laughed at the anti-prom fatwa and that meant that as soon as the imam sat cross-legged in front of us on the short dais, he began to talk about sending undercover Muslim men to the prom in order to guard the virginity of young Muslim girls and that was when I realized that I understood what the imam was saying since he was saying it in English, a fucked-up broken English just like my dad, and I definitely had the language skill for that, but the intimidating FBI agent didn't believe me at first when I told him about undercover Muslims at the prom but he changed his tune when the agents following the imam called to tell him that the imam came out of the tuxedo rental shop with a baby-blue number, so the Fresno FBI went into an insane frenzy because the prom was only three days away, and I knew that because my baby sister had stolen all the condoms I had hidden under the mattress, and when I tried to confront her she said, "Fuck off, you imperialist tool," and to get back at her, I laced her Diet Coke with K but then thought what a waste and drank it myself, but it wasn't my fault that her plans for the prom blew up because eleven undercover FBI agents went to the school gym, including a hostage negotiator and a diffuser, although why they would want to diffuse potpourri in a large gym is beyond me, and they were joined by the imam and another Muslim guy even though they were supposed to be five but the other three had eaten burritos at Taco Bell and became indisposed, and the poor girl at the entrance couldn't stop any of them from going in, and the FBI thought they would have it easy since there was only two undercover Muslims but once in the gym, they saw all these Muslim kids dancing and drinking and making out in corners, with each other and with non-Muslim kids, the intermingling kissing offending both the undercover FBI agents and the undercover Muslim, and then my sister saw me, punched me in the shoulder, demanding to know what I was doing at the prom, but before I could tell her that I was with the FBI, she dragged me under the bleachers, where we were shocked to see Adam daisy-chained between Mohammad A. and Mohammad K., their pants around their ankles, and I envied homosexuals for being able to go from making out to full-fledged fucking in less than six seconds, and while pulling their pants back up, Adam, Mohammad A., and Mohammad K. asked us not to judge because they were in love and wanted to move in together and live as a throuple when they graduated in a couple of years, and I said cool, but they didn't pull up their pants fast enough because the imam, looking kinda not bad in the baby-blue tux, showed up out of nowhere next to us under the bleachers and began to yell at both Mohammads, then he called my baby sister a slut because he assumed they were making out with her and that was when she slugged him and he staggered back and fell in front of the entire prom and was out cold, a baby-blue lake on the hardwood floor, and my baby sister came out from under the bleachers still yelling at the unconscious imam, and there was a big brouhaha, and the undercover FBI went into action, trying to intimidate anyone into confessing whether there was a bomb or not, and the police got involved and so many people were taken to the station, and I don't have to tell you the rest because you must have read about the weapons of prom destruction jokes online and the FBI tried and failed to hush things up, and my baby sister is still so angry because everyone at school thought she was doing sinful things under the bleachers and all she wanted was to get fucking laid and I ruined everything for her and I didn't even get the fifty dollars the FBI promised me.

♦ ♦ ♦ **FROM THE AUTHOR** ♦ ♦ ♦

About twenty years ago, the filmmaker Omar Naim suggested we collaborate on a screenplay. He told me that the FBI was sending out letters to people with Arabic-sounding names, suggesting that they could have a good career with the bureau because of their language skills. Unfortunately, Omar and I didn't end up collaborating, but the idea percolated in my head. What if whoever received that letter didn't speak another language and desperately needed a job? I kept imagining this sweet screwup, an Arab pothead, becoming an FBI informant, and his young sister who just wants to get laid. I'd considered writing the story as a script, as a novel, but it never took hold. It was only when I was asked to write a short-short story to be read aloud that I realized that what had been floating in my head for those twenty years might work for that.

BEDTIME STORY

◆ VICTOR LaVALLE ◆

Who knew an eight-year-old could get depressed? Maybe you did, but I didn't. My son, Malachi Martin. The kids at school call him Kai for short. Or they did. Before school closed. Before the whole city put up a CLOSED FOR BUSINESS sign. New York, New York. The city that never sleeps. Well, that's officially bullshit now. We went into hibernation on March 20. It's been eight weeks since then. Which leads us back to Malachi, my depressed child.

He's the first one who noticed our building had emptied out. He said the neighbors had gone away, and I dismissed it. "They're just staying in," I told him. But once he said it, I became aware of the silent streets; our hallways and landings were quieter, too.

I knew plenty of our neighbors; it wasn't unusual for me to be late getting Kai to school because I'd been catching up with someone in the lobby. But we stopped running into folks, and I was getting him to school on time. And then, you know, the schools closed.

I promised we'd figure out a way to keep up with his friends, but it turned out my kid didn't get much pleasure out of yapping with buddies on a screen. No privacy, no contact, and with all the Internet glitches freezing their conversations, he might as well make small talk with a painting. I scheduled remote playdates, but Kai declined the invitations.

Here's the way he was before: Kai could make friends with anyone, eight years old or eighty. He'd walk right up and tell you about the book he was reading or the dream he'd had the night before. Not everybody loved this, but most bloomed before his attention like a flower opens up to the sun. He gets that from his mother. She had to leave us four weeks into quarantine because her mom wasn't doing well. That didn't help Kai either.

So imagine my surprise when he tells me he has an idea; how we could have some fun. I'm ready for anything, or so I think. Then he tells me he wants to go camping.

Now, I am born and raised in Queens, New York, and the closest I've ever come to camping is when I learned to spell the word correctly in the second grade. But still I propose sleeping in the living room, or maybe the kitchen. And honestly that's about all the choices I have to offer in our two-bedroom apartment. Not unless I'm going to propose we sack out by the toilet, and I wasn't going to do that.

But he's already got a plan. He doesn't want to sleep in the apartment. He wants to sleep in the hallway, on the *landing*. Under normal circumstances, this would be the time I ask my eight-year-old what on earth he could be thinking. What about when people walk on our heads as they step out of the elevator? But Kai points out the new reality: none of our neighbors are here. Six apartments on this floor, but only one is occupied. Everyone escaped except us. If his mother had seen me hauling blankets, pillows, and a pile of books into the hallway, she would've threatened to call Child Protective Services on me.

But she wasn't here.

It felt strange to lie down beside him out there. We were utterly unguarded. It felt like lying flat on a raft in the middle of the sea. Who knew what might appear from the depths. A sudden wave could capsize us.

I knew I wouldn't fall asleep; I hoped he would.

I brought my iPad out with us. I'd downloaded an app called Hearth. You could pick from a hundred different fireplaces, and the wood inside burned and crackled until you closed the screen. Kai chose "Soapstone." He lay on his stomach, watching the fire. I felt like he wanted me to speak, but I struggled, searching for the soothing thing to say.

"When Grandma was only a little older than you," I finally began, "she got hit by a car. Broke both her legs, fractured her hip. Bad stuff. Bad stuff. She was ten."

I looked to him, but he remained transfixed by the fire. I turned over on my stomach.

"She spent a whole year laid up. Her dad, my grandpa, worked at the post office and he made a special trip once a week to the library picking up books for her. She cleaned out the whole branch before she could walk healthy again. She learned so much American history she knew more than the teachers when she went back to school."

Kai lay his head down, looking toward me. Now I could see he wanted to speak, so I stayed quiet long enough to let him.

"While she was laid up," he began, "did she ever get scared? Scared that things would never get better?"

I was about to say something obvious, weave the connection between what she went through then and what we were going through now, but he looked at me with a kind of warning: don't mess things up by trying to teach *me* a *lesson*.

Instead, I lay beside him, listened as his breathing slowed, watched his body shift into easefulness. He fell asleep, and I refused every urge I had to pick him up, give him a kiss; all that soothing would've been for my sake, not his. That caught me by surprise, that I needed reassuring, too. I'd been so focused on giving it to him.

Kai shifted where he slept, and I watched his face. He glowed, and I lay there in his light, letting it warm me. Tomorrow night I'd tell him about his grandfather; then about his mother, as a girl, and what it took to reach this country. Tell him all of it so he would know his people—that he and I—would survive.

◆ ◆ ◆ **FROM THE AUTHOR** ◆ ◆ ◆

My story began with COVID-19. That will be obvious. We live in Washington Heights and our building did clear out. Some of our neighbors had second homes, or family living elsewhere, but we were a hotspot neighborhood so more than a few of our older neighbors fell ill, or died in their homes. We stayed and the building took on the quality of a haunted house. Our older son, eight years old, took the isolation hard. But I didn't just want to write about his trouble; instead I marveled at all the ways he tried to keep his spirits up: walks to the park, once that was safe; playing in the alley; running up and down the stairs. He did a lot of good for himself, and for the rest of the family, too.

SUCH SMALL ISLANDS

◆━━━━◇━━━━◆

◆ LAUREN GROFF ◆

They came to the summerhouse in May. There was still a bite to the salty air, and the hydrangeas clenched their fists, wary of blooming. Through the windows, the pool glinted malignantly, and at the edge of the beach, a tiny gardener moved his clipper hands down the hedge. Aura sat under the dining table in the last slab of oceanlight as her mother and Phyllis, the housekeeper, spoke in the kitchen. Because her mother was just coming into her glory at work—because Aura was sickly and taxing—Aura's half sister on her father's side was coming to watch her all summer. Now her mother was asking the housekeeper to make sure the girl's bedroom would be ready when she arrived in the early morning. Then, Aura watched her mother carry a glass of wine out to the veranda, where dinner was cooling. She called, Aura! Aura! the anger growing in her voice, but Aura ignored her.

She crept along with the lash of sunlight that swiftly diminished over the floor. The sky bled purplish orange. At last, her mother stopped calling, covered her face with both hands, and gently screamed into them.

In the morning, there was a strange voice downstairs when Aura slid in her socks down the stairs. She came into the kitchen to find her mother at the table in her suit, tapping at her phone with her thumbs. Beside her, a girl with lustrous black hair down to her hips was licking the sugar off the top of her split grapefruit. This was Augusta, but everyone called her Gus. Gus held out her arms, but Aura said, No, you're a stranger.

Silly, of course you know me. Gus laughed. We're sisters. We saw each other all the time before our dad and your mom got divorced. But Aura's mother, who brooked no fools, said that Aura had been only two then, of course she couldn't remember, and their dad barely had time to see her. Then she smiled tightly, as if in conciliation, and said, You haven't been out to the island before? No, Gus said, my mom wouldn't ever let me come. That's right, Aura's mother said, and in her face Aura saw first dislike then a slow victory, because Gus was here; Aura's mother had won. She loved winning.

Well, her mother said, standing. As they'd discussed over the phone, she would be gone a lot this summer and there would be times she probably wouldn't make it back to the island for a few days at a time. Phyllis would take care of food and whatever else they needed. Her assistant had sent Gus the information about the jeep, Aura's medications, the beaches they could go to with their badges; still, for good measure, she handed Gus a thick printout. Be good, love you, she said, kissing her daughter's head. So fast, she was out the door, in the car, gone.

Uncertainly, Aura looked at Gus. She was pretty, Aura saw now. Her lips were thin but she had a smile that spread so broadly it seemed to touch her tiny earlobes, and her teeth gleamed like pearls. Don't worry, we'll figure everything out, little sis, Gus said, and picked her up. Aura pressed her face into her neck and inhaled her marvelous smell, like apples and pine trees and the kind of candies that look like colored glass. That was when something in her began to burn.

The days became bright and smooth. Gus's long limbs browned, her black hair spread like a wing over Aura's face when, in the afternoons, stinging with sun and salt and the tiny abrasions of sand, the girl went down for her nap. There were days of blowsy pink peonies full of ants, bike rides through the golden meadows to the children's beach, coconut sun lotion, Gus in a blue bikini on the pool float when Aura came yawning into the afternoon, rubbing sleep from her eyes. They ate strawberry ice cream, watching the sun set over the private beach. Aura refused to go to bed at night anywhere but in Gus's bed, but woke in her own room with the rocking horse in the corner gazing at her with boggled horror. One day down on the sand, as Aura wove strange landscapes out of bladder wrack and eelgrass, Gus sighed and said, This is heaven. She sat up and opened a beer she'd stolen from the fridge and said, You're a lucky kid. Your whole life is what people like me pinch our pennies to have for a single measly week every year. Aura tried to think what this would mean but couldn't. But you *are* people like me, Aura said. Gus looked at her and smiled a little. Maybe, she said. I will be.

Soon Aura's mother's absences went from just a few days at a time to four, then five days. Each night when she called to apologize, Aura heard the city bleating behind her, and Aura felt relieved that she, too, wasn't in the city; that her mother was. It's okay, Aura told her, Gus and me are perfect without you. Gus and I, Honey, her mother said but absently; she hadn't even been listening.

By mid-June, they began to go to the beach cafe to eat dinner once or twice a week, and soon Gus had friends, the boys who had ropy muscles in their legs from carrying trays over sand, the boys who sat at the bar with their collars turned up against their sunburned necks. Gus leaned back in her chair, in her jean cutoffs and bikini top, and laughed up at those who came by to talk to her, and played with her hair and drank the beers they slipped her because she wasn't yet legal to drink in public. When they rode their bikes home through the thick dark, she sang songs; and hearing her made Aura feel as though the whole night were somehow bursting out of her, the sleek marshlands covered with darkness, the cobbled streets, the giant pale moon, Gus singing and gliding in great smooth arcs back and forth across the dark path, her black hair flicking behind her body.

But one morning as Aura slid thumping down the stairs, there was a disturbance of voices and she came into the breakfast room to find a boy in a pink shirt soft with age, an expensive constellation of holes on one shoulder, leaning close to Gus and murmuring. Phyllis put down plates of eggs before them, shooting spikes out of her eyes. Thanks! Gus said in a strange voice. The housekeeper gave a sniff and went out. The boy saw Aura, and said, What weak, writhled shrimp is this? because at his expensive college he was studying drama. Gus flushed and said too loudly, My little sister! and opened her arms, and Aura clutched her, hiding her face from the boy. There was a new smell to Gus's body, a swollenness to her lip that Aura wanted to pinch thin again. The boy was called Oz, short for Oscar, and when he finally walked off, Aura was relieved to have gotten rid of him. But she watched him from the front porch because Gus did, and felt outraged when he went only to the house next door, a giant gray thing with turrets. Gus said, in a low voice, Oh, I like him so much. Aura turned away to make a face. She wasn't surprised when he was back hours later, and again they watched from the front porch as he jogged up the drive. Aura willed her eyes to hurt him, his giant limbs, his lacrosse hands, his bare, shining chest. He had a fanny pack at his waist with a pen in it for his nut allergies. It seems like that little bag should look stupid, Gus said as though to herself, watching him; but I don't know, he somehow pulls it off. Oz leapt up the steps, palmed Aura's head like a ball, came into the house, and later kissed Gus in the pool for the entire time they thought she was napping.

Now it wasn't just Gus and Aura, it was Gus and Aura and Oz. He drove the kind of car that had no walls, so their whole bodies were terrifyingly exposed to the wind. He picked Aura up and threw her in the pool, though she screamed and kicked and, when she surfaced, wept. During hide-and-seek, he didn't even try to find Aura, just pressed Gus against the pool house while, crouched in the hydrangeas, Aura ripped up handfuls of grass. He was too much, too large, too loud, something about him ate up all the air and left others gasping. After Oz, Aura wasn't allowed to fall asleep in Gus's bed; she was bullied into sleep by that hateful rocking horse in her own room. At the Fourth of July water fight in the center of town, Aura watched, hopeful, as the firefighters turned their great hoses in Oz's direction, but he wasn't knocked down, and when things became too wild, he tucked Aura under his arm as though she were a rugby ball and pushed through the crowds. When she couldn't stop crying at the indignity of being carried like that, Gus said in a hard voice, Looks like someone needs her nap.

Aura felt so wounded she was inconsolable, and not even Popsicles would help.

That night in bed Aura chanted in an endless stream all of the terrible things of the world that she knew: earthquakes and snakes and broken bones and pinches, car crashes and heart attacks and zits and head lice, and sent the black stream in the direction of Oz's huge, stupid house. But of course when, in the middle of the night, the noises woke her from Gus's room, they told her that he'd been with Gus just beyond her wall, not in his own house, all along.

The coolness of early summer bled out, and heat poured into the days like liquid in cups, overflowing into the nights. Aura woke in her bedroom to see a glow in the window and knew it was a bonfire down at their private beach, that Gus had left the house to be down there with Oz and his friends and their booze and music, and that Aura's mother would be angry if she knew. In the dawn, her face ugly in its puffiness, Gus went down with a trash bag that clanked when she dragged it back up to the garage. Aura watched her and saw how the pink flowers were all gone, and now the world was filled with aggressive yellow, tiger lilies and daisies and sunflowers. She heard Gus come up the stairs, her voice and Oz's murmuring, and then they slept again, long past the time that Aura was supposed to have breakfast. Aura refined her list of terrible events until it felt like a tarry ball choking her. Finally, Phyllis came up with a tray, muttering things under her breath that sounded like curses. Aura ignored the food and lay in her bed alone, her tears so hot they seared the skin of her temples as they fell.

At last Gus came for her, brushing her wet hair, a floral dress showing the outline of her body as she stepped through the bands of sun from the windows. Hello, sleepyhead, she said. You slept so late it's almost lunchtime. We're going on a picnic! And she leaned over Aura and dripped her wet hair on the girl's face until Aura loosened her anger and let it fly away. She reached up to Gus's face, the wide smile and teeth, the eyebrows like bird wings, and took her cheeks in her hands and squeezed them until Gus's mouth puckered fishily. The day had been reset. The hydrangeas wore great heavy blue-green globes. The sunlight was honey. Best of all, there was no Oz with them when they rode their bikes to the sandwich shop. Every part of Aura rejoiced that this would be a day like the beginning of summer, slow and clean and soft, just Gus and her, their serious talks and the long gentle silences. But there he was, Oz, waiting at the store with his bare chest and his fanny pack, his enormous feet in his flip-flops. Ahoy, pathetical nit, he said, tugging at one of Aura's braids. She felt the bitter ball rise into her throat again.

Inside, they picked out cut watermelon, beers, a cherry soda for Aura. Don't tell your mom, she hates sugar, Gus said, twinkling. And fun, Oz said, but Gus hushed him. Aura turned away in hatred. She watched the boy in the kitchen making their sandwiches through the vitrine where the salads waited lonely under their shining wrap. The boy made Aura's peanut-butter-and-jelly first, then wrapped it in white paper. When he went to spread the mustard on Gus and Oz's sandwich, he took up the knife that he had used for Aura's, absentmindedly wiped it on a cloth, and used it to spread and flatten and cut. Aura thought of the peanut butter still on the knife, how it was now on the bread. The world came to a hot point in her. The boy wrapped up the sandwiches, put tape on them, checked them out. Aura watched, she knew, she said nothing.

The ride out to the hidden cove was hot. There was a smashed cat with blood on its teeth at an intersection and it smelled like panic. Oz was impatient with how slowly Aura rode and kept shouting, Come on, Pokey, over his shoulder. Aura looked only at the blacktop rushing by and emptied her head of thoughts and made her legs go even slower. At last, they got off their bikes. The ocean was a strange dark blue, and the wind had picked up and was blowing tiny pieces of sand in their faces. They climbed down the cliffs to the beach, where Gus spread a blanket. At this time of day, the beach was in shadow and the little caves in the cliffs seemed endlessly deep. Oz kicked off his shoes and dropped the fanny pack and sprinted into the waves, and soon he stood shining with water and saying, Come on, Gus, my sweet. Gus flushed and bit back a laugh and told Aura to make her a giant sandcastle, then took off her dress and joined him, and they held hands until they were past where the breakers crashed, in the smoother waves beyond. Then their heads were close together. Aura knew they were doing that thing again, even though she was there to see them, even though they had left her all by herself on the beach, and she was still a little child and should never be left alone. The thing in her grew so large it blinded her. She began to dig with her metal shovel, wildly, like a dog, throwing sand everywhere, on the blanket, on the basket of food, on their clothes, on their shoes, on their cell phones, she dug and dug and hours or even days probably passed, she thought, until she was in a hole so deep her eyes were at water level and there were heaps of sand everywhere. At last Gus and Oz stood over her hole, panting and dripping, saying how incredible it was that such a tiny girl could dig so fast, and such a deep hole, too.

Gus shook out the blanket and unearthed the basket. Oz pulled Aura out of the hole and into the colder wind. She saw with satis-faction that the sand had buried everything, clothing, shoes, fanny pack, cell phones. Lunchtime, he said. I'm starved. Aura stood with a finger in her mouth, tasting salt and sand, watching Gus unpack the forks, the watermelon, the drinks. When she took the sand-wiches out, Aura yelled, Not hungry, and ran off toward the caves in the cliffs. Gus called after her, but Oz said, If she wants to be like that, just let her go.

In Aura's cave, the stone was cold and smooth and it was chill-ier here, though out of the wind. There were seashells heaped in a corner, a pulsing black to her back. Way up the beach, Gus and Oz were tiny, the size of her pinky finger. She couldn't hear them or see what they were doing. She watched but only out of the corner of her eye. For a long time nothing happened, and the knowledge she'd held like a little flame in her dwindled and almost blew out. But then suddenly Gus leapt up. She began kicking frantically at the mounds of sand. She fell to her knees and dug with her hands, she ran back to Oz, she bent over him, she ran off. Oz slowly laid his body down. Aura closed her eyes. The cool rock cupped her, the seagulls screamed, the waves beat a steady time. She didn't mean to but she fell asleep.

When she woke, it was much later, the beach had filled with afternoon light, the blanket was empty, and a red light was flash-ing up where they had parked the bikes. Up and down the beach there were strangers walking along, calling her name. Aura! they called, Aura! But not one of them was Gus, not one wore her hair flicking in the wind, her cool face, her long smile. So Aura stayed quiet, crouched. She was just a tiny thing, after all, at least when measured against the weight of so much rock around her. She was just a little nothing beside the grasping, hissing ocean stretched all the way to the edge of the sky.

◆ ◆ ◆ **FROM THE AUTHOR** ◆ ◆ ◆

Sometimes place suggests a story, and this one came out of a strange visit to my sister-in-law's cottage in Nantucket, which was a week of bicycles and blue hydrangeas and beach bars and sand everywhere. But the collision, the thing that made this a short story and not a piece of travel writing, was I had just reread Saki's "Sredni Vashtar," and was seized by the passion of the child protagonist; the profound love, the shocking hatred.

ALMOST EVERYTHING

◆ ETGAR KERET ◆

[Translated from the original Hebrew by Jessica Cohen]

To Shira

For her forty-ninth birthday, Schleifer bought her forty-nine gifts. They each came from a different country: perfume from France, sake from Japan, a hair clip from the Ivory Coast. He wrapped each present separately, in the colors of the respective country's flag. On the morning of her birthday he got up early, arranged everything on the coffee table, and between the curtain rod and the chandelier he hung a silk banner on which he'd embroidered her name in forty-nine gold-threaded hearts.

When Aviva woke up and walked into the living room, her eyes welled with tears of joy, and within seconds he was weeping too, with happiness and relief.

Schleifer's surprise birthday production became the talk of the town. Several people complimented him for being so creative and industrious. Even the busty cashier at the grocery store, who never said anything more personal than "It's buy one, get one free," smiled and asked where she could get herself a husband like him. Schleifer gave her a nonchalant wink and remarked self-assuredly, "If you're going to celebrate, you may as well go all out."

But not everyone was supportive. "Dude, you dug us all into a hole," Haimon grumbled. "You raised the bar so high, there's no way I can get away with buying Lizzy a bunch of flowers and a card at the gas station anymore." And when Schleifer stopped by the nursery for some fertilizer, Albert snorted: "Bro, if that's what you came up with for her forty-ninth, I don't even want to think about the production you'll put on for her fiftieth." After a minute he put his calloused hand on Schleifer's shoulder and asked, "Are you okay? You look pale."

Like a prisoner who digs a tunnel from his cell and discovers it ends up in the prison yard, like a warrior returning triumphantly from the battlefield only to be sent back to the front, like a gazelle that narrowly escapes a forest fire straight into a pride of hungry lions—that's exactly how Schleifer felt when he got home from the nursery. Aviva's birthday was a grueling challenge that he'd managed to complete, a character test he'd passed while knowing that even the slightest deviation from the fantasy she'd concocted would lead to sorrow and bitter disappointment. Yet through all the months during which he'd clambered up that steep and slippery mountain, he hadn't given so much as a moment's thought to the fact that after he conquered the summit, awaiting him beyond it, only one year away, there would be another one, far higher and more precipitous.

"Then leave her," said Yana in her indifferent tone, as if she were scheduling him for a dentist appointment. That, by the way, was how they'd met. Yana was the receptionist for Dr. Miklos, his and Aviva's dentist. The first time he met her at the clinic she'd told him a really dirty joke, and when she laughed loudly, as if it were the first time she'd heard it, she revealed two rows of glistening white teeth. Clean teeth and a filthy mouth—was there any sexier combo? "I asked you to help me think of a gift," Schleifer grumbled, and pulled on his pants, "not give me couples counseling." "Okay," Yana said, and inserted a long fingernail between her teeth to pull out a pubic hair, "then buy her some expensive jewelry. Or a luxury hotel getaway. She'll love it." "Aviva doesn't like jewelry," Schleifer said as he finished tying his shoelaces, and on the way out he added, "and when I suggest a vacation she always says going abroad is for people who aren't happy at home." "Yeah," Yana called after him, "and are you?"

That night, after Aviva fell asleep, Schleifer sat with his laptop for almost five hours, searching for something special. While in the past he'd made do with stale search terms like "gift," "surprise," or simply "expensive," he was now savvy enough to try concrete things like "endangered animals" (a clouded leopard could have made her happy, but since it was a feline she might be allergic), "illegal cosmetic treatments" (he found a hospital in Albania that offered innovative surgery to lengthen your legs by two inches, but whenever Aviva had gone under anesthesia she'd suffered terrible nausea), or "blissful orgasm" (a Latin robot-lover sounded interesting, but if he knew Aviva, she'd view that as an attempt to shirk his duties. And besides, with all due respect to Latins, they excelled in many areas but robotics was not one of them). Finally, after all other efforts had failed, he typed in "asteroid" and discovered that for thirty or forty thousand shekels you could get one named after you. Schleifer copied down the phone number with the US area code and decided to look into the matter. At first he imagined Aviva, perfectly in character, saying, "This is what you got me? A piece of rock?" But he also knew it was important to her that the gift be original and imaginative, and there was no denying that having an asteroid named for you was not the kind of gift you got every day.

It was 4 a.m. when Schleifer dialed the number. He went out to the balcony, so as not to wake Aviva, and was surprised when a deep, gravelly voice answered in a heavy Southern accent. The man on the other end of the line introduced himself as Galileo, and when Schleifer asked if that was his real name, the guy snickered and said, "No, genius, it's not my real name." Galileo explained to Schleifer that the whole field of naming astronomical objects was still wide-open and that outer space was "the twenty-first century's Wild West." Officially, it turned out, astronomical bodies were supposed to be named for their discoverers, and the authorities were strongly opposed to commercializing things. But gravelly Galileo knew how to get around that. "By your wife's fiftieth birthday," he promised Schleifer, "I guarantee I'll find a new asteroid and give it her weird name."

"It's not a weird name," Schleifer said defensively. "Aviva is a very acceptable name in Israel. Common, even. It comes from the Hebrew word *aviv*, which means—"

"Honestly?" Galileo cut him off. "I don't give a shit. Just get the ten thou' ready, yeah? Because from the minute I locate the asteroid, everything's gotta run like clockwork so I can register it fast. Neither of us would be thrilled if while I'm waiting for you to come up with the 10k, some fucking Chinaman cuts in and names the asteroid after his granny."

The next eleven months were calm. They were not, however, uneventful. Aviva's parents both died of COVID-19, and Schleifer's business suffered a blow when his partner, François, skipped the country, leaving a pile of debt behind. Yana left him too, and started going out with a fitness coach who'd trained half the commandos in the army's elite squads and could have sex for eight hours straight without stopping for a second, not even for a glass of water. Or so Yana claimed. But when it came to the preparations for Aviva's fiftieth birthday, Schleifer felt supremely calm. It was as if that brief, peculiar phone call in the middle of the night with a man who lived on the other side of the world and called himself Galileo was more reliable than the bank account emptied out by the conniving François before he disappeared. Thoughts such as "Maybe he won't be able to find an asteroid in time" or "He might just be a crackpot American who likes lying to people on the phone" never even crossed Schleifer's normally skeptical mind. Perhaps it was because Galileo had sounded so confident, or perhaps because Schleifer's facade of serenity was hiding such colossal terror that he was afraid to let it crack.

His second talk with Galileo was also at 4 a.m. This time it was Galileo who called. Aviva woke up when the phone rang, but Schleifer told her it was a Canadian lawyer who was trying to help him sort things out with François, and she went back to sleep. Schleifer stepped out onto the balcony, and Galileo informed him that he'd found the promised asteroid and that Schleifer was lucky he wasn't charging by weight, because this one was almost as big as the moon. Galileo said he would text Schleifer his bank account info, and as soon as the wire transfer was confirmed he would register the asteroid in Aviva's name. Schleifer thanked him and was about to hang up, but Galileo said there was one more little detail—"full disclosure," he called it: "When you find an asteroid, it's not enough to know where it is now. Those fuckers are always in motion, you know, so you have to calculate their course."

"And . . . ?" Schleifer asked when Galileo's silence stretched out.

"And the thing is," Galileo went on, "that based on my calculations, this asteroid is on track to strike Earth. This isn't going to have any bearing on the naming, see? Our transaction is unaffected, but still, I felt I should share this information with you."

"Okay . . . So when exactly is this supposed to happen?"

"When did you say your wife's birthday is?"

"April thirtieth," Schleifer replied.

"Great. The asteroid should only collide with us the next day. For a second there I was afraid it would work out exactly on her birthday, which would, you know, put a damper on the party."

"And this collision . . . could it be serious?"

"Serious?" Galileo snorted. "Hombre, based on the tragic fate befallen by our friends the dinosaurs, I'd say that when an asteroid this big hits planet Earth, it's pretty serious."

On the evening of April 29, when he stopped to fill up the car, Schleifer went into the empty convenience store and bought a frozen Swiss roll and a card. Aviva was still in her year of mourning over her parents, which absolved him from the need to organize a party or even make reservations at a restaurant. She'd loved her parents dearly. So had he. They were stand-up people, people from the pre-scum era, and they'd really loved each other. Aviva told him once that they'd never celebrated birthdays when she was growing up, and that's why she'd always felt deprived. Her dad used to say, "What would you prefer—one day with parties and lots of attention, or for us to love you year-round?" Every time her dad said that, little Aviva had felt stupid and guilty. But when she grew up, her therapist explained that the need to celebrate birthdays was universal and ingrained, like needing sleep or food, and that she shouldn't feel bad about never forgiving her parents for it.

The birthday card Schleifer bought had a picture of a shooting star, and underneath it said in gold letters *Make a wish*. He added in his lopsided handwriting: *For the woman who has (almost) everything*. Aviva found the gilded card and the Swiss roll with a lit candle on the kitchen table on the morning of her birthday, and right on cue, exactly as she and Shleifer were biting into the cake, a news flash on the radio reported that the asteroid called Aviva would reach Earth in less than twenty-four hours. Schleifer sipped his coffee and waited patiently. The first two times they said the name of the asteroid, Aviva didn't seem to make the connection. But when the newscaster relayed predictions of tens of millions of casualties from Aviva and then outlined various catastrophic scenarios, she looked at the shooting star on the birthday card again and a faint smile came to her lips. "You nutcase," she said in a shaky voice, and put her warm hand on the hairy back of his neck. "You really shouldn't have." Instead of answering, Schleifer shut his eyes and submitted, like a cat, to the touch of her hand.

◆ ◆ ◆ **FROM THE AUTHOR** ◆ ◆ ◆

My wife always takes birthdays seriously, while I come from a lineage who saw in a birthday an arbitrary date in which one was forced to relocate from his mother's womb to somewhere way less pleasant. Birthday celebrations were always a big deal in my wife's family, a tsunami of creativity and love that required from its organizers true stamina and dedication, and through the years I was able to raise my helium-balloon-filling techniques and socks-drawing abilities to the required standard, but as my wife's forty-ninth birthday grew closer I found myself more and more anxious. We were in the middle of a lockdown and the difficult task of coming up with original and unique presents becomes even more difficult when you are not allowed to leave your home. Seeing how anxious I'd become, my wife suggested that this year, instead of going for the standard birthday celebration, we'll have a simple and minimalistic one with no cakes, balloons, or wrapped presents, and that instead I'll just write to her as a gift a special birthday story. "Sure, why not," I said, trying to hide my relief. "Does it have to have a happy ending?"

WHERE THE CANDLES ARE KEPT

◆ DAVE EGGERS ◆

Oisín

OISÍN WAS AT the airport to pick up two wayward young people, cousins to each other, grand-niece and grand-nephew to him. One was Calla, who he knew a bit. Haunted eyes, twig-thin, freckled, languid. She was probably nineteen by now, and was somehow entangled in drugs. A classmate of hers had overdosed, or almost overdosed, and Calla was involved. Or to blame. She'd thrown the party.

The other kid was Torin, a few years younger than Calla. He was what—maybe fifteen by now? Oisín remembered him from the last reunion, a shy boy, always on the periphery, his eyes watchful behind a tangle of black hair. His mother, Evie, had a stroke three months ago, and the idea was that a month in Idaho would help both kids. Clear their heads, give their parents some respite.

"As long as I don't have to feed them," Oisín had told their parents.

"Of course you have to feed them," their parents said.

Eventually they agreed that Oisín would buy them food but would not cook. He didn't even cook for himself, subsisted on sandwiches and did not eat out. He loathed the concept of restaurants, serving, ordering—all the groveling and tipping and complaining. His approach was to get food, eat food, eliminating all of the attendant ceremony and supplication. This was the kind of thing the extended family expected of him, anyway—eccentricities of an old man who lived like a woodland hermit.

"They won't have phones," Calla's mother said, and Oisín couldn't decide if that was a good thing or not. He didn't want to plan a month of activities for two LA teenagers. Had they ever seen a tree? A river unbound by concrete?

He sat at the baggage claim, nursing a dull dread. These two could be awful. They could be terrible individually and far worse together. What if they fought with each other? He hadn't heard a raised voice in years. If they quarrelled, he'd send them away and burn the cabin down.

Evie had mailed him photos of Calla and Torin, and he brought the photos with him, like a hitman. Each plane landing at the Hailey Airport only had twenty or so people on it, so he didn't think he'd have difficulty sorting the two of them out. While he waited, he flipped through a free magazine, a guide to the Wood River Valley region, and stopped at an article about the local theater group.

My God, he thought. That's her.

Fayaway Yount. He'd seen her in *As You Like It* a few years ago, the only play he'd been to since college. She was magnetic. Wry, lithe, with a mane of rich auburn hair. And the name! *Fayaway*. He assumed it was a stage name. Only twice had he fallen in love from afar, and each time he coveted the feeling, telling no one, forgetting nothing. The first time was with a woman crossing the street in Hartford, Connecticut, in 1989. She was in some kind of security-guard uniform, and was carrying a white umbrella in the sun.

Oisín had never married, had never been a romancer, and did not romance women now. He was seventy-two, and Fayaway Yount couldn't be more than fifty. Even the thought of it was pitiable, distasteful—his sagging, pasty flesh next to her taut olive skin. Look at that face! In the magazine, she was posing behind a rough-hewn fence, her arms resting on it in an effort to look at ease. She was wearing a kind of cowgirl outfit, brand-new, totally unconvincing and no doubt the photographer's idea. And yet her eyes bore into the viewer. *I have swallowed worlds*, they said.

"That's really my given name!" she said in the article. "They assume because I'm an actor that it's a play on Faye Dunaway. But really, my parents got it from Melville. There was a young woman in the Marquesas named Fayaway, a beautiful girl who captured his heart. My parents fell in love with the name after Melville fell in love with her."

The article said Fayaway, the Idaho Fayaway, was single.

"Oisín?"

He startled and looked up. It was them. Calla was in overalls, cloth bracelets up and down her arms. Torin wore a black hoodie and long baggy shorts. Headphones dangled from their ears.

"Good magazine?" Calla asked. "Who's the lady?"

Oisín put the magazine back in the rack, though immediately wished he hadn't. He wanted to finish the article at home, to reread it, to have that photo of Fayaway Yount, her eyes boring into him. He grabbed the magazine, rolled it up, and put it under his arm.

"How was the flight?" he asked.

"It was a triumph," Calla said. "And now I'm in Idaho."

Torin giggled in a falsetto.

Thus far they were insufferable. With divine clarity, Oisín knew the best thing for all involved would be for the two of them to take the next plane home.

"These yours?" he asked, reaching for the two roller bags next to Calla.

"We'll get 'em," Calla said. "You carry your magazine."

Oisín eyed his van in the distance. He pictured driving away in it, alone. Who would fault him?

"Thank you for picking us up," Torin said.

Ah, Oisín thought. He's the polite one.

"His mom told him to always thank people at the start, like right when you get in the car," Calla said. "That way you don't forget. He told me that on the plane."

Oisín saw that Torin was horrified, as if suddenly realizing that nothing he would ever tell Calla would remain private. And then Oisín remembered something Torin's father had said. It was Calla who needed the quiet month in Idaho. Torin, a shy kid, was there as a kind of buffer. "She's a strong dose," he'd said. "If Torin comes, they can entertain each other so you don't have to."

"This is it," Oisín said when they arrived at his van. It had once belonged to an electrician friend of his. It was long and cavernous.

"Shotgun," Calla said, and took the front seat.

She rolled down her window and spoke to Oisín with her elbow on the window frame.

"I don't drive," she said, and looked into the largely empty hull of the van. "But if I did, I would never drive something like this."

Torin

TORIN HAD NEVER been anywhere and had never seen anything. This was the longest trip he'd ever taken, and it was only two hours by plane. He'd met Oisín twice at family reunions and had had only cursory conversations with him. He did not know or like old people, and did not look forward to spending time with this one. He was in Idaho for Calla.

"This can't be it," she said.

They were standing in front of Oisín's cabin.

"It'll be tight," Oisín said. He made a barely audible *hmm* sound, as if just now realizing he would be sharing it with two full-sized people.

Torin had no reaction at all. It didn't look possible that anyone lived there, let alone that the three of them would cohabitate for the month. It was not quite a cabin. Set below a steep mountain dense with pines, it looked like the decaying dwelling of an ancient wizard. There was something about the pitched roof, crooked and covered in moss, that hinted at fading magic. A ladder leaned against its side, further confusing the geometry.

"Do you have tents?" Calla asked. "I'd almost rather stay in a tent. What about you?" She turned to Torin, who thought the idea of sharing a tent with Calla wildly intoxicating.

"I actually think you'll like it inside," Oisín said, and walked across the gravel to the clearing around the cabin.

Torin followed Calla in, and the smell hit him first—pine and lacquer and the airless scent of all-day sun on old wood. The whole of the cabin was one room, about the size of a standard bedroom, with a tiny kitchen in the back, facing the river. The walls were cluttered with random things—old snowshoes, a photo of Roberto Clemente, and what looked like a conquistador's sword.

"Can I ask why you live out here?" Calla asked.

Torin almost laughed, because Calla's form of humor had everything to do with saying the wrong thing, and suddenly. But this time he resisted. He had no living grandparents, and had been brought up to treat the elderly with a deference approaching condescension.

"Remember what T. E. Lawrence said about the desert?" Oisín asked. "He liked it because it was clean."

"But your place isn't clean," Calla said.

"I said *Idaho* was clean," Oisín said. "Not my place. And my place is not unclean. You think it's unclean? I spent all yesterday fixing it up."

"It looks good," Torin said, and watched as Calla made a more thorough assessment.

She drew her finger across the mantle, surprised to find it free of dust. "I guess it's just cluttered. It reminds me of a guitar. It's like living inside a guitar." She turned to Torin. "Isn't it like the inside of a guitar?"

Torin thought this harmless enough. "Sort of," he said.

"And there's no bathroom?" Calla said.

They knew there was no bathroom. This had been emphasized during every mention of the summer plan. Oisín had no indoor plumbing at all. But she seemed to be stating this most unconscionable fact in the hope that it wasn't true.

"Follow me," Oisín said, and he led them across the gravel drive to the outhouse, a moon and a trio of stars cut into its higher regions.

Torin expected the odor to be overwhelming, but when he opened the plywood door, it just smelled like more wood. There was a toilet seat embedded into a wooden shelf, and next to the seat, there was a tube of hand sanitizer and a tall tower of toilet paper rolls.

"Got those when the bus station in Hailey ordered too many," Oisín said.

"Score," Calla said. "And look!" She pointed to a small plaque commemorating the fact that it had been built in 1941. "Torin, you get to shit in a historical landmark."

With sudden clarity, Torin realized that Calla wasn't planning to stay. She would call home, make up an excuse, or flat-out escape.

Oisín let the door close with a smack.

"Let's go to the lake," he said.

Calla

CALLA DID PLAN to escape. Oisín was far older than she remembered, and far stranger, and his cabin was not habitable. She would feel bad for Torin, would feel momentarily guilty about leaving him to the old wizard. But she couldn't take him with her. That would be kidnapping, and statutory something, and beyond that, her parents and Torin's would murder her if she made him into any kind of accomplice.

"This is the most beautiful alpine lake you'll ever see," Oisín said. They were rumbling down the two-lane road in his rickety, ugly-ass van, and cars were periodically passing them as if they were standing still. The speed limit was sixty-five, but the van didn't seem capable of breaking fifty.

Calla had no interest in this lake. Lakes were for people who didn't live near the ocean, and alpine lakes were just lakes too cold to swim in. She had no interest in the bald black hills Oisín kept pointing to, the site of this or that forest fire. Burn, Idaho, burn, she thought, and wished she had someone near who would appreciate her joke. Torin was too innocent, too good; she'd seen his horrified face when she'd hazed Oisín about his filthy home.

"I rented a boat," Oisín said as they pulled into the parking lot. All around were corny log cabins and fat families waddling around carrying paddleboards and rafts.

"Wow," Calla said. "This is the most beautiful alpine lake I've ever seen."

Torin laughed; they hadn't seen the lake yet.

Oisín looked at her in a way she took to mean disappointment. He was actually an interesting old guy, she thought. Not scolding. Not grumpy. There was something in his eyes, in fact, that implied he understood her sarcasm but found it unfunny.

They made their way past the main lodge, and then the vista opened up. The lake was a bright blue mirror with a jagged white mountain range at the end. It looked like a screen saver. There was a wide lawn, then a small beach bright with umbrellas and rafts, then the tiny waves of the lake rushing to the shore like mad, happy mops. A musical trio was playing something folky on the lawn, a few dozen older fans watching from folding chairs. Calla had never been to Switzerland, but her idea of Switzerland was this—everything clean and orderly and full of families in bright clothing acting appropriately and not too loud.

"I'll go deal with the boat," Oisín said, and made his way toward the docks. Calla got her first clear look at him. He walked purposefully, not at all frail, wearing long faded-blue shorts and canvas sneakers. From a distance he could have been forty, fifty, the father of one of her friends.

Oisín stopped at the rental desk, around which there were

a handful of pedal boats and kayaks and motorboats for rent, bobbing in the clear water. Calla thought that it would be kind of fun to see what it was like out on the lake; she hadn't been in a boat in years. But then again, if she said she'd get seasick, and that she'd stay on the beach while Oisín and Torin took the boat out, it would give her time to disappear. She could hitch, call a taxi, run through the woods, anything. She'd have hours before they knew.

When Oisín was out of earshot, Calla turned to Torin. "I'm leaving," she said. "I hope you understand. Obviously I can't stay."

"Leaving for where?" he asked.

"Back home, probably. I don't know. I have an aunt in Minneapolis. Maybe I go that direction."

Torin's big eyes were wet. "I'll go with you," he said.

"You're fifteen," she said. "It'd be like kidnapping. I'd go to jail."

He seemed on the verge of tears. "I'll explain it to anyone," he said in a desperate rush. "That it was my choice. I can be useful. You're much safer if you're not alone."

This kid! Calla thought. He loved her, that much was obvious. "You're cute, but no," she said. "I'd get arrested. I'm nineteen, so . . ."

"You can't drive," he said. "I know how. How will you get anywhere when you can't drive?"

Good point, she thought. "I'll hitch," she said. "My mom used to. She did it all over the country, all over fucking Greece. Apparently she was allowed to do shit like that and I'm not."

Now Oisín was walking back from the dock. He looked far older from the front, his face carved from the bark of a gnarled tree. He waved to them, a pair of keys in his hand.

Torin

NO ONE KNEW Torin was Machiavellian and he preferred it that way. He was both a good kid and also knew he was a good kid, and knew how to bring about events in his favor. He didn't want Calla to leave him alone with this strange old man, and he had no idea how to prevent her from leaving. For now, though, he only had to postpone her escape. He had to get her on the boat. Oisín was drawing near.

"I totally get it," he whispered to Calla, "but you can't do it now. There's nothing here. No buses, trains, taxis. There's damned sure no Ubers at Redfish Lake." Already he saw her face softening into recognition. She seemed impressed, too, by his use of "damned sure." He'd never sworn in her presence before.

"Wait till we go into town," he said. "We have to. Probably later today, for groceries. That'll be the place. Go there, get on a truck. Or catch a bus out of town. Do it there. You'll have options."

She smiled. He had her.

Oisín

IT WAS UNCANNY. What was she doing here? Oisín had made his way back from the dock, and when he crossed the green lawn to get the kids, he'd seen her. Fayaway Yount! She was singing in a trio on the lawn. He didn't know she sang, but of course all actresses sing, and of course she would be singing in a trio in a place like this. Everyone around here had four jobs. She was probably a pharmacist, too.

He moved closer to the small stage, and as he did, he tuned out the squeals of children on the beach and yaps of dogs in the shallow water. It was her. She was wearing a red linen button-down over a long cotton skirt, and she stood barefoot on the grass, singing with her eyes closed. Somehow she was more winsome this way, in the daylight, her hair pulled back, her toes in the grass. And then her eyes opened, and fell on Oisín, briefly but unmistakably, before she looked up to the sky, where the corpulent clouds pulsed with kept sun.

"It's her, isn't it?" Calla was right behind him. "I recognize her from the magazine! Jesus, Oisín, you're in love!"

Oisín was growing less fond of this Calla by the minute. Torin was straightforward and shy—two admirable traits in a teenager—while this older one was acidic, maybe even cruel.

"We should get going," Oisín said. "We only have the boat for two hours." But he badly wanted to stay.

"One more song," Calla said, lowering her voice, trying to contain her glee. "Seriously. I didn't mean to be annoying. If you like her, you know, *music*, then we should stay." She was trying to suppress a grin.

"We're going," Oisín said.

Calla and Torin followed him up the narrow dock and to the boat he'd rented. He glanced one more time toward Fayaway. He actually didn't care that Calla knew his feelings. And what were his feelings? His feelings were that he found Fayaway very beautiful, and she sang with a gorgeous low mezzo-soprano, like the rush of a shallow river, but he had no intentions beyond listening to her. He loved beauty, needed to always be near beauty, and when an unusual beauty was near, he found himself gripped, immobilized. It had always been this way. But he'd never needed to possess this beauty. Nearness was always enough.

Calla

SHE WAS GIDDY. She'd correctly diagnosed the crush of a seventy-two-year-old man on a fifty-year-old woman. Yes! It was adorable, and now she wondered if she really could leave when such delicious work was to be done here, and she the only one to do it.

She followed Oisín to the small motorboat at the end of the dock. Silver and dented, it looked like army surplus. Two teenaged boys, a year or two younger than Calla, showed them the mechanical features of the boat, handed them their vests, and then stood on the dock, inspecting Calla from behind, their wraparound sunglasses giving them cover.

Oisín dropped their bag into the boat with a dull thump and started the engine. Torin sat dutifully by his side and Calla took the bow. They puttered through the no-wake zone, passing candy-colored kayaks and paddleboards, and when they passed the last buoy, Oisín put the base of his hand to the throttle. The bow lifted, they gained speed and unzipped the lake lengthwise. They sped toward the Sawtooth Mountains, which rose from the glassy surface of the lake like gray men in white shawls. When they arrived at the lake's far end, they were alone, no vessels or people in sight. Oisín cut the engine and turned to them.

"So which of you had the pills?" he asked.

"Me," Calla said. "I had some friends over. They found a prescription bottle in the garbage that had three pills still in it. You know Dilaudud?"

"Dilaudid," Oisín corrected.

"Okay, Dilaudid," she said. "That just started things. They found more pills upstairs. I helped, actually."

Calla did not expect him to be scandalized. She'd heard stories about Oisín. He'd been a hippie, and a soldier, and a hermit. He'd worked as a welder, a long-haul trucker, a river guide. She was unsure what would shock him. For the time being, he simply stared at the mountains as she spoke.

"I'd stashed a few bottles of champagne from Christmas," she said. "So we had a party, and everyone got sick, and one girl got scared and called her mom, and she ended up getting her stomach pumped even though she'd taken less than anyone else. The rest of us—someone should have died."

"*Could* have died," Oisín said.

"Could have died," Calla repeated.

"Not *should* have died," he said, turning back to her. "Don't say *should have*."

"Okay, okay," Calla said. She didn't know what to do with his attention focused on her like this. She found it disorienting, annoying, thrilling.

They hadn't dropped an anchor, so the gentle current was push-ing them toward the shore, where a tangle of downed pines were wedged between a trio of people-high boulders. The wind picked up.

"And Torin, I'm sorry about your mom," Oisín said. Coming from anyone else, pivoting so quickly from one personal shitshow to the next, it would have sounded false and perfunctory. "I know she'll get better."

"Thanks," Torin said.

"When she was a girl, she went up Mount Lassen with me and Patrick. She must have been ten. In sandals! And she never com-plained. She ever tell you that?"

Torin

"I THINK SO," Torin said, though he had no recollection of a story like that. His mother was what to Oisín? Niece? Something about the story unsettled him. Was it the kind of thing you said about someone dead or dying? Every day since her stroke, Torin flung himself between defending her and being disgusted by her—half her face fallen, numb, her constant drooling, the thick-tongued way she spoke now.

He was avoiding Oisín's eyes, looking into the lake, when he saw it: a diaper, floating on the surface. "Look," he said, relieved to change the subject.

"Huh," Oisín said. "You never see garbage on this lake. See if you can grab it."

Torin reached down to get it. The diaper was heavy with lake water. He dropped it onto the boat floor with a wet slap.

"A whole bunch of stuff over here," Calla said. She was looking over the other side of the boat. "A sandal. A bag of chips. Oh shit, a life preserver."

There was a dark snaking object that Torin took to be a shirt. A Styrofoam cooler, open, with an apple core inside. A plastic water bottle, half-full. It was as if someone had dumped the contents of a beach bag.

"Grab as much as you can," Oisín said.

"What do you think happened?" Calla asked.

"Looks like it fell off a boat," Oisín said, his voice wavering. "Maybe they were going fast and didn't realize they'd lost this stuff."

Torin leaned down, pulling from the lake a dark sweater wound around a life vest. He dropped it on the boat's deck.

"Over here," Calla said, and grabbed a plastic carton of baby wipes. "Shit. Why is there a diaper and wet wipes? I'm freaking out now."

Torin's heart hammered. He scanned the water, expecting to see a baby.

"Look!" Calla yelled. "Bonnet! Baby bonnet!" She held it up, horrified, flinging it back into the water. "What the fuck is all this?"

"Calm down," Oisín said.

Torin was still leaning over the edge, reaching for a pair of goggles, when he saw, a few feet under the surface, the ghostly white triangle of the bow of a boat.

Oisín

OISÍN RUSHED TO Torin's side. The bow was sticking straight up, not three feet from the surface. To be positioned that way, and with all their possessions still close, the sinking must have been recent.

"Look for people," he said evenly.

"People? Where?" Calla said.

Oisín searched the shoreline, hoping to find a family shivering there. He could see one of the smaller campsite beaches, not more than two hundred yards away. There were a few families lounging in the shallows, oblivious. Whoever had been in this boat was not on shore. Which meant they were still inside the boat. But none of this made sense. A single boat, sunk in twenty feet of water? And no one else near?

Oisín was staring down, furious at himself that he hadn't already jumped in, when he heard a splash. He turned to see Calla's ankles disappear.

Calla

IT FELT LIKE crashing through plate glass. The water was hard, cold, clear, and she touched the boat immediately. It was so close she'd struck it at nearly full force. She felt its smooth white bow and took the railing and pulled herself down the side, hand over hand. She saw no people, no sign of people. The boat was the same kind Oisín had rented. It had no cabin. She wanted no cabin. A cabin could mean there were people trapped inside—a baby even.

A hand gripped her calf. She screamed underwater. Bubbles exploded from her mouth. A second hand appeared in front of her and she screamed again. Finally she saw a face. It was Oisín.

Oisín

HE'D JUMPED IN after her and thought he should let her know he was there, too—so she wouldn't be startled if she saw him. But his plan had produced the opposite effect.

He saw her point herself toward the surface and kick her way up to the light. Oisín's lungs were on fire. He had about thirty seconds of air left, so he grabbed the windshield of the boat and used it to pull himself downward.

It was the same boat they'd rented. No cabin. There was nothing visible, nothing but a towel that had been tied to the stern. He pulled himself farther down, determined to reach the outboard, thinking there was a chance that someone was stuck underneath. The boat could have hit chop, gone airborne, flipped, sunk.

He pulled himself down, hand over hand on the side rail, until he was at the bottom. The water was thick with sand and muck, but he saw nothing near the motor. Whatever happened to the people on this boat, they were no longer here.

Just as he was ready to return to the surface, he heard a dull crash above, and looked up to see Torin's body like an arrow, shooting downward.

Torin

OISÍN HAD BEEN under too long. Calla had flung herself up from the lake and was gasping, holding on to the back ladder. "Go check on him," she'd said, and Torin had thrown off his shirt, shaped

himself into a dagger and dove, finding himself instantly at the
bottom of the lake.

Oisín was struggling under the boat. It looked like a tug-of-war,
with Oisín violently pulling away from the outboard. Torin swam
closer and waved to Oisín. Oisín pointed to his shorts, which were
tangled in the motor's corkscrew. Torin tried to unweave the fabric
but it was no use, Oisín's struggling had drawn it too taut. Torin
began instead to pull down on the shorts, with an aim to take them
off completely.

Oisín understood. He fumbled at the drawstring but it wouldn't
give. Torin needed scissors or a blade. Oisín could die this way,
Torin thought—this old man could die while trying to untie his
shorts. But then he did it, Oisín loosened the knot. Torin pulled
down, the shorts went slack, and Oisín went free and upward, and
Torin followed.

Calla

THEY DRAGGED OISÍN into the boat, his naked body bony and blue,
and now the sky was a low iron ceiling. The sun was gone, the wind
was slashing. They raced across the lake and to the docks. Close
to shore, while Torin steered, Calla waved her arms wildly. She
wanted people to worry, to panic, to scream. She got the attention
of the two boys working at the dock. They ran to the slip closest
and began guiding Torin in.

"Cut the engine! Cut the engine!" they yelled. Torin didn't
know what that meant.

"Turn the keys in the ignition," Oisín said. "Left." He lay in the
back of the boat, Torin's T-shirt draped over his midsection. Calla
was startled to hear him speak. She'd assumed he was dying or dead.

Torin turned the keys left. The engine died. They drifted into the dock. One of the dock boys jumped into their boat and steered it into a slip.

"Is he dead?" he asked, staring at Oisín's blue face.

"Just cold," Oisín said.

Calla jumped from the boat. A young couple was getting out of another rental, and she pulled their towels from their shoulders. "Need these!" she said, and ran back to Oisín. She put one towel under his head and the other over his waist.

"Can you sit up?" she asked.

"In a minute," he said. "Tell them about the capsized boat."

"We saw a boat," Torin said. "Sunk. On the other end of the lake, by the mountains. You know anything about it?"

"It's fine," one of the boys said. "It sunk yesterday. Everyone's fine."

"What about the baby?" Oisín asked.

"The baby wasn't on the boat," the boy said. "It was my aunt who rented the boat. The baby wasn't there. They left the baby on shore."

Oisín laughed. "They left the baby on shore," he said, and passed out.

Oisín

HE COULDN'T GET warm. He'd been brought into the lodge and installed in a giant leather chair by the fire, but he couldn't get warm. The lodge's staff huddled around him, laid blankets upon blankets upon him. Calla wanted to call the paramedics, but he refused. He begged Calla and Torin and the lodge manager, Helen, not to call anyone. He'd walked himself off the boat, he noted, off the dock, across the beach, and into the lodge, talking all the while.

He did not need a hospital, he said. He needed to catch his breath, stare at the fire, get warm.

Soon the staff floated away, watching him from across the amber-colored room, leaving him to Calla and Torin. They were sitting on the fireplace hearth, their backs to the fire, talking to Oisín, watching him warily.

"Don't worry," he told them.

Oisín was worried. Not worried, concerned. Concerned because he couldn't get warm. He'd been inside the lodge for thirty minutes but was still shivering uncontrollably. The lake had been cold but it was the naked ride back that had done it. The wind had cut through him, made him feel featherlight and porous. If not for that ride back, with that icy wind, he would have been fine.

Now he was fighting violent chills. Just when he muffled one, another came on. He looked at the clock. Four-thirty. If he wasn't better by five he'd let the kids call a doctor. But a doctor meant an ambulance, and a hospital, and a gown, and a building full of infections, and everyone he knew—everyone his age who'd gone in—had never come out.

Torin

TORIN DROVE THEM home. At six, just as the dinner rush began to crowd the lodge, Oisín's chills subsided and he said he wanted to go home.

They had to sneak out of the lodge, really, for otherwise there would have been questions. Aren't you too young to drive? Where are you all going? Are you sure he's okay? What's your address, your phone number, so we can check up on him?

Oisín was in the front seat, leaning against the window, wearing sweatpants and wool socks and a knit cap and a hoodie, all donated by the Redfish Lake gift shop. There were no turns on the road from the lake to Oisín's cabin, so Torin kept his hands at 10 and 2, feeling godlike, urgent, Calla's bare thigh against his.

Calla

IN THE MORNING, Calla felt sure that Oisín might die. She and Torin were outside the cabin, debating next steps. They'd been up all night, taking turns watching him, feeling his forehead, covering him with every blanket and sheet in the cabin. They'd wrapped his feet in needlepoint pillowcases.

"He's, like, eighty," she said. "At that age, anything goes. They get a cold and then they're dead. He's still clammy and feverish."

"Then let's call the hospital," Torin said.

"No hospital," she said. "But we can find a doctor."

Oisín

HE LAY INSIDE, on his bed, hearing their muffled conversation, very much amused. He was not close to death, and had told them this all through the night, whenever they checked on him.

He was sure they had not slept all night. Each time he woke up, one of them was by his side, sitting on the hard Quaker chair he used to stack kindling. It was not made for long sits. One time he woke to find Calla holding his hand, the bones in her knuckles so smooth and so cold, like river stones. Another time he found Torin standing on the other side of the room, hands behind his back, looking out the window like a general before battle. All along, the room had been illuminated by candles. How had they found the candles? Even he didn't know where the candles were kept.

And now it was morning and Oisín felt much better, was hungry in fact, and these two were outside, considering his imminent death.

Torin

IT WAS TORIN'S idea to return to the lake. By midmorning, Oisín seemed much better. His face had gone from gray to pink and his temperature seemed close to normal, but it would not hurt to bring a doctor back to the cabin. Calla had convinced Torin a hospital, if against Oisín's wishes, was out of the question. But simply going to the lake and bringing a doctor back, they agreed, would not violate any pact. The lake was close enough, and full of people, and surely one of them was a doctor or nurse. And it was the only place they knew how to get to.

Torin drove with arms stiff, breathing tensely through his nose, occasionally glancing at the sky, the mountains, the half-burned forests all around them.

"You're doing good," Calla said, and Torin felt triumphant.

Calla

WHEN THEY ARRIVED at the lake, immediately she felt silly. How would they find a doctor? They couldn't go to Helen, the lodge manager, and ask who among their guests was a doctor. Helen would know what was up and would call an ambulance. Walking the beach asking for a doctor would have the same effect. There would be inquiries and fuss.

"This," Calla told Torin, "was not a good idea."

But then she saw the actress.

Torin

HE DID NOT think they should talk to the actress. She was singing in her band again, on the wide lawn with the jagged mountains behind her.

"Let's ask her to come back with us," Calla said, and let loose a mad soliloquy about death and desire. Oisín might die, she said, might die that day, and that if they could not get a doctor for him, they might give him purpose by arranging a visit from this woman.

Torin was aghast. Calla had lost her mind. They came to get a doctor but were bringing home a singer?

"Let's at least ask her," Calla said.

"I won't do it," Torin said.

"I will," Calla said.

Calla

SHE WAITED TILL the end of the band's set, which might have been cut short because she was lingering in front, staring at Fayaway with unsettling intensity.

"We need a favor," Calla said.

Fayaway

IT WAS NOT a bother for Fayaway. Unusual, yes, but not so unusual for this region. She'd been in this part of Idaho on and off for thirty years, and she'd met more than a few off-grid oddballs. One noted hermit, Salmon River Sal, had come to a production of *Three Days of Rain* on three consecutive nights. He had introduced himself politely afterward, and she'd never heard from him again. Some years later, she read that he'd died in his lair. Among his few belongings was a program from the play.

So this did not seem so different. The two kids acting as intermediary was a new one, but otherwise she was accustomed to the attention of older men, gentlemanly men who rarely wanted anything more than a moment's proximity.

She was surprised when the younger, smaller one got into the driver's seat of the long white van—the girl was taller, seemed older and more capable. But Fayaway got in her truck and followed them the twenty miles to the old man's cabin. It was this kind of thing that had brought her, and kept her, in these small towns, these jumbled Idaho towns that had, it seemed, rolled down the mountains to settle like stones on the valley floor.

Through the van's rear windows, she watched the two kids, the backs of their heads as they looked steadily at the winding road ahead. Such purpose! At the lodge, she'd taken them to be the same kind of listless, scowling kids that her friends had produced, but then they laid out their request and had provided a short biography of their uncle—or great-uncle?—and their vision seized her. This kind of thing never happened in the suburbs of Atlanta where she was raised. Only in the emptiness of Idaho could you see people one by one, and breathe a bit, and ask a favor like this. She felt at home in their dream.

Oisín

HE WAS HOME and awake and feeling fine. Earlier, he'd gotten up, fixed himself a bowl of mush, and changed into his own clothes. That operation had tuckered him out, though, so when he heard the van come in, spitting gravel and stopping in a rush of white dust, he was reclining again, covered in a light wool blanket. There was no window that faced the driveway, so he couldn't see them coming in, but he heard a solicitousness in the voices of the kids that was new. Then he heard a third voice, flutelike, almost familiar.

The door opened and Torin's face appeared, his brow furrowed, apologetic. Calla followed, chin up, grinning, eyes alight.

"You look good!" she said. She seemed surprised.

"You do," Torin said. "And you changed clothes."

"I am good," Oisín said. "And I did change."

"We brought a guest," Calla said. "Just to cheer you up. It's not a priest."

Oisín laughed, Calla gestured to the open door, and Fayaway Yount entered his cabin. Fayaway Yount was in his cabin, and immediately he saw it through her eyes. He was an animal living in a cave, a burrow. He was not fully human. He watched as she looked around briefly, her eyes adjusting to the darkness and the clutter, and then she found him, the old man in the corner. She smiled and came to him.

"How are you?" she asked, sitting in the hard Quaker chair. She was gorgeous up close, far more radiant than onstage or in any photo. Everything about her, even the whites of her eyes, was polished bright.

She stayed for ten minutes or so, looking at Oisín like a nurse, as if she were playing a nurse—a nurse who knew just the effect she had on the blubbering men in her care. There was nothing in her demeanor that said she would ever consider Oisín a man for her to kiss and love, but still, he adored her for coming all this way. For following these two kids to him. Oisín looked over her shoulder and found them, Calla and Torin. They had become a kind of parental couple, leaning into each other as they watched, biting their nails, hoping they'd done something right.

There is still courage among us, Oisín thought. It only has to be urged forth. From the depths of our selfish selves, it has to be called upon. These two, who had seemed to him so flimsy yesterday, turned out to be monumental. They had gorgeous butterfly hearts beating hard within ribs of gold, and they could be trusted with the world.

◆ ◆ ◆ **FROM THE AUTHOR** ◆ ◆ ◆

I figured the world needs more stories set in Idaho, so I wrote one.

ABOUT THE AUTHORS

◆ **RABIH ALAMEDDINE** is the author of the novels *Koolaids*; *I, the Divine*; *The Hakawati*; *An Unnecessary Woman*; *The Angel of History*; and the story collection *The Perv*. His novel *The Wrong End of the Telescope* was released in September 2021.

◆ **JENNY ALLEN** is a writer and performer whose works include the fable collection *The Long Chalkboard* and, most recently, *Would Everybody Please Stop?* a finalist for the Thurber Prize for American Humor. She wrote and starred in the award-winning one-woman show *I Got Sick Then I Got Better*. Allen's writing has been featured in several anthologies, including *Disquiet, Please!: More Humor Writing from the New Yorker* and *The 50 Funniest American Writers*, edited by Andy Borowitz.

◆ **LESLEY NNEKA ARIMAH** is the author of the short-story collection *What It Means When a Man Falls From the Sky*, winner of the Kirkus Prize for Fiction, the Minnesota Book Award for Fiction, and the New York Public Library's Young Lions Fiction Award. Her stories have won a National Magazine Award, the

Caine Prize, and the O. Henry Prize, and she has been a National Book Foundation 5 Under 35 honoree.

◆ **AIMEE BENDER** is the author of *The Girl in the Flammable Skirt, An Invisible Sign of My Own, Willful Creatures, The Particular Sadness of Lemon Cake, The Color Master*, and most recently, *The Butterfly Lampshade*. Her short fiction has appeared in *Granta, GQ, Harper's, Tin House, McSweeney's*, and the *Paris Review*, among other publications. Bender's work has been honored with two Pushcart Prizes.

◆ **MARIE-HELENE BERTINO** is the author of the novels *Parakeet* (a *New York Times* Editors' Choice) and *2 a.m. at the Cat's Pajamas* (NPR Best Books, 2014), and the story collection *Safe as Houses* (Iowa Short Fiction Award). Her work has received an O. Henry Prize and a Pushcart Prize, and in 2017 she was the Frank O'Connor International Short Story Fellow in Cork, Ireland. She teaches in the MFA programs at NYU and the New School. Her fourth book, the novel *Beautyland*, is forthcoming from Farrar, Straus and Giroux.

◆ **JAI CHAKRABARTI** is the author of *A Play for the End of the World* and the forthcoming story collection *A Small Sacrifice for an Enormous Happiness*, published by Knopf Doubleday. His short fiction has appeared in numerous journals and has been anthologized in *The O. Henry Prize Stories* and *The Best American Short Stories* and awarded a Pushcart Prize. Jai was an Emerging Writer's Fellow with *A Public Space* and received his MFA from Brooklyn College.

◆ **JESSICA COHEN** is a freelance translator based in Denver. She translates contemporary Israeli prose and other creative work. In 2017, she shared the Man Booker International Prize with David Grossman, for her translation of *A Horse Walks Into a Bar*. She has also translated works by other major Israeli writers, including Etgar Keret, Amos Oz, Ronit Matalon, and Nir Baram. She is a past board member of the American Literary Translators Association.

◆ **PATRICK COTTRELL** is the author of *Sorry to Disrupt the Peace*, published by McSweeney's. He is the winner of a Whiting Award in Fiction and a Barnes and Noble Discover Award. Most recently, he guest-edited a queer-fiction issue of *McSweeney's Quarterly*. He teaches at University of Denver.

◆ **ELIZABETH CRANE** is the author of several short-story collections, including *Turf* and *When the Messenger Is Hot*, which was adapted for the stage by Chicago's Steppenwolf Theater Company, as well as the novels *The History of Great Things* and *We Only Know So Much*, which was adapted into a feature film. Crane teaches in the UCR–Palm Desert low-residency MFA program, and a memoir is forthcoming in 2022.

◆ **MICHAEL CUNNINGHAM** is the author of the Pulitzer Prize–winning novel *The Hours*, which was adapted into an award-winning film. His works also include the novels *A Home at the End of the World*, *Flesh and Blood*, *Specimen Days*, *By Nightfall*, *The Snow Queen*, and the short-story collection *A Wild Swan*, as well as the nonfiction *Land's End: A Walk in Provincetown*. Cunningham has received the Whiting Award, the PEN/Faulkner Award, and a Guggenheim Fellowship, and is a Senior Lecturer in English and Creative Writing at Yale University.

◆ **PATRICK DACEY** is the author of the short-story collection *We've Already Gone This Far* and the novel *The Outer Cape*. His work has been featured in the *Paris Review, Zoetrope All-Story, Harper's, LitHub, Guernica*, and *BOMB Magazine*, among other publications. Dacey currently lives and writes in Richmond, Virginia.

◆ **EDWIDGE DANTICAT** is the author of several books, including *Breath, Eyes, Memory, Claire of the Sea Light*, and *The Dew Breaker*. She is a 2009 MacArthur Fellow and a 2020 winner of the Vilceck Prize. Her most recent work, the story collection *Everything Inside*, is a 2020 winner of the Bocas Fiction Prize, the Story Prize, and the National Books Critics Circle Award for Fiction.

◆ **DAVE EGGERS** is the author of many books, including *The Every, The Monk of Mokha, A Hologram for the King, What Is the What*, and *The Museum of Rain*. He is the cofounder of 826 National, a network of youth writing centers, and of Voice of Witness, an oral history book series that illuminates the stories of those impacted by human rights crises. Born in Boston and raised in Illinois, he has now lived in the San Francisco Bay Area for three decades.

◆ **OMAR EL AKKAD** is an award-winning journalist and author whose debut novel, *American War*, was listed as one of the best books of the year by the *New York Times, Washington Post, GQ, NPR, Esquire*, and was selected by the BBC as one of a hundred novels that changed our world. He is a recipient of Canada's National Newspaper Award for investigative reporting and the Goff Penny Memorial Prize for Young Canadian Journalists, as well as three National Magazine Award honorable mentions.

◆ **NEIL GAIMAN** is the *New York Times* bestselling author and creator of books, graphic novels, short stories, films, and television for all ages, including *Norse Mythology, Neverwhere, Coraline, The Graveyard Book, The Ocean at the End of the Lane, The View from the Cheap Seats, The Sandman* comic series, and *The Neil Gaiman Reader*, which contains fifty-two short stories and selections from his novels. His fiction has received many awards and honors, including the Newbery and Carnegie medals, and the Hugo, Nebula, World Fantasy, and Will Eisner awards. Several of his novels have been adapted for film and television, winning an Oscar nomination for *Coraline*, an Emmy nomination for *American Gods*, and two writing awards for his work on the scripts of *Good Omens*, a novel he wrote with the late Sir Terry Pratchett. Gaiman's books have been translated into forty languages worldwide. In 2017, he became a Goodwill Ambassador for UNHCR, the UN Refugee Agency.

◆ **LAUREN GROFF** is the author of six books, including *Fates and Furies* and *Florida*, both of which were finalists for the National Book Award; her latest, the novel *Matrix*, was published in September 2021. She is a winner of the Story Prize, a Guggenheim Fellow, and in 2017, she was named one of the Best of Young American Novelists by the literary magazine *Granta*. Her work has been translated into over thirty languages.

◆ **JACOB GUAJARDO** lives and writes in Michigan. His fiction has appeared in places such as *Midwestern Gothic, Necessary Fiction, Hobart, Passages North,* and *The Best American Short Stories 2018.* He is a graduate of the University of Florida creative writing program and a MacDowell Fellow.

◆ **A. M. HOMES** is the author of the novels *Jack, In a County of Mothers, The End of Alice, Music for Torching, This Book Will Save Your Life,* and *May We Be Forgiven,* winner of the Orange/ Women's Prize for Fiction. Homes is also the author of the memoir *The Mistress's Daughter* and the short-story collections *The Safety of Objects, Things You Should Know,* and *Days of Awe.* She teaches in the Program in Creative Writing at Princeton.

◆ **MIRA JACOB** is a novelist, memoirist, illustrator, and cultural critic. Her graphic memoir, *Good Talk: A Memoir in Conversations,* was shortlisted for the National Book Critics Circle Award and longlisted for the PEN Open Book Award, and her novel, *The Sleepwalker's Guide to Dancing,* was named one of the best books of the year by *Kirkus Reviews, Boston Globe, Goodreads, Bustle,* and *The Millions.* She lives in Brooklyn.

◆ **JAC JEMC** is the author of the novels *My Only Wife,* winner of the Paula Anderson Book Award, and *The Grip of It*; and the short-story collections *A Different Bed Every Time* and *False Bingo,* winner of the *Chicago Review of Books* Award for Fiction and longlisted for the Story Prize. Jemc currently teaches creative writing at UC–San Diego.

◆ **ETGAR KERET** was born in Ramat Gan and now lives in Tel Aviv. A recipient of the French Chevalier des Arts et des Lettres, the Charles Bronfman Prize, and the Caméra d'Or at the Cannes Film Festival, he is the author of the memoir *The Seven Good Years* and story collections including *Fly Already*, *The Bus Driver Who Wanted to Be God*, *The Nimrod Flipout*, and *Suddenly, a Knock on the Door*. His work has been translated into over forty-five languages and appeared in the *New Yorker*, the *Wall Street Journal*, *Paris Review*, and the *New York Times*, among other publications.

◆ **LISA KO**'s first novel, *The Leavers*, was a national bestseller that won the 2016 PEN/Bellwether Prize for Socially Engaged Fiction and was a finalist for both the 2017 National Book Award for Fiction and the 2018 PEN/Hemingway Award. Her short fiction has appeared in *Best American Short Stories* and her essays and nonfiction in the *New York Times*, the *Believer*, and elsewhere. She lives in New York City.

◆ **VICTOR LaVALLE** is the author of the short-story collection *Slapboxing with Jesus*, four novels—*The Ecstatic*, *Big Machine*, *The Devil in Silver*, and *The Changeling*—two novellas, *Lucretia and the Kroons* and *The Ballad of Black Tom*, and is the creator and writer of the comic book *Victor LaValle's Destroyer*. He is the recipient of numerous awards, including a Whiting Writers' Award, a United States Artists Ford Fellowship, a Guggenheim Fellowship, a Shirley Jackson Award, an American Book Award, and the key to Southeast Queens.

◆ **J. ROBERT LENNON** is the author of *Familiar*, *Broken River*, *Subdivision*, and other novels, and the story collections *Pieces for* *the Left Hand*, *See You in Paradise*, and *Let Me Think*. He teaches creative writing at Cornell University.

◆ **BEN LOORY** is the author of *Tales of Falling and Flying* and *Stories for Nighttime and Some for the Day*, as well as a picture book for children, *The Baseball Player and the Walrus*. His fables and tales have appeared in the *New Yorker*, *Tin House*, *Fairy Tale Review*, and *A Public Space*; been anthologized in *The New Voices of Fantasy* and *Year's Best Weird Fiction*; and been heard on *This American Life*. Loory lives in Los Angeles and teaches short-story writing at the UCLA Extension Writers' Program.

◆ **CARMEN MARIA MACHADO** is the author of the National Book Award finalist short-story collection *Her Body and Other Parties*; the bestselling memoir *In the Dream House*; and the limited-run comic series *The Low, Low Woods*. Her fiction and essays have appeared in the *New Yorker*, *Granta*, *Tin House*, the *Believer*, *McSweeney's*, *Guernica*, and elsewhere.

◆ **JUAN MARTINEZ** is the author of the short-story collection *Best Worst American*, winner of the Neukom Institute Literary Arts Award. His work has appeared in various literary journals and anthologies, including *Glimmer Train*, *McSweeney's*, *TriQuarterly*, *Conjunctions*, Norton's *Sudden Fiction Latino: Short-Short Stories from the United States and Latin America*, and *The Perpetual Engine of Hope: Stories Inspired by Iconic Vegas Photographs*.

◆ **MAILE MELOY** is the author of the novels *Liars and Saints*, *A Family Daughter*, and *Do Not Become Alarmed*, the short-story collections *Half in Love* and *Both Ways Is the Only Way I Want It*, and

a middle-grade trilogy that begins with *The Apothecary*. She has
received the PEN/Malamud Award, the E. B. White Award, and a
Guggenheim Fellowship.

◆ **JOE MENO** is the author of seven novels: *Marvel and a Wonder*,
Office Girl, *The Great Perhaps*, *The Boy Detective Fails*, *Hairstyles
of the Damned*, *How the Hula Girl Sings*, and *Tender as Hellfire*.
His short-story collections are *Bluebirds Used to Croon in the Choir*
and *Demons in the Spring*. His short fiction has been published
in *McSweeney's*, *One Story*, *Swink*, *LIT*, *TriQuarterly*, *Other Voices*,
and *Gulf Coast*, and have been broadcast on NPR.

◆ **SUSAN PERABO** is the author of the short-story collections
Who I Was Supposed to Be and *Why They Run the Way They Do* and
the novels *The Broken Places* and *The Fall of Lisa Bellow*. Her fiction has been anthologized in *Best American Short Stories*, *Pushcart
Prize Stories*, and *New Stories from the South* and has appeared in
numerous magazines, including *One Story*, *Glimmer Train*, the
Iowa Review, the *Missouri Review*, and the *Sun*. She is Writer in
Residence and Professor of Creative Writing at Dickinson College
and on the faculty at Queens University.

◆ **HELEN PHILLIPS** is the author of five books, including
the novel *The Need*, which was a nominee for the 2019 National
Book Award, a *New York Times* Notable Book of 2019, and a
Time Magazine Top 10 Book of 2019. Her collection *Some Possible
Solutions* received the 2017 John Gardner Fiction Book Award. Her
novel *The Beautiful Bureaucrat*, a *New York Times* Notable Book
of 2015, was a finalist for the *Los Angeles Times* Book Prize and the
New York Public Library's Young Lions Award. Her collection *And*

Yet They Were Happy was named a notable collection by the Story Prize. She is the recipient of a Guggenheim Foundation Fellowship, a Rona Jaffe Foundation Writers' Award, and the Italo Calvino Prize in Fabulist Fiction. Her work has appeared in the *Atlantic* and the *New York Times*, and on *Selected Shorts*. She is an associate professor at Brooklyn College.

◆ **NAMWALI SERPELL** is a Zambian writer and a professor of English at Harvard University. She's a recipient of a 2020 Windham-Campbell Prize for fiction and the 2015 Caine Prize for African Writing. She was selected for the Africa39 in 2014 and received a 2011 Rona Jaffe Foundation Writers' Award. Her first novel, *The Old Drift* (Hogarth, 2019), won the Anisfield-Wolf Book Award for fiction "that confronts racism and explores diversity," the Arthur C. Clarke Award for Science Fiction, and the *Los Angeles Times* Art Seidenbaum Award for First Fiction in 2020. It was shortlisted for the *Los Angeles Times* Ray Bradbury Prize for Science Fiction, Fantasy, and Speculative Fiction; longlisted for the Center for Fiction First Novel Prize; and named one of the year's 100 Notable Books by the *New York Times Book Review*.

◆ **RIVERS SOLOMON** is a dyke, an anarchist, a she-beast, an exile, a shiv, a wreck, and a refugee of the Transatlantic Slave Trade. In addition to appearing on the Stonewall Honor List and winning a Firecracker Award, Solomon's debut novel, *An Unkindness of Ghosts*, was a finalist for a Lambda, a Hurston/Wright, a Tiptree, and a Locus Award, among others. Solomon's second book, *The Deep*, was the winner of the 2020 Lambda Award and is on the shortlist for a Nebula, Locus, and Hugo award. Faer third book, *Sorrowland*, was published in May 2021.

◆ **ELIZABETH STROUT** is the #1 *New York Times* bestselling author of *Olive Kitteridge*, winner of the Pulitzer Prize; *Olive, Again*, an Oprah's Book Club pick; *Anything Is Possible*, winner of the Story Prize; *My Name Is Lucy Barton*, longlisted for the Man Booker Prize; *The Burgess Boys*, named one of the best books of 2013 by the *Washington Post* and NPR; *Abide with Me*, a national bestseller; and *Amy and Isabelle*, winner of the *Los Angeles Times* Art Seidenbaum Award for First Fiction and the *Chicago Tribune* Heartland Prize.

◆ **HANNAH TINTI** was the literary commentator on *Selected Shorts* from 2010 to 2013. She is the author of the bestselling novel *The Good Thief*, which won the Center for Fiction's First Novel Prize, and the story collection *Animal Crackers*, a runner-up for the PEN/Hemingway Award. Her novel *The Twelve Lives of Samuel Hawley* was a national bestseller and has been optioned for television. Tinti is also the co-founder and executive editor of *One Story* magazine, which won the AWP Small Press Publisher Award, a 2020 Whiting Prize, CLMP's Firecracker Award, and the PEN/ Nora Magid Award for Excellence in Editing. She teaches creative writing at New York University's MFA program and co-founded the Sirenland Writers Conference.

◆ A finalist for the Pulitzer Prize for his landmark work of nonfiction *The Devil's Highway*, **LUIS ALBERTO URREA** is the bestselling author of the novels *The Hummingbird's Daughter*, *Into the Beautiful North*, *Queen of America*, and most recently, *The House of Broken Angels*, as well as the story collection *The Water Museum*, a PEN/Faulkner Award finalist. He has won the Lannan Literary

Award, an Edgar Award, and a 2017 American Academy of Arts and Letters Award in Literature, among many other honors.

◆   **JESS WALTER** is the author of seven novels, most recently the 2020 national bestseller *The Cold Millions*. Among his other novels are *Beautiful Ruins*, a 2012 #1 *New York Times* bestseller; *The Zero*, a 2006 finalist for the National Book Award; and *Citizen Vince*, winner of the 2005 Edgar Award. His short fiction has appeared three times in *Best American Short Stories*, as well as *Harpers, Esquire*, and many others, and is collected in the books *We Live in Water* (2013) and the forthcoming *Famous Actors*.

◆   **WEIKE WANG** is the author of the novels *Chemistry* and *Joan Is Okay*. Her work has appeared in *Glimmer Train, Kenyon Review, Ploughshares, Alaska Quarterly Review, Redivider*, and the *New Yorker*, among other publications, and her fiction has been anthologized in *The Best American Short Stories* and *The O. Henry Prize Stories*. She is the recipient of the 2018 Pen/Hemingway Award, a Whiting Award, and a National Book Foundation 5 Under 35 Prize.

ABOUT SELECTED SHORTS

ON A WARM summer night in 1984, in the back of a darkened theater at Symphony Space, Kay Cattarulla had an idea. The concept was a simple but powerful one—our greatest actors transporting us through the magic of fiction, one short story at a time. She brought it to Isaiah Sheffer, Symphony Space's co-founder and co–artistic director, and through their visionary partnership, a groundbreaking new series was born: Selected Shorts.

Selected Shorts premiered at Symphony Space in 1985, and with that, the "literature in performance" genre was born. The series expanded to include a popular public radio show, national tours, and a podcast. Whether featuring stories around a curated theme, the favorite works of a guest author, or a unique collaboration, each Selected Shorts continues to be a special experience and a celebration of the written word.

The Selected Shorts Commissioning Project was inspired by the arrival of the series' thirty-fifth anniversary. We knew of no better way to celebrate this landmark than by inviting an extraordinary array of writers—some long in the Symphony Space fold, some recent additions to our ever-growing community of artists—to create new work. This project has been a joyful collaboration, and we are deeply grateful to each and every writer for their contribution.

ABOUT SYMPHONY SPACE

THE BIRTH OF Symphony Space is the quintessential New York story. In 1978, Isaiah Sheffer and Allan Miller threw open the doors to an abandoned and dilapidated theater and invited the community to be part of something magical. Friends, colleagues, families, shopkeepers, and neighbors all rallied together to help Isaiah and Allan transform that old theater for a free, twelve-hour marathon of music and community called *Wall to Wall Bach*. Since that first *Wall to Wall*, Symphony Space has grown to become a beacon that has welcomed, nurtured, and championed generations of artists and audiences alike. It remains a magical place where meaningful and adventurous programming thrives and radiates far beyond our beloved corner of 95th and Broadway.

ACKNOWLEDGMENTS

WORDS MATTER. DIVERSE voices matter. Storytelling matters. Symphony Space and Selected Shorts are thrilled to have worked alongside a partner in this project who shares these convictions— Algonquin Books. Under the leadership of Executive Director Kathy Landau, and with Director of Literary Programs Jennifer Brennan at the helm, Symphony Space gratefully acknowledges the contributions of our extraordinary team, with special thanks to Matthew Love, Sarah Montague, Drew Richardson, Mary Shimkin, Miles B. Smith, Johanna Thomsen, Hannah Tinti, Vivienne Woodward, Peg Wreen, and Magdalene Wrobleski. Each played a unique and pivotal role in bringing this book to fruition.

And none of this would have been possible without Katherine Minton, an unparalleled champion of fiction and the Director of Literary Programs at Symphony Space for twenty-five years.

We are all eternally indebted to Isaiah Sheffer and Kay Cattarulla for their legacy of passion for the short story, which will continue to inspire writers, readers, and audiences for generations to come.